Quag Keep

Tor Books by Andre Norton

Quag
Keep

ANDRE NORTON

TOR®

A TOM DOHERTY ASSOCIATES BOOK
NEW YORK

QUAG KEEP

First published in the United States by Atheneum Books

A Tor Book
Published by Tom Doherty Associates, LLC
175 Fifth Avenue
New York, NY 10010

www.tor.com

Tor® is a registered trademark of Tom Doherty Associates, LLC.

Library of Congress Cataloging-in-Publication Data
Norton, Andre.
Quag keep / Andre Norton.
"A Tom Doherty Associates book."
Summary: Seven strangers, each wearing a
similar bracelet, meet and become pawns in the
continuing struggle between the forces of good and evil.
ISBN-13 978-0-765-31302-7
ISBN-10 0-765-31302-2
1. Good and evil—Fiction. 2. Fantasy games—Fiction. 3. Fantasy.

PZ7.82 Qa 2003
[Fic] 22   2006040367

First Tor Trade Paperback Edition: May 2006

Printed in the United States of America

0 9 8 7 6 5 4 3 2 1

The author wishes to express appreciation for the invaluable aid of E. Gary Gygax of TSR, expert player and creator of the war game, DUNGEONS AND DRAGONS, on which the background of QUAG KEEP is based. I wish also to acknowledge the kind assistance of Donald Wollheim, an authority and collector of fantasy miniatures, whose special interest was so valuable for my research.

Contents

Contents

Quag Keep

1

Greyhawk

ECKSTERN PRODUCED THE PACKAGE WITH AN EXAGGERATED FLOUR-ish and lifted the lid of the box to pluck out shredded packing with as much care as if he were about to display the crown jewels of some long-forgotten kingdom. His showmanship brought the others all closer. Eckstern liked such chances to focus attention, and tonight, as the referee chosen to set up the war game, his actions were backed with special authority.

He unwrapped a length of cotton and set out on the table, between the waiting game sheets, a two-inch figure, larger than any they habitually played with. It was, indeed, a treasure. A swordsman—complete with shield on which a nearly microscopic heraldic design blazed forth in brilliant enamel paints. The tiny face of the figure was sternly set above the rim of the shield, shadowed by a helmet with a small twist of spike rising from it. There was an indication of mail on the body which had been modeled as if the figure were advancing a step in grim determination. The sword in the hand was a length of glittering metal, more like well-polished steel than lead which was the usual material for playing figures.

Martin stared at it in fascination. He had seen many expertly painted and well-positioned war-game figures but this—this gave him a queer feeling, as if it had not been turned out of a mold, but rather had been designed by a sculptor in the form of a man who once had lived.

"Where—where did you get that?" Harry Conden's slight hesitation of speech was more pronounced than usual.

"A beauty, isn't it?" Eckstern purred. "A new company—Q K Productions—and you wouldn't believe the price either. They sent a letter and a list—want to introduce their pieces to 'well-known' players. After we won those two games at the last convention, I guess they had us near the top of their list . . ."

To Martin, Eckstern's explanation was only a meaningless babble. His hand had gone out without his conscious willing, to touch fingertip on that shield, make sure it did exist. It was true that the makers of playing pieces for the fantasy war games were starting to try to outdo each other in the production of unusual monsters, noble fighters, astute elves, powerful dwarves, and all the other characters a player might call for, identify with while playing, even keep on display like some fabulous antique chessmen between games. Martin had envied those able to equip themselves with the more ornate and detailed figures. But the best he had seen in displays could not compare to this. Within him came a sudden compulsion: he must have this one. It was beyond any doubt meant for him.

Eckstern was still talking as he unwrapped other figures, set them out, his elbow firmly planted meanwhile on the referee notes for the coming game. But Martin's attention never wavered from the swordsman. This was his! He grasped it lovingly.

THERE WERE GOOD SMELLS AND STALE ONES FIGHTING FOR DOMinance in a room lit only by baskets of fire wasps, one of which was close enough so that he could see every old stain on the table at which he sat. By his right hand stood a drinking horn mounted on a base of dull metal. His right hand . . .

He stared at both hands, the fists lightly clenched and lying on the scored board. This was (it seemed that his mind had skipped something of importance as a heart might skip a beat), this was, of course, the Sign of Harvel's Axe, a dubious inn on the edge of the Thieves' Quarter in the city of Greyhawk. He frowned, troubled. But there had been something else—something of importance—of which only a hint slithered so swiftly through his brain that he could not fasten on it quickly enough.

His name was Milo Jagon, a swordsman of some experience, now unemployed. That much was clear. And the hands before him were bare below sleeves of very supple, dark-colored mail which had a hint of copper in it, yet was darker brown. Turned back against his wrists were mitts fastened to the sleeves. And about each of his thumbs was the wide band of a ring. The one to the right was set with an oblong stone of dull green, across which, in no discernible pattern, wandered tiny red veins and dots. The setting on the left was even more extraordinary—an oval crystal of gray, clouded and filmed.

On the right wrist there was a glint of something else; again that faintest hint of other memory—even of alarm—touched Milo's mind. He jerked down the right mitt and saw, banded over the mail itself, a wide bracelet of a metal as richly bright as newly polished copper. It was made of two bands between which, swung on hardly visible gimbals, were a series of dice—three-sided, four-sided, eight-sided, six-sided. They were of the same bright metal as the bracelet that supported them. But the numbers on them were wrought in glistening bits of gem-stones, so tiny he did not see how any gem smith could have set them in so accurately.

This—with his left hand he touched that bracelet, finding the metal warm to his fingertips—this was important! His scowl grew deeper. But why and how?

And he could not remember having come here. Also—he raised his head to stare about uneasily—he sensed that he was watched. Yet there were none in that murky room he was quick enough to catch eyeing him.

The nearest table to his own was also occupied by a single man. He had the bulk, the wide shoulders and thick, mail-covered forearms, of a man who would be formidable in a fight. Milo assessed him, only half-consciously, with the experienced eye of one who had needed many times in the past to know the nature of an enemy, and that quickly.

The cloak the other man had tossed to the bench beside him was of hide covered with horny bristles. And his helmet was surmounted with a realistic and daunting representation of a snarling boar brought dangerously to bay. Beneath the edge of it, his face was wide of the cheekbone and square of jaw, and he was staring, as Milo had been, at his hands on the tabletop before him. Between them crouched a bright, green-blue pseudo-

dragon, its small wings fluttering, its arrow-pointed tongue darting in and out.

And on his right wrist—Milo drew a deep breath—this
stranger wore a bracelet twin to his own, as far as the swordsman could see without truly examining it.

Boar helm, boar cloak—memories and knowledge Milo did
not consciously search for arose. This other was a berserker,
and one with skill enough to turn were-boar if he so desired.
Such were chancy companions at the best, and the swordsman
did not wonder now that their two tables, so close together,
were theirs alone, that the rest of the patrons, eating and drinking, had sought the other side of the long room. Nor was he surprised that the stranger should have the pseudo-dragon as a
traveling companion or pet, whichever their relationship might
be. For the weres, like the elves and some others, could com-
municate with animals at will.

Once more Milo gave a searching, very steady survey of the
others in the room. There were several thieves, he guessed, and
one or two foreigners, who, he hoped for their own sakes, were
tough enough to defend themselves if they had wandered into
Harvel's Axe without due warning. A cloaked man who, he
thought, might be a druid (of low rank) was spooning up stew
with such avidity that spattering drops formed gobbets of grease
on his clothing. Milo was paying particular attention to right
wrists. Those he could see were certainly innocently bare of any
such banding as he and the berserker wore. At the same time,
the impression that he was being watched (and not with any
kindness) grew in him. He dropped hand to sword hilt and, for
the first time, noted that a shield leaned against the table. On it
was emblazoned an intricate pattern which, though dented in

places and plainly weatherworn, had once been skillfully done. And he had seen that . . . where?

The vagrant curl of memory grew no stronger for his trying to grasp it. He grinned sourly. Of course he had seen it many times over—the thing was his, wasn't it? And he had callouses from its weight along his arm to prove that.

At least he had had the wisdom to pick a table where he sat with his back to the wall. Now there flowed through his mind half memories of other times when he had been in just such uncertain lodgings. A table swung up and forward could serve as a barrier to deter a rush. And the outer door? . . .

There were two doors in the room. One led, uncurtained, to the inner part of the inn. The other had a heavy leather drape over it. Unfortunately, that was on the opposite side of the room. To reach it he would have to pass a group he had been watching with quick glances, five men gathered close together whispering. They had seemed to show no interest in him, but Milo did not depend on such uncertain reassurance of innocence.

The eternal war between Law and Chaos flared often in Greyhawk. It was in a manner of speaking a "free city"—since it had no one overlord to hold it firmly to his own will. For that reason it had become a city of masterless men, a point from which many expeditions, privately conceived and planned for the despoiling of ancient treasures, would set out, having recruited the members from just such masterless men as Milo himself, or perhaps the berserker only an arm's length away.

But if those on the side of Law recruited here, so did the followers of Chaos. There were neutrals also, willing to join with either side for the sake of payment. But they were never to be wholly depended upon by any man who had intelligence, for they might betray one at the flip of a coin or the change of the wind itself.

As a swordsman Milo was vowed to Law. The berserker had more choice in such matters. But this place, under its odors of fresh and stale food, stank to Milo of Chaos. What *had* brought him here? If he could only remember! Was he spell-struck in some fashion? That idea caught and held in his mind to worry him even more. No man, unless he had won to high adeptship and therefore was no longer entirely human, could even begin to reckon the kinds and numbers of spells that might be set to entangle the unwary. But he knew that he was waiting—and he again tested the looseness of his sword within its sheath, keeping his other hand close to the edge of the table, tense as a man may be before he reaches a position he has chosen for his own defense.

Then—in the light of the fire wasps he caught the flashes from his wrist. Dice—moving! Again he half remembered a fast, fleeting wisp of some other knowledge he should have and did not—to his own danger.

But it was not the suspected men in the corner who were a threat. Instead the berserker got to his feet. Up the mighty thickness of his mailed arm fluttered the pseudo-dragon, to perch upon his shoulder, its spear tongue darting against the cheekpiece of his heavy helmet. He had caught up his cloak but he did not turn to the leather curtain of the outer door. Instead he took two strides and stood towering over Milo.

Under the brush of his brows his eyes held a red glint like those of an angry boar, and he thrust out his hand and wrist to match Milo's. There, too, showed the glint of the dice, turning by themselves on their almost invisible gimbals.

"I am Naile Fangtooth." His voice was close to a low grunting. And, as his lips moved to form the words, they betrayed the reason for his self-naming—two teeth as great as tusks set on either side of his lower jaw. He spoke as if compelled to, and Milo found that he answered as if he must offer some password, lest the danger that made his flesh crawl break forth. Yet at the same moment he knew that his sensed danger did not come from this mighty fighting machine.

"I am Milo Jagon. Sit you down, fighting man." He moved his shield, slid farther along the bench to make room for the other.

"I do not know why, but—" Fangtooth's eyes no longer held those of the swordsman. Rather he was looking with an open expression of perplexity at their bracelets. "But," he continued after a moment's pause, "this is what I must do: join with you. And this"—he attempted to slip the bracelet from his thick wrist but could not move it—"is what commands me—after some fashion of its own."

"We must be bespelled." Milo returned frankness with frankness. Berserkers seldom sought out any but their own kind. Among their fellows, they had comradeships that lasted to the shores of death and beyond, for the survivor of a fatal encounter was then aware always of only one driving force, the need for revenge upon those who had slain his other self in battle-kinship.

The berserker scowled. "Spells—they have a stink to 'em. And, yes, swordsman, I can pick up that stink a little. Afreeta"—the pseudo-dragon flickered its thread of tongue like a signal—"has already sniffed it. Yet it is not, I think, one sent by a dark-loving devil." He had kept his voice low with a visible effort as if his natural tone was more of a full-throated roar.

Milo noted that the eyes beneath those heavy brows were

never still, that Naile Fangtooth watched the company in the room with as keen an eye for trouble as he himself had earlier. Those who whispered together had not once made any move to suggest that the two were of interest to them. The shabby druid licked his spoon, then raised the bowl to his lips to sup down the last of the broth it contained. And two men wearing the shoulder badges of some merchant's escort kept drinking steadily as if their one purpose in life was to see which first would get enough of a skinful to subside to the rush-strewn, ill-swept floor.

"They—none of them—wear these." Milo indicated the bracelet on his own wrist. The dice were now quiet on their gimbals. In fact when he tried to swing one with his fingernail, it remained as fixed as if it could never move, yet it was the same one he had seen turn just before Naile had joined him.

"No." The berserker blinked. "There is something—something that nibbles at my mind as a squirrel worries away at a nut. I should know, but I do not. And you, swordsman?" His scowl did not lighten as he looked directly at Milo. There was accusation in it, as if he believed the swordsman knew the secret of this strange meeting but was purposefully keeping it to himself.

"It is the same," Milo admitted. "I feel I must remember something—yet it is as if I beat against a locked door in my mind and cannot win through that to the truth."

"I am Naile Fangtooth." The berserker was not speaking to Milo now, but rather affirming his identity as if he needed such assurance. "I was with the Brethern when they took the Mirror of Loice and the Standard of King Everon. It was then that my shield brother, Engul Widehand, was cut down by the snake-skins. Also it was there later that I picked Afreeta from a cage so she joined with me." He raised a big hand and gently stroked the back of the dragon at a spot between its continually fluttering wings. "These things I remember—yet—there was more. . . ."

"The Mirror of Loice . . ." Milo repeated. Where had he heard of that before? He raised both fists and pressed them against his forehead, pushing up the edge of the helmet he wore. The edges of the two thumb rings pressed against his skin, giving him a slight twinge of pain. But nothing answered in his memory.

"Yes." There was pride now in his companion's voice. "That was a mighty hosting. Orcs, even the Spectre of Loice herself, stood against us. But we had the luck of the throws with us for that night. The luck of the throws—!" Now it was Fangtooth's turn to look at the bracelets on his own wrist. "The throws—" he repeated for the second time. "It means . . . it means . . . !"

His face twisted and he beat upon the table board with one calloused fist, so mighty a blow that the horn cup leaped though it did not overturn. "What throws?" The scowl he turned upon Milo now was as grim as a battle face.

"I don't know." Milo wet his lips with his tongue. He had no fear of the berserker even though the huge man might well be deliberately working himself into one of those rages that transcended intelligence and made such a fighter impervious to weapons and some spells.

Once more he struggled to turn the dice on the bracelet. Far back in his mind he knew them. They had a very definite purpose. Only here and now he was like a man set down before some ancient roll of knowledge that he could not read and yet knew that his life perhaps depended upon translating it.

"These," he said slowly. "One turned just before you joined me. They are like gamers' dice, save that there are too many shapes among them to be ordinary."

"Yes." Naile's voice had fallen again. "Still I have thrown such—and for a reason, or reasons. But why or where I cannot remember. I think, swordsman, that someone thinks to play a game with *us*. If this be so, he shall discover that he has chosen not tools but men, and therefore will be the worse for his folly."

"If we are bespelled . . ." Milo began. He wanted to keep the berserker away from the battle madness of his kind. It was useful, very useful, that madness, but only in the proper place and time. And to erupt, not even knowing the nature of the enemy, was rank folly.

"Then sooner or later we shall meet the spell caster?" To Milo's relief, Fangtooth seemed well able to control the power of were-change that was his by right. "Yes, that is what I believe we wait for now."

The druid, without a single glance in their direction, had set by his now empty bowl and got to his feet, ringing down on the table top a small coin. He wore, Milo noted as he turned and his robe flapped up a little, not the sandals suitable for city streets, but badly cured and clumsily made hide boots such as a peasant might use for field labor in ill weather. The bag marked with the runes of his training was a small one and as shabby as his robe. He gave a jerk to bring his cowl higher over his head and started for the outer door, nor did he make any attempt to approach their table. Milo was glad to see the last of him. Druids were chancy at best, and there were those who had the brand of Chaos and the powers of the Outer Dark at their call, though this one was manifestly lowly placed in that close-knit and secret fraternity.

Fangtooth's lips pursed as if he would spit after the figure now tugging aside the door curtain.

"Cooker of spells!" he commented.

"But not the one who holds us," Milo said.

"True enough. Tell me, swordsman, does your skin now prickle, does it seem that, without your helm to hold it down, your very hair might rise on your head? Whatever has netted us comes the closer. Yet a man cannot fight what he cannot see, hear, or know is alive."

The berserker was far more astute than Milo had first thought him. Because of the very nature of the bestial ferocity such fighters fell into upon occasion, one was apt to forget that they had their own powers and were moved by intelligence as well as by the superhuman strength they could command. Fangtooth had the right of it. His own discomfort had been steadily growing. What they awaited was nearly here.

Now the five whisperers also arose and passed one by one beyond the curtain. It was as if someone, or something, were clearing the stage for a struggle. Yet still Milo could not locate any of the signs of Chaos. On the berserker's shoulder the pseudo-dragon chittered, rubbing its head back and forth on the cheekplate of the boar-crowned helmet.

Milo found himself watching, not the small reptile, but rather the bracelet on his wrist. It seemed to have loosened somewhat its grip against his mail. Two of the dice began slowly to spin.

"Now!"

Naile got to his feet. In his left hand he held a deadly battle axe of such weight that Milo, trained though he was to handle many different weapons, thought he could never have brought to shoulder height. They were alone in the long room. Even those who had served had gone, as if they had some private knowledge of ill to come and would not witness it.

Still, what Milo felt was not the warning prick of normal fear—rather an excitement, as if he stood on the verge of learning the answer to all questions.

As Naile had done, he got to his feet, lifted his shield. The dice on his bracelet whirred to a stop as the hide door curtain was drawn aside, letting in a blast of late fall, winter-touched air. A man, slight and so well cloaked that he seemed merely some shadow detached from a nearby wall to roam homelessly about, came swiftly in.

2

Wizard's Wiles

THE NEWCOMER APPROACHED THEM DIRECTLY. HIS PALE FACE above the high-standing collar of his cloak marked him as one who dwelt much indoors by reason of necessity or choice. And, though his features were human enough in their cast, still Milo, seeing their impassivity, the thinness of his bloodless lips, the sharp-beak curve of his nose, hesitated to claim him as a brother man. His eyelids were near closed, but, as he reached the table, he opened them widely and they could see that his pupils were of no human color, rather dull red like a smoldering coal.

Save for those eyes, the only color about him was the badge sewn to the shoulder of his cloak. And that was so intricate that Milo could not read its meaning. It appeared to be an entwining of a number of wizardly runes. When the newcomer spoke, his voice was low-pitched and had no more emotion than the monotone of one who repeated a set message without personal care for its meaning.

"You are summoned—"

"By whom and where?" Naile growled and spat again, the flush on his broad face darkening. "I have taken no service—"

Milo caught the berserker's arm. "No more have I. But it would seem that this is what we have awaited." For in him that expectancy which had been building to a climax now blended into a compulsion he could not withstand.

For a moment it seemed that the berserker was going to dispute the summons. Then he swung up his fur cloak and fastened it with a boar's head buckle at his throat.

"Let us be gone then," he growled. "I would see an end to this bedazzlement, and that speedily." The pseudo-dragon chittered shrilly, shooting its tongue at the messenger, as if it would have enjoyed impaling some part of the stranger on that spear-point.

Again Milo felt the nudge of spinning dice at his wrist. If he could only remember! There was a secret locked in that arm-let and he must learn it soon, for as he stood now, he felt helplessness like a sharp-set wound.

They came out of Harvel's Axe on the heels of the messenger. Though the upper part of the city was well lighted, this portion was far too shadowed. Those who dwelt and carried out their plans here knew shadows as friends and defenses. However, as three of them strode along, they followed a crooked alley where the houses leaned above them as if eyes set in the upper stories would spy on passersby. Milo's overactive imagination was ready to endow those same houses, closed and barred against the night and with seldom a dim glow to mark a small-paned window, with knowledge greater than his own, as if they snickered slyly as the three passed.

Before they reached the end of the Thieves' Quarter a dark form slipped from an arched doorway. Though he had had no warning from the armlet, Milo's hand instantly sought his sword hilt. Then the newcomer fell into step with him and the very dim light showed the green and brown apparel of an elf. Few, if any, of that blood were ever drawn into the ways of Chaos. Now better light from a panel above the next door made it plain that the newcomer was one of the Woods Rangers. His long bow, unstrung, was at his back and he bore a quiver full of arrows tight packed. In addition both a hunter's knife and a sword were sheathed at his belt. But most noticeable to the swordsman, on his wrist he, too, wore the same bracelet that marked the berserker and Milo himself.

Their guide did not even turn his head to mark the coming of the elf, but kept ahead at a gliding walk which Milo found he must extend his stride to match. Nor did the newcomer offer any greeting to either of the men. Only the pseudo-dragon turned its gem-point eyes to the newcomer and trilled a thin, shrill cry.

Elves had the common tongue, though sometimes they disdained to use it unless it was absolutely necessary. However, besides it and their own speech, they also had mastery over communication with animals and birds—and, it would seem, pseudo-dragons. For Naile's pet—or comrade—had shrilled what must be a greeting. If the elf answered, it was by mind-talk alone. He made no more sound than the shadows around them; far less than the hissing slip-slip of their guide's footgear which was oftentimes drowned out by the clack of their own boot heels on the pavement.

They proceeded into wider and less winding streets, catching glimpses now and then of some shield above a door to mark a representative of Blackmer, a merchant of substance from Urnst, or the lands of the Holy Lords of Faraaz.

So the four came to a narrow way between two towering walls. At the end of that passage stood a tower. It was not impressive at first, as were some towers in Greyhawk. The surface of the stone facing was lumpy and irregular. Those pocks and rises, Milo noted, when they came to the single door facing the alley that had brought them and could see the door light, were carving as intricately enfolded and repeated as the patch upon their guide's cloak.

From what he could distinguish, the stone was not the local grayish-tan either, but instead a dull green, over which wandered lines of yellow, adding to the confusion of the carven patterns in a way to make the eyes ache if one tried to follow either carving or yellow vein.

He whom they followed laid one hand to the door and it swung immediately open, as if there was no need for bars or other protection in this place. Light, wan, yet brighter than they had seen elsewhere, flowed out to engulf them.

Here were no baskets of fire wasps. This light stemmed from the walls themselves, as if those yellow veins gave off a sickly radiance. By the glow Milo saw that the faces of his companions looked as palely ghostlike as those of some liche serving Chaos. He did not like this place, but his will was bound as tightly as if fetters enclosed his wrists and chains pulled him forward.

They passed, still in silence, along a narrow corridor to come at the end of it to a corkscrew of a stairway. Because their guide flitted up it, they did likewise. Milo saw an oily drop of sweat streak down the berserker's nose, drip to his chin where the bristles of perhaps two days of neglected beard sprouted vigorously. His own palms were wet and he had to fight a desire to wipe them on his cloak.

Up they climbed, passing two levels of the tower, coming at last into a single great room. Here it was stifling hot. A fire burned upon a hearth in the very middle, smoke trailing upward through an opening in the roof. But the rest of the room . . . Milo drew a deep breath. This was no lord's audience chamber. There were tables on which lay piles of books, some bound in wooden boards eaten by time, until perhaps only their hinges of metal held them together. There were canisters of scrolls, all pitted and green with age. Half the floor their guide stepped confidently out upon was inlaid with a pentagon and other signs and runes. The sickly light was a little better here, helped by the natural flames of the fire.

Standing by the fire, as if his paunchy body still craved heat in spite of the temperature of the chamber, was a man of perhaps Milo's height, yet stooped a little of shoulder and completely bald of head. In place of hair, the dome of his skin-covered skull had been painted or tattooed with the same unreadable design as marked the cloak patch of his servant.

He wore a gray robe, tied with what looked like a length of plain yellowish rope, and that robe was marked with no design or symbol. His right wrist, Milo was quick to look for that, was bare of any copper, dice-set bracelet. He could have been any age (wizards were able to control time a little for their own benefit) and he was plainly in no cheerful mood. Yet, as the swordsman stepped up beside Naile, the elf quickly closing in to make a third, Milo for the first time felt free of compulsion and constant surveillance.

The wizard surveyed them critically—as a buyer in the slave market might survey proffered wares. Then he gave a small hacking cough when smoke puffed into his face and waved a hand to drive away that minor annoyance.

"Naile Fangtooth, Milo Jagon, Ingrge." It was not as if he meant the listing of names as a greeting, but rather as if he were reckoning up a sum important to himself. Now he beckoned and, from the other side of the fire, four others advanced.

"I am, of course, Hystaspes. And why the Great Powers saw fit to draw me into this meeting. . . ." He scowled. "But if one deals with the Powers it is a two-way matter and one pays their price in the end. Behold your fellows!"

His wave of the hand was theatrical as he indicated the four who had come into full sight. As Milo, Naile, and the elf Ingrge had instinctively moved shoulder to shoulder, so did these also stand.

"The battlemaid Yevele." Hystaspes indicated a slender figure in full mail. She had pushed her helmet back a little on her forehead, and a wisp of red-brown hair showed. For the rest, her young face was near as impassive as that of their guide. She wore, however, Milo noticed, what he was beginning to consider the dangerous bracelet.

"Deav Dyne, who puts his faith in the gods men make for themselves." There was exasperation in the wizard's voice as he spoke the name of the next.

By his robe of gray, faced with white, Deav Dyne was a follower of Landron-of-the-Inner-Light and of the third rank. But a bracelet encircled his wrist also. He gave a slight nod to the other three, but there was a frown on his face and he was plainly uneasy in his present company.

"The bard Wymarc—"

The red-headed man, who wore a skald's field harp in a bag on his back, smiled as if he were playing a part and was slyly amused at both his own role and the company of his fellow players.

"And, of course, Gulth." Hystaspes's visible exasperation came to the surface as he indicated the last of the four.

That introduction was answered by a low growl from Naile Fangtooth. "What man shares a venture with an eater of carrion? Get you out, scale-skin, or I'll have that skin off your back and ready to make me boots!"

The lizardman's stare was unblinking. He did not open his fanged jaws to answer—though the lizard people used and understood the common tongue well enough. But Milo did not like the way that reptilian gaze swept the berserker from head to foot and back again. Lizardmen were considered neutral in the eternal struggles and skirmishes of Law and Chaos. On the other hand a neutral did not awake trust in any man. Their sense of loyalty seldom could be so firmly engaged that they would not prove traitors in some moment of danger. And this specimen of his race was formidable to look upon. He was fully as tall as Naile, and in addition to the wicked sword of bone, double-edged with teeth, that he carried, his natural armament of fang and claw was weaponry even a hero might consider twice before facing. Yet on his scaled wrist, as on that of the bard and the cleric, was the same bracelet.

Now the wizard turned to the fire, pointed a forefinger.

Phrases of a language that meant nothing to Milo came from his lips in an invoking chant. Out of the heart of the flames spread more smoke but in no random puff. This was a serpent of white which writhed through the air, reaching out. It split into two and one loop of it fell about Milo, Naile and the elf before they could move, noosing around their heads, just as the other branch noosed the four facing them.

Milo sputtered and coughed. He could see nothing of the room now or of those in it. But . . .

"ALL RIGHT, YOU PLAY THAT ONE THEN. NOW THE PROBLEM IS . . ."

A room, misty, only half seen. Sheets of paper. He was . . . he was . . .

"WHO ARE YOU?" A VOICE BOOMED THROUGH THE MIST WITH THE resonance of a great bell.

Who was he? What a crazy question. He was Martin Jefferson, of course.

"Who are you?" demanded that voice once more. There was such urgency in it that he found himself answering it:

"Martin Jefferson."

"What are you doing?"

His bewilderment grew. He was—he was playing a game. Something Eckstern had suggested that they practice up on for the convention using the new Q K figures.

That was it—just playing a game!

"No game." The booming voice denied that, leaving him bewildered, completely puzzled.

"Who are you?"

Martin wet his lips to answer. There was a question of two of his own for which he wanted an answer. The mist was so thick he could not see the table. And that was not Eckstern's voice— it was more powerful. But before he could speak again he heard a second voice:

"Nelson Langley."

Nels—that was Nels! But Nels had not come tonight. In fact he was out of town. He hadn't heard from Nels since last Saturday.

"What are you doing?" Again that relentless inquiry.

"I'm playing a game . . ." Nels' voice sounded odd—strong enough and yet as if this unending fog muffled it a little.

"No game!" For the second time that curt answer was emphatic.

Martin tried to move, to break through the fog. This was like one of those dreams where you could not get away from an ever-encoaching shadow.

"Who are you?"

"James Ritchie."

Who was James Ritchie? He'd never heard of him before. What *was* going on? Martin longed to shout out that question and discovered that he could not even shape the words. He was beginning to be frightened now—if this was a dream it was about time to wake up.

"What are you doing?"

Martin was not in the least surprised to hear the same answer he and Nels had given—the same denial follow.

"Who are you?"

"Susan Spencer." That was a girl's voice, again that of a stranger.

Then came three other answers: Lloyd Collins, Bill Ford, Max Stein.

The smoke was at last beginning to thin. Martin's head hurt. He was Martin Jefferson and he was dreaming. But . . .

As the smoke drifted away in ragged patches he was—not back at the table with Eckstern—no! This was—this was the tower of Hystaspes. He was Milo Jagon, swordsman—but he was also Martin Jefferson. The warring memories in his skull seemed enough for a wild moment or two to drive him mad.

"You see." The wizard nodded as his gaze shifted from one of the faces to the next.

"Masterly—masterly and as evil as the Nine and Ninety Sins of Salzak, the Spirit Murderer." The wizard seemed divided, too, as if he both hated and feared what he might have learned from them. Still, a part of him longed for the control of such a Power as had done this to them.

"I am—Susan." The battlemaid took a step forward. "I know I am Susan—but I am also Yevele. And these two try to live within me at once. How can this thing be?" She flung up her arm as if to ward off some danger and the light glinted on her bracelet.

"You are not alone," the wizard told her. There was no warmth of human feeling in his voice. It was brisk in tone as if he would get on to other things at once, now that he had learned what he wished of them.

Milo slipped off his helm, let his mail coif fall back against his shoulders like a hood so he could rub his aching forehead.

"I was playing—playing a game. . . ." He tried to reassure himself that those moments of clear thought within the circle of the smoke were real, that he would win out of this.

"Games!" spat the wizard. "Yes, it is those games of yours, fools that you are, that have given the enemy his chance. Had it not been that I, I who know the Lesser and the Larger Spells of Ulik and Dom, was searching for an answer to an archaic formula, you would already be *his* things. Then you would play games right enough, *his* games and for *his* purpose. This is a land where Law and Chaos are ever struggling one against each other. But the laws of Chance will let neither gain full sway. Now this other threat has come to us, and neither Law nor Chaos are boundaries for him—or them—for even yet we know not the manner or kind of what menaces us."

"We are in a game?" Milo rubbed his throbbing head again. "Is that what you are trying to tell us?"

"Who are you?" snapped the wizard as if he struck with a war axe and without any warning.

"Martin—Milo Jagon." Already the Milo part of him was winning command—driving the other memory far back into his mind, locking and barring doors that meant its freedom.

Hystaspes shrugged. "You see? And that is the badge of your servitude that you set upon yourselves in your own sphere of life, with the lack of wit only fools know."

He pointed to the bracelet.

Naile dug at the band on his wrist, using his great strength. But he could not move it. The elf broke the short silence.

"It would seem, Master Wizard, that you know far more than we do concerning this matter. And that also you have some hand in it or we would not be gathered here to be shown what you deem to be sorcery behind it. If we were brought to this world to serve your unknown menace, then you must have some plan—"

"Plan!" The wizard near shouted. "How can a man plan against that which is not of his world or time? I learned by chance what might happen far enough in advance so that I was able to take precautions against a complete victory for the enemy. Yes, I gathered you in. He-it-them are so confident that there was no part ready and waiting for you to play. The mere fact that you were here perhaps accomplished the first purpose toward which the enemy strives. By so little am I in advance of what is to come."

"Tell us then, follower of sorcerous ways," the cleric spoke up, "what you know, what you expect, and—"

The wizard laughed harshly. "I know as much as those who serve those faceless gods of yours, Deav Dyne. If there are any gods, which is problematical, why should they concern themselves with the fates of men, or even of nations? But, yet, I will tell you what I know. Chiefly because you are now tools of mine—*mine*! And you shall be willing tools, for this has been done to you against your will, and you have enough of the instincts of lifekind to resent such usage.

"Karl!" He clapped his hands. From the darker end of the room moved the messenger who had led Milo and his comrades. "Bring stools and drink and food—for the night is long and there is much to be said here."

Only Gulth, the lizardman, disdained a stool, curling up on the floor, his crocodile-snouted head supported on his hands, with never a blink of his eyelids, so that he might have been a grotesque statue. But the rest laid their weapons down and sat in a semicircle facing the wizard, as if they were a class of novices about to learn the rudiments of a charm.

Hystaspes settled himself in a chair Karl dragged forward, to watch as they drank from goblets fashioned in the form of queer and fabulous beasts and ate a dark, tough bread spread with strong-smelling, but good-tasting cheese.

Though Milo's head still ached, he had lost that terrible sense of inner conflict, and for that he was glad. Still he remembered, as if that were the dream, that once he had been someone else in another and very different world. Only that did not matter so much now, for this was Milo's world and the more he let Milo's memory rule him the safer he was.

"The dreams of men, some men," the wizard began, smoothing his robe across his knees, "can be very strong. We know this, we seekers out of knowledge that has been found, lost, hidden, and found again, many times over. For man has always been a dreamer. And it is when he begins to build upon his dreams that he achieves that which is his greatest of gifts.

"We have discovered that it may be entirely possible that what a man dreams in one world may be created and given substance in another. And if more than one dream the same dreams, strive to bring them to life, then the more solid and permanent becomes that other world. Also dreams seep from one space-time level of a world to another, taking root in new soil and there growing—perhaps even to great permanence.

"You have all played what you call a war game, building a world you believe imaginary in which to stage your adventures and exploits. Well enough, you say, what harm lies in that? You know it is a game. When it is done, you put aside your playthings for another time. Only—what if the first dreamer, who 'invented' this world according to your conception, gathered, unknowingly, dream knowledge of one that did and does exist in another time and space? Have you ever thought of that—ha?" He leaned forward, a fierceness in his eyes.

"More and more does this dream world enchant you. Why should it not? If it really is a pale, conscious-filtered bit of another reality, therefore it gains in substance in your minds and in a measure is drawn closer to your own world. The more players who think about it—the stronger the pull between them will be."

"Do you mean," Yevele asked, "that what we imagine can become real?"

"Was not playing the game very real to you when you played it?" countered Hystaspes.

Milo nodded without thought and saw that even the lizard head of Gulth echoed that gesture.

"So. But in this there is little harm—for you play but in a shadow of our world and what you do there does not influence events that happen. Well and good. But suppose someone— something—outside both of our spaces and times sees a chance to meddle—what then?"

"You tell us," Naile growled. "You tell us! Tell us why we are here, and what you—or this other thing you do not seem to know very much about—really wants of us!"

3

Geas Bound

IN SO FAR AS I HAVE LEARNED, IT IS SIMPLE ENOUGH." THE WIZARD waved his hand in the air. His fingers curved about a slender-stemmed goblet that appeared out of nowhere. "You have been imported from your own time and space to exist here as characters out of those games you have delighted in. The why of your so coming—that is only half clear to me. It would seem that he—or it—who meddles seeks thus to tie together our two worlds in some manner. The drawing of you hither may be the first part of such a uniting—"

Naile snorted. "All this your wizardry has made plain to you, has it? So we should sit and listen to this—"

Hystaspes stared at him. "Who are you?" His voice boomed as it had earlier through the smoke. "Give me your name!" That command carried the crack of an order spoken by one who was entirely sure of himself.

The berserker's face flushed. "I am—" he began hotly and then hesitated as if in that very moment some bemusement confused him. "I am Naile Fangtooth." Now a little of the force was lost from his deep voice.

"This is the city of Greyhawk," went on the wizard, an almost merciless note in his voice. "Do you agree, Naile Fangtooth?"

"Yes." The heavy body of the berserker shifted on his stool. That seat might suddenly become not the most comfortable perch in the world.

"Yet, as I have shown you—are you not someone else also? Have you no memories of a different place and time?"

"Yes . . ." Naile gave this second agreement with obvious reluctance.

"Therefore you are faced with what seems to be two contrary truths. If you are Naile Fangtooth in Greyhawk—how can you also be this other man in another world? Because you are prisoner of *that*!"

His other hand flashed out as he pointed to the bracelet on the berserker's wrist.

"You, were-boar, fighter, are slave to that!'

"You say we are slaves," Milo cut in as Naile growled and plucked fruitlessly at his bracelet. "In what manner and why?"

"In the manner of the game you chose to play," Hystaspes answered him. "Those dice shall spin and their readings will control your movements—even as when you gamed. Your life, your death, your success, your failure, all shall be governed by their spin."

"But in the game"—the cleric leaned forward a little, his gaze intent upon the wizard, as if to compel the complete attention of the other—"we throw the dice. Can we control these so firmly fixed?"

Hystaspes nodded. "That is the first sensible question," he commented. "They teach you a bit of logic in those dark, gloomy abbeys of yours, do they not, after all, priest? It is true you cannot strip those bits of metal from your wrists and throw their attachments, leaving to luck, or to your gods, whichever you believe favor you, the result. But you shall have a warning an instant or two before they spin. Then—well, then you must use your wits. Though how much of those you can summon"—he shot a glance at Naile that was anything but complimentary— "remains unknown. If you concentrate on the dice when they begin to spin, it is my belief that you will be able to change the score which will follow—though perhaps only by a fraction."

Milo glanced about the half-circle of his unsought companions in this unbelievable venture. Ingrge's face was impassive, his eyes veiled. The elf stared down, as if he were not looking outward at all, at the hand resting on his knee, the bracelet just above that. Naile scowled blackly, still pulling at his band as if strength and will could loose it.

Gulth had not moved and who could read any emotion on a face so alien to humankind? Yevele was not frowning, her gaze was centered thoughtfully on the wizard. She had raised one hand and was running the nail of her thumb along to trace the outline of her lower lip, a gesture Milo guessed she was not even aware she made. Her features were good, and the escaped tress of hair above her sun-browned forehead seemed to give her a kind of natural aliveness that stirred something in him, though this was certainly neither the time nor place to allow his attention to wander in *that* direction.

The cleric had pinched his lips together. Now he shook his head a little, more in time, Milo decided, to his own thoughts than to what the wizard was saying. The bard was the only one who smiled. As he caught Milo's wandering eyes, the smile became an open grin—as if he might be hugely enjoying all of this.

"We have been taught many things," the cleric replied with a faint repugnance. He had the countenance of one forced into speaking against his will. "We have been taught that mind can control matter. You have your spells, wizard, we have our prayers." He drew forth from the bosom of his robe a round of chain on which dull silver beads were set in patterns of two or three together.

"Spells and prayers," Hystaspes returned, "are not what I speak of—rather of such power of mind as is lying dormant within each of you and which you must cultivate for yourselves."

"Just when and how do we use this power?" For the first time, the bard Wymarc broke in. "You would not have summoned us here, Your Power-in-Possession," (he gave that title a twist which hinted at more than common civility, perhaps satire) "unless we were to be of use to you in some manner."

For the first time the wizard did not reply at once. Instead he gazed down into the goblet he held, as if the dregs of the liquid it now contained could be used as the far-seeing mirror of his craft.

"There is only one use for you," he stated dryly after a long moment.

"That being?" Wymarc persisted when Hystaspes did not at once continue.

"You must seek out the source of that which had drawn you hither and destroy it—if you can."

"For what reason—save that *you* find it alarming?" Wymarc wanted to know.

"Alarming?" Hystaspes echoed. Now his voice once more held arrogance. "I tell you, this—this alien being strives to bring together our two worlds. For what purpose he desires that, I cannot say. But should they so coincide—"

"Yes? What will happen then?" Ingrge took up the questioning. His compelling elf stare unleashed at the wizard as he might have aimed one of the deadly arrows of his race.

Hystaspes blinked. "That I cannot tell."

"No?" Yevele broke in. "With all your powers you cannot foresee what will come then?"

He flashed a quelling look at the girl, but she met that as she might a sword in the hands of a known enemy. "Such has never happened—in all the records known to me. But that it will be far more evil than the worst foray which Chaos has directed, that I can answer to."

There was complete truth in that statement, Milo thought.

"I believe something else, wizard," Deav Dyne commented dryly. "I think that even as you had us brought here to you, you have wrought what shall bind us to your will, we having no choice in the matter." Though his eyes were on the wizard, his hands were busy, slipping the beads of his prayer string between his fingers.

Ingrge, not their captor-host, replied to that. "A geas, then," he said in a soft voice, but a voice that carried chill.

Hystaspes made no attempt to deny that accusation.

"A geas, yes. Do you doubt that I would do everything within my power to make sure you seek out the source of this contamination and destroy it?"

"Destroy it?" Wymarc took up the challenge now. "Look at

us, wizard. Here stands an oddly mixed company with perhaps a few minor arts, spells, and skills. We are not adepts—"

"You are not of this world," Hystaspes interrupted. "Therefore, you are an irritant here. To pit you against another irritant is the only plausible move. And remember this—only he, or it, who brought you here knows the way by which you may return. Also, it is not this world only that is menaced. You pride yourself enough upon your imaginations used to play your game of risk and fortune—use that imagination now. Would Greyhawk—would all the lands known to us—be the same if they were intermingled with your own space-time? And how would *your* space-time suffer?"

"Distinctly a point," the bard admitted. "Save that we may not have the self-sacrificing temperament to rush forth to save our world. What I remember of it, which seems to grow less by the second, oddly enough, does not now awake in me great ardor to fight for it."

"Fight for yourself then," snapped the wizard. "In the end, with most men, it comes to self-preservation. You are committed anyway to action under the geas." He arose, his robe swirling about him.

"Just who stands against us, save this mysterious menace?" For the first time Milo dropped his role of onlooker. The instincts that were a part of the man he had now become were awake. Know the strength of your opposition, as well as the referee might allow, that was the rule of the game. It might be that this wizard was the referee. But Milo had a growing suspicion that the opposition more likely played that role. "What of Chaos?"

Hystaspes frowned. "I do not know. Save it is my belief that they may also be aware of what is happening. There are adepts enough on the Dark Road to have picked up as much as if not more than I know now."

"What of the players?" Yevele wanted to know. "Are there dark players also?"

A very faint shadow showed for an instant on the wizard's face. Then he spoke, so slowly that the words might have been forceably dragged from his lips one by one.

"I do not know. Nor have I been able to discover any such."

"Which does not mean," Wymarc remarked, "that they do not exist. A pleasant prospect. All you can give us is some slight assurance that we *may* learn to control the roll of these"—he shook his hand a little so that the dice trembled on their gimbals but did not move—"to our advantage."

"It is wrong!" Naile's deep voice rang out. "You have laid a geas on us, wizard. Therefore give us what assistance you can— by the rule of Law, which you purport to follow, that is our right to claim!"

For a moment Hystaspes glared back at the berserker as if the other's defiant speech offered insult. Visibly he mastered a first, temper-born response.

"I cannot tell you much, berserker. But, yes, what I have learned is at your service now." He arose and went to one of the tables on which were piled helter-skelter the ancient books and scrolls. Among these he made a quick search until he located a strip of parchment perhaps a yard long that he flipped open, to drop upon the floor before their half-circle of stools. It was clearly a sketchy map, as Milo began to recognize by that queer mixture of two memories to which he privately wondered if he would ever become accustomed.

To the north lay the Grand Duchy of Urnst, for Greyhawk was clearly marked nearly at the edge of the sheet to his right. Beyond that swelled the Great Kingdom of Blackmoor. To the left, or west, were mountains scattered in broken chains, dividing smaller kingdoms one from the other. Rivers, fed by tributaries, formed boundaries for many of these. This cluster of nations ended in such unknown territories as the Dry Steppes which only the Nomad Raiders of Lar dared venture out upon (the few watering places therein being hereditary possessions of those clans). Farther south was that awesome Sea of Dust from which it was said no expedition, no matter how well equipped, had ever returned, though there were legends concerning its lost and buried ships and the treasures that still might exist within their petrified cargo holds.

The map brought them all edging forward. Leaning over the parchment, Milo sensed that perhaps some of this company recognized the faded lines, could identify features that to him were but names, but that existed for them in the grafted-on memories of those they had become.

"North, east, south, west!" exploded Naile. "Where does your delving into the Old Knowledge suggest we begin, wizard? Must we wander over half the world, perhaps, to find this menace of yours in whatever fortress it has made for itself?"

The wizard produced a staff of ivory so old that it was a dull yellow and the carving on it worn by much handling to unidentifiable indentations. With its point he indicated the map.

"I have those who supply me with information," he returned. "It is only when there is a silence from some such that I turn to other methods. Here—" The point of the staff aimed a quick, vicious thrust at the southwestern portion of the map, beyond the last trace of civilization (if one might term it that) represented by the Grand Duchy of Geofp, a place the prudent avoided since civil warfare between two rivals for the rule had been going on now for more than a year, and both lords were well known to have formally accepted the rulership of Chaos.

The Duchy lay in the foothills of the mountain chain and from its borders, always providing one could find the proper passes, one might emerge either into the Dry Steppes or the Sea of Dust, depending upon whether one turned either north or south.

"Geofp?" Deav Dyne spat it out as if he found the very name vile, as indeed he must since it was a stronghold of Chaos.

"Chaos rules there, yes. But this is not of Chaos. Or at least such an alliance has not yet come into being. . . ." Hystaspes moved the pointer to the south. "I have some skill, cleric, in my own learning. What I have found is literally—nothing."

"Nothing?" Ingrge glanced up sharply. "So, you mean a void." The elf's nostrils expanded as if, like any animal of those woods his people knew better than Hystaspes might know his spells, he scented something.

"Yes, *nothing*. My seekings meet with only a befogged nothingness. The enemy has screens and protections that answer with a barrier not even a geas-burdened demon of the Fourth Level can penetrate."

Deav Dyne spun his chain of prayer beads more swiftly, muttering as he did so. The wizard served Law, but he was certainly admitting now to using demons in his service, which made that claim a little equivocal.

Hystaspes was swift to catch the cleric's reaction and shrugged as he replied. "In a time of stress one uses the weapon to hand and the best weapon for the battle that one can produce, is that not so? Yes, I have called upon certain ones whose very breath is a pollution in this room—because I feared. Do you understand that?" He thumped the point of his staff on the map. "I feared! That which is native to this world I can understand, this menace I cannot. All non-knowledge brings with it an aura of fear.

"The thing you seek was a little careless at first. The unknown powers it called upon troubled the ways of the Great Knowledge, enough for me to learn what I have already told you. But when I went searching for it, defenses had been erected. I think, though this is supposition only, that it did not expect to find those here who could detect its influences. I have but recently come into possession of certain scrolls, rumored to have once been in the hands of Han-gra-dan—"

There was an exclamation from both the elf and the cleric at that name.

"A thousand years gone!" Deav Dyne spoke as if he doubted such a find.

Hystaspes nodded. "More or less. I know not if these came directly from a cache left by that mightiest of the northern adepts. But they are indeed redolent of power and, taking such precautions as I might, I used one of the formulas. The result"—his rod stabbed again on the map—"being that I learned what I learned. Now this much I can tell you: there is a barrier existing somewhere here, in or about the Sea of Dust."

For the first time the lizardman croaked out barely understandable words in the common tongue.

"Desert—a desert ready to swallow any venturing into it." His expression could not change, but there was a certain tone in his croaking which suggested that he repudiated any plan that would send them into that fatal, trackless wilderness.

Hystaspes frowned at the map. "We cannot be sure. There is only one who might hold the answer, for these mountains are his fortress and his range. Whether he will treat with you—that will depend upon your skill of persuasion. I speak of Lichis, the Golden Dragon."

Memory, the new memory, supplied Milo with identification. Dragons could be of Chaos. Such ones hunted men as men might hunt a deer or a forest boar. But Lichis, who was known to have supported Law during thousands of years of such struggles (for the dragons were the longest lived of all creatures) must have a command of history that had become only thin legend as far as men were concerned. He was, in fact, the great lord of his kind, though he was seldom seen now and had not for years taken any part in the struggles that swept this world. Perhaps the doings of lesser beings (or so most human kind would seem to him) had come to bore him.

Wymarc hummed and Milo caught a fragment of the tune. "The Harrowing of Ironnose," a saga or legend of men, once might have been true history of a world crumbled now into dust and complete forgetfulness. Ironnose was the Great Demon, called into being by early adepts of Chaos, laboring for half a lifetime together. He was intended to break the Law forever. It was Lichis who roused and did battle. The battle had raged from Blackmoor, out over Great Bay, down to the Wild Coast, ending in a steaming, boiling sea from which only Lichis had emerged.

The Golden Dragon had not come unwounded from that encounter. For a long time he had disappeared from the sight of men, though before that disappearance, he had visited the adepts who had given Ironnose being. Of them and their castle was left thereafter only a few fire-scorched stones and an evil aura that had kept even the most hardy of adventurers out of that particular part of the land to this very day.

"So we seek out Lichis," Ingrge remarked. "What if he will have no word with us?"

"You"—Hystaspes swung to Naile—"that creature of yours." Now he pointed the staff at the pseudo-dragon curled against the berserker's thick neck just above the edging of his mail, as if it had turned into a torque, no longer a living thing. Its eyes were mere slits showing between scaled lids. And its jaws were now firmly closed upon that spear-pointed tongue. "In that creature you may have a key to Lichis. They are of one blood, though near as far apart in line as a snake and Lichis himself. However—" Now he shrugged and tossed the ivory rod behind him, not watching, as it landed neatly on a tabletop. "I have told you all I can."

"We shall need provisions, mounts." Yevele's thumb again caressed her lower lip.

Hystaspes's lips twisted. Perhaps the resulting grimace served the wizard for a smile of superiority.

The elf nodded, briskly. "We can take nothing from you, save that which you have laid upon us—the geas." With that part of Power Lore born into his kind, he appeared to perceive more than the rest of their company.

"All I might give would bear the scent of wizardry." Hystaspes agreed.

"So be it." Milo held out his hand and looked down at the bracelet. "It would seem that it is now time for us to test the worth of these and see how well they can serve us." He did not try to turn any of the dice manually. Instead he stared at them, seeking to channel all his thought into one command. Once, in that other time and world, he had thrown just such dice for a similar purpose.

The sparks which marked their value began to glow. He did not try to command any set sum from such dealing, only sent a wordless order to produce the largest amount the dice might yield.

Dice spun—glowed. As they became again immobile, a drawstring money bag lay at the swordsman's feet. For a moment or two the strangeness, the fact that he had been able to command the dice by thought alone, possessed him. Then he went down on one knee, jerked loose a knotting of strings, to turn out on the floor what luck had provided. Here was a mixture of coins, much the same as any fighter might possess by normal means. There were five gold pieces from the Great Kingdom, bearing the high-nosed, haughty faces of two recent kings; some cross-shaped trading tokens from the Land of the Holy Lords struck out in copper but still well able to pass freely in Greyhawk where so many kinds of men, dwarves, elves, and others traveled. In addition he saw a dozen of those silver, half-moon circles coined in Faraaz, and two of the mother-of-pearl disks incised with the fierce head of a sea-serpent which came from the island Duchy of Maritiz.

Yevele, having witnessed his luck, was the next to concentrate on her own bracelet, producing another such purse. The coins varied, but Milo thought that approximately in value they added up to the same amount as his own effort had procured. Now the others became busy. It was Deav Dyne, who through his training as a clerk was best able to judge the rightful value of unusual pieces (Gulth had two hexagons of gold bearing a flaming torch in high relief—these Milo could not identify at all) and tallied their combined wealth.

"I would say," he said slowly, after he had separated the pieces into piles, counted and examined those that were more uncommon, "we have enough, if we bargain skillfully. Mounts can be gotten at the market in the foreign quarter. Our provisions—perhaps best value is found at the Sign of the Pea Stalk. We should separate and buy discreetly. Milo and—shall we say you, Ingrge, and Naile—to the horse dealers, for with you lies more knowledge of what we need. Gulth must have his own supplies—" He looked to the lizardman. "Have you an idea where to go?"

The snouted head moved assent as the long clawed hand picked up coins Deav Dyne swept in his direction, putting them back into the pouch that had appeared before him. Unlike those of the others it was not leather, but fashioned of a fish that had been dried, its head removed, and a dull metal cap put in its place.

Milo hesitated. He was armed well enough—a sword, his shield, a belt knife with a long and dangerous blade. But he thought of a crossbow. And how about spells? Surely they had a right to throw also for those?

When he made his suggestion Deav Dyne nodded. "For myself, I am permitted nothing more than the knife of my calling. But for the rest of you—"

Again Milo was the first to try. He concentrated on the bracelet, striving to bring to the fore of his mind a picture of the crossbow, together with a quota of bolts. However, the dice did not fire with life and spin. And, one after another, saving only

Wymarc and Deav Dyne—the bard apparently already satisfied with what he had—they tried, to gain nothing.

The wizard once more favored them with grimace of a smile. "Perhaps you had already equipped yourselves by chance before *that* summoned you," he remarked. "I would not waste more time. By daylight it would be well for you to be out of Grey-hawk. We do not know what watch Chaos may have kept on this tower tonight, nor the relation of the Dark Ones to our enemy."

"Our enemy—" snorted Naile, swinging around to turn his back on the wizard with a certain measure of scorn. "Men under a geas have one enemy already, wizard. You have made us *your* weapons. I would take care, weapons have been known to turn against those who use them." He strode toward the door without looking back. His mighty shoulders, with the boar helm riding above, expressed more than his words. Naile Fangtooth was plainly beset by such a temper as made his kind deadly enemies.

4

Out of Greyhawk

PARTS OF GREYHAWK NEVER SLEPT. THE GREAT MARKET OF THE merchants, edging both the Thieves' Quarter and the foreign section of the free city, was bright with the flares of torches and oil lanterns. People moved about the stalls, a steady din of voices arose. You could bargain here for a bundle of noisome rags, or for a jewel that once topped some forgotten king's crown of state. To Greyhawk came the adventurers of the world. The successful brought things that they showed only behind the dropped curtains of certain booths. The prospective buyers could be human, elvish, dwarf—even orc or other followers of Chaos as well as of Law. In a free city the balance stood straight-lined between Dark and Light.

There were guards who threaded among the narrow lanes of the stalls. But quarrels were settled steel to steel. In those they did not meddle, save to make sure riot did not spring full born from some scuffle. A wayfarer here depended upon his own weapons and wits, not upon any aid from those guardians of the city.

Naile muttered to himself in such a low whisper that the words did not reach Milo through the subdued night roar of the market. Perhaps the swordsman would not have understood them even if he had heard, for to a berserker the tongues of beasts were as open as the communication of humankind. They had gone but a short way into the garish, well-lighted lines of booths, when Fangtooth stopped, waiting for the other two, swordsman and elf, to come up with him.

The pseudo-dragon still lay, perhaps sleeping, curled about the massive lift of his throat. Under his ornately crowned helmet his own face was flushed, and Milo could sense the heat of anger still building in the other. As yet that emotion was under iron control. Should it burst the dam, Naile might well embroil them all in quick battle, picking some quarrel with a stranger to vent his rage against the wizard.

"Do you smell it?" The berserker's voice sounded thick, as if his words must fight hard to win through that strangling anger. Under the rim of his helmet, his eyes swept back and forth, not to touch upon either of his companions, but rather as if in that crowd he sought to pick out some one his axe could bring down.

There were smells in plenty here, mainly strong, and more than half-bordering on the foul. Ingrge's head was up, his nostrils expanded. The elf did not look about him. Rather he tested the steamy air as if he might separate one odor from all the rest, identify it, lay it aside, and try again.

To Milo the slight warning came last. Perhaps because he had been too caught up in the constant flow of the scene about them. His sense for such was, of course, far less acute than that of either of his companions. But now he felt the same uneasiness that had ridden him in the inn, as well as along the way the wizard's guide had taken them. Somewhere in this crowd there existed interest in—them!

"Chaos," Ingrge said, and then qualified that identification. "With something else. It is clouded."

Naile snorted. "It is of the Dark and it watches," he returned. "While we walk under a geas! I wish I had that damn wizard's throat between my two hands, to alter the shape of it—for good! It would be an act of impiety to foul my good skull-splitter"—he touched his axe where it hung at his belt—"with his thin and treacherous blood!"

"We are watched." Milo did not address that as a question to either elf or berserker. "But will it come to more than watching?" He surveyed the crowd, now not seeking the identity of the foe (for unless the enemy made an overt move he knew his skills could not detect the source of danger) but rather noting those places where they might set their backs to a solid wall and face a rush—should that materialize.

"Not here—or yet." There was firm confidence in Ingrge's answer.

Seconds later the berserker grunted an assent to that.

"The sooner that we ride out of this trap of a city," he added, "the better." His hand rose and he touched with a gentleness that seemed totally alien to his shaggy and brutal strength the head of the pseudo-dragon. "I do not like cities and this one stinks!"

The elf was already on the move, threading a way through the market crowd. Milo had an odd feeling that the three of them were nearly invisible. No hawker or merchant called them to look at his wares, though those about them were sometimes even seized by the cloak edges and urged to view this or that marvel so cheaply offered that no man could resist.

He would have liked to linger by one display where the seller did not raise his head from his work as they pushed past. Here were dwarf-wrought arms—swords, throwing knives, daggers, a mace or two—one large enough even to fit into Naile's paw. The owner stood with his back to them, his forge fire glowing so that the heat reached out as his hammer rose and fell in a steady beat upon metal.

If what Hystaspes had said was true (and Milo felt it was), even if he had carried twice as heavy a purse as that which the bracelet had brought him, he could not have spent a single piece at this booth. Those rules, dim and befogged, but still available in part to his memory, told Milo that he was already equipped with all that fate—or the sorcery of this world—would allow him.

"This way." Just a little past the temptation of the sword-smith's forge, the elf took a sharp turn to the right. After passing between two more rows of booths (these smaller, less imposing than those they had earlier viewed), they came upon the far side of the market itself where there were no more stalls, rather rope-walled corrals and picket lines and some cages set as a final wall. Here the live merchandise was on view.

Camels, kneeling and complaining (placed by market regulation as far from the horse lines as possible), puffed out their foul breath at passersby. Beyond them was a small flock of oriths, their mighty wings pinned tight up their feathered sides by well-secured restraints. Oriths were hard to handle and must be eternally watched. They just might answer to an elf's commands but for a man to attempt to ride these winged steeds was folly.

There were hounds, their leashes made fast to stakes driven deeply into the ground. They raised snarling lips as Naile passed, but backed away and whimpered when he looked upon them. A berserker was not their meat for the hunt, their instinct told them that.

Some feline squalled from a cage but kept to the shadows so only a dusky outline of its crouched body could be seen. It was onto the horses that Milo, now in the lead, moved eagerly. He began at once to study the mounts, which ranged from a trained war steed, its front hooves already shod with knife-edged battle shoes, to ponies, whose ungroomed hides were matted with mountain weeds and who rolled their eyes and tried to strike out with their hind feet at anyone reckless enough to approach them unwarily. To tame such as those was a thankless task.

Milo wanted the war horse. It was seldom one of those came into the open marketplace for sale, unless some engagement had left an army or a raiding party so bloated with loot they could afford to cull captured animals. But for such an expedition as faced them now—no, that fighting-trained stallion could not last in a long wilderness or mountain haul. They were not even ridden, except in a battle, their owners having them led instead, while riding a smaller breed until the trumpets sounded.

Resolutely Milo turned from that prize, began eyeing critically the animals on a middle line. Beyond was thick-legged, uncurried farm stock—some already worn out and useless, better put out of their misery by a quick knock on the head. But on the outer line he spotted about a dozen ragged-maned, dark grays. Steppe mounts! What chance had brought those here? They were raider-taken probably, passed along across the more civilized country because they had long-use stamina. They would be considered too light for battle except for irregular calvary and too hard to control for farm service. Add to a careful choice from among them some of the better-tempered of the mountain ponies for packing. . . .

Ingrge had already moved forward toward the very horses Milo had marked down. Elves had the animal speech, he could be communicating with the Steppe mounts.

"Those?" Naile asked. There was a dubious note in his voice and Milo could understand why. In the first place the berserker was the heaviest of their company. There was need for a powerful horse, one used to the weight of a large man, to carry him. Second, allied though such as Naile were, through their own particular magic, to the animal worlds, some horses would not accept a were near them at all—going mad at the scent which no human nose could pick up until the Change—but which seemed always present to animals.

There was swift movement at Naile's throat. The pseudo-dragon uncoiled with one lithe snap of her slender body. Spreading her nearly transparent wings, she took off before the berserker could reach her with a futile grab, to sail with lazy wing beats through the air toward the horses. She hovered over and between two of the largest. Suddenly, as she had taken to flight, she folded wings again, settling on the back of the mount to the right.

The horse flung up its head with a loud whinny, jerked against the lead rope and turned its head as far as it could, endeavoring to see what had alighted. Then the mount stood still, its wild roll of eye stopped.

Naile laughed. "Afreeta has chosen for me."

"Your servant, sirs. You would deal?"

Ingrge passed among the horses, slipping his hand lightly

over haunch, down shoulder. Those he touched nickered. Milo
looked to the speaker.

The man wore leather, with an over-jacket of spotted black
and white pony hide. A piece of his long, tousled hair flopped
down on his forehead like a ragged forelock, and his teeth
showed large and yellowish in a wide grin.

"Prime stock, warriors." He waved a hand at the horse lines.

"Steppe stock," Milo answered neutrally. "Trained to a single
rider's call—"

"True enough," the trader conceded without losing his grin.
"Brought them out of Geofp. There was a manhood raid over
the border. But the young whelps who tried that had no luck.
Forstyn of Narm was doing a little raiding himself along the
same general strip. He got some Nomad skins to cover his stor-
age chests and I got the horses. Forstyn heard the old tales,
too—'bout a Steppe man and his chosen horse. But you've an
elf with you. Never heard tell that any one of them couldn't get
into the skulls of anything that flew, crawled, or trotted, always
supposing they were both of the Law. And the Nomads—they
give lip service to Thera. Not since I heard tell has the Maned
Lady ever bowed head to Chaos."

"How much?" Milo came directly to the point.

"For how many, warrior?"

An old trick of the mountain country, again a memory that
was only a part of him, took over Milo's mind. There were seven
of them, a dozen of the Steppe mounts. For two reasons it
might be well to buy them all. First, it might possibly confuse
that watcher or watchers, whom they all sensed, about the even-
tual size of their own party, though that, Milo decided, was

probably a very faint hope. Second, once out in the wilderness, the loss of a single horse might mean disaster unless they had a spare, for none of them, even the cleric who wore no armor, could be mounted on a pack pony.

"For the lot," Ingrge, back from his inspection, returned quietly.

Naile stood to one side, it would seem that they were willing to leave this bargaining to the swordsman.

"Well, now . . ." There was a slyness near open malice in the dealer's never-ending grin. "These are seasoned stock, good for open country traveling. Also, this is a town where there are a-many who come to outfit a company—"

"Steppe stock," repeated Milo stolidly. "Are all your buyers then elves—or dwarves, perhaps?"

The trader laughed. "Now you think you got me by the short hairs with that one, warrior? Maybe, just maybe. I say ten gold for each; you won't find their like this far east. Of course, if you plan to take them west—I'd go south of the Steppes. The Nomads are blood feuding and won't take kindly to see a kinsman's mount carrying a stranger."

"Five pieces," Milo returned. "You've just talked yourself into another ill thought with that warning, trader. The Nomads may have already taken sword oath for the trail. Keep these and they could be willing to hunt the new riders down to meet Thera's Maidens."

"Not even sword oaths are going to bring them to Greyhawk, warrior. And I don't propose to ride west again neither. But you've a tongue on you, that's true. Say eight pieces and I am out of purse in this bargain."

In the end Milo got the mounts for six. He had a suspicion

that he could have beaten that price lower, but the uneasiness that was growing in him (until it was all he could do to not look over one shoulder or the other for that watcher or watchers) weakened his resolve to prolong the bargaining. He also bought five pack ponies, those Ingrge methodically selected, counting upon the elf's skill to control that wilder, mountain-born stock.

Naile's Afreeta returned to sit on his shoulder, crouching there alert, her bright beads of eyes missing nothing. Ingrge had indicated his choices and Milo was counting out a mixture of strange coins to equal the price of their purchases, when the elf's head swung left, his large green eyes set aslant in his narrow face opened wide, his nostrils flared.

There had been other men, among them a dwarf and a cloaked figure, whose species was well concealed by his body covering, drifting or walking with purpose through the animal lines. Neither Ingrge nor Naile had shown any interest in these. Now a man approached them directly, and it was plain he was seeking them in particular.

His clothing was made of supple leather, not unlike that worn by the elf. However, it was not dyed green or dull gray-brown such as became a ranger. Rather it was a shiny, glossy black from the high boots on his feet to a tunic which had a flaring collar standing up so high about the back of his head as to form a dark frame for his weather-browned face. Over those garments (which reminded Milo of the shiny body casing of some great insect and might have been fashioned from such, as far as the swordsman knew) he wore a single splash of vivid color—a sleeveless thigh-length vest, clipped together slightly below the throat with a round metal clasp, and made of short, plushy fur of a bright orange-red. A skull cap of the same fur covered the crown of his head, allowing to escape below its edging oily strands of hair as dark as his jerkin.

There was an odd cast to his features, something that hinted of mixed blood, perhaps of the elven kind. Yet his eyes were not green but dark, and he wore a half-smile as he came up to them with the assurance of one certain of welcome.

Milo glanced at Ingrge. The elf presented his usual impassive countenance. Yet even without the use of any recognition spell, Milo knew (just as he had been able to sense the watchful waiting that had dogged them through the market) that this new-comer did not have elf favor.

The stranger sketched a gesture of peace—his open palm out. He wore weapons—a blade, which was not quite as long as a fighting sword nor short as a dagger, but somewhat between the two, and a throwing axe, both sheathed at his belt. Coiled on his right hip, showing only when his vest swung open a bit, was something else, a long-lashed whip.

"Greetings, warriors." He spoke with an assurance that matched his open approach. "I am Helagret, one who deals in rare beasts . . ."

He paused as if awaiting introductions from the three in turn. Naile grunted, his big hand had gone up to stroke Afreeta, and there was certainly no welcome in his lowering scowl.

Milo tried to sharpen his sense of uneasiness. Was this their watcher come at last into the open? He glanced at Ingrge. From a fleeting change of expression on the elf's face, the swordsman knew that this was not the enemy.

The swordsman dropped the last counted piece into the trader's grimy palm. Then he answered, since it would seem that the others left reply to him.

"Master Helagret, we have no interest in aught here save mounts."

"True," the other nodded. "But I have an interest in what your comrade has, swordsman." He raised his hand, gauntleted in the same glossy leather, to point a forefinger at Afreeta. "I am gathering specimens for my Lord Fon-du-Ling of Faraaz. He would have in his out-garden the rarest of beasts. Already"— now he waved towards the line of cages—"I have managed to find a griff-cat, a prim lizard, even a white sand serpent. Warrior." Now he addressed Naile directly. "To my Lord, money is nothing. A year ago he found the hidden Temple of Tung and all its once-locked treasures are under his hand. I am empowered to draw upon them to secure any rarity. What say you to a sword of seven spells, a never-fail shield, a necklet of lyra gems such as not even the king of the Great Kingdom can hope to hold, a—"

Naile's hand swept from cupping Afreeta to the haft of his axe. The pseudo-dragon flickered out of sight within the collar of his boar-skin cape.

"I say, trapper of beasts, shut your mouth, lest you find steel renders it unshutable for all time!" There were red sparks in the berserker's deep-set eyes. His own lips pulled back, showing fangs that had given him his war name.

Helagret laughed lightly. "Temper your wrath, were-man. I shall not try to wrest your treasure from you. But since this is my mission there lies no great harm in my asking, does there?" His tone was faintly derisive, suggesting that Naile was too closely akin to those bristled and tusked beasts, whose fury he could share, to be treated with on the true human level.

"If you will not deal with me on one matter, warriors, perhaps we can bargain on another. I must transport my animals to Faraaz. Unfortunately, my hired guards indulged too deeply in the wine the Two Harpies is so noted for. They now rest in the Strangers' Tower where they have been given a period to reflect upon their sin of indulgence. I have cart men, but they are no fighters. If your passage is westward I can pay fighting wages until we reach the castle of my lord. Then he may well be so delighted with what I bring him that he will be even more openhanded."

He smiled, looking from one to another of them. Milo smiled in return. What game the other might be playing he had no guess, but no one could possibly be as stupid as this beast trainer presented himself. Though Ingrge had passed the sign that this was not their watcher, yet the very way he attempted to force himself upon their company was out of character.

"We do not ride to Faraaz." Milo tried to make his voice as guilelessly open as the other's.

Helagret shrugged. "It is a pity, warriors. My lord has had unusual luck in two of his recent quests. It is said that he is preparing for a third. He has been given a certain map—a southward map . . ."

"I wish him luck for the third time then," Milo returned. "We go our own way, Master Trainer. As for your guards—there are those in plenty here who need fill for their purses and are willing to take sword oath for the road."

"A pity," Helagret shook his head. "It is in my mind we might have dealt well together, swordsman. You may discover that pushing away the open hand of Fortune may bring ill in return."

"You threaten—beast chaser?" Naile took a step forward.

"Threaten? Why should I threaten? What have you to fear

from me?" Helagret moved both his hands wide apart as if dis-
playing that he was not in the least challenging a short-
tempered berserker.

"What indeed." Ingrge spoke for the first time. "Man of
Hither Hill."

For the first time that smile was lost. There was a spark for a
second in the dark eyes—quickly gone. Then Helagret nodded
as one who has solved a problem.

"I am not ashamed of my blood, elf. Are you of yours?" Yet he
did not wait for any answer but turned abruptly and moved
away.

Milo felt a faint warmth at his wrist and looked hurriedly to
the bracelet. It was glowing a little but none of the dice swung.
An exclamation from Naile brought his attention elsewhere. Ingrge held out his hand. There was a bright blaze of color and he
was staring hard at the dice which were awhirl for him, using,
Milo guessed, every fraction of control he could summon to aid
in their spin.

The glow flashed off, yet Ingrge continued for a long moment
to watch the dice. Then he raised his head.

"The half-blood did not succeed—in so much is the wizard
right."

"What was it?" Milo was irritated at his own ignorance. It
was plain that Ingrge had encountered, or perhaps they had all
faced, some unknown danger. But the nature of it—

"He keeps company." Naile had softened his usual heavy
growl to a mutter. From under the shadow of his helm he stared
across the length of the market. There the circle of flares and
lanterns gave a wavering light—perhaps not enough to betray
some lurkers. But the burnished shine of Helagret's clothing

had caught a gleam. He must have retreated very quickly to reach that distance. He stood before another now, who wore a loose robe that was nearly the same color as the drab shadows. Since the hood of the robe was pulled well forward, he was only a half visible form.

"He speaks with a druid," Ingrge returned. "As to what he tried—he is of the half-blood from the Hither Hills." The cold note of repudiation in that was plain enough to hear. "He sought to lay upon us a sending—perhaps to bend us to his will. But not even the full-blood can work such alone. There must be a uniting of power. Therefore, this Helagret merely furnished a channel through which some other power was meant to flow. He established eye contact, voice contact—then he struck!"

"What power? The druid?" hazarded Milo. "Chaos?"

Slowly Ingrge shook his head. "The druid—perhaps. But this was no spelling I have ever heard of. He carried on him some talisman which had its own smell, and that was alien. However," once more the elf regarded his wrist and the bracelet on it, "alien though that was—I could defeat it. Yes, the wizard was right. Brothers"—there was more animation in his usually calm voice than Milo had heard before—"we must hone and sharpen our minds, even as the dwarf swordsmiths hone and sharpen their best of blades. For it is that power which may be both shield and weapon to us, past our present knowing!"

"Well enough," Naile said. He clenched his huge fist. "With my hand—thus—or with the axe or with the likeness I have won to"—now he raised his fist to strike lightly against his helmet with its crowning boar—"there are few who dare face me. Yet to use the mind so—that will be a new experience."

"They have gone." Milo had been watching Helagret and the

shadowy figure beyond him. "I think it is well we follow their example and that speedily."

Ingrge was already moving toward the horses the trader had loosed from his picket lines, stringing halter ropes together. It was apparent that the elf was of a similar mind to the swordsman.

5

Ring of Forgotten Power

DAWN WAS MORE THAN JUST A STRIP OF COLD GRAY ACROSS THE sky when they at last rode out of the maingate southward. Milo, knowing that wastes and mountains lay before them, had bought light saddles that were hardly more than pads equipped with loop stirrups and various straps to which were attached their small bundles of personal clothing and the water bottles needed in the wilderness. He had questioned Ingrge carefully as to the countryside before them, though the elf, for all his woodcraft and ranger-scout training, admitted freely that what little he knew of the territory came through the rumors and accounts of others. Once they were across the river and into the plains of Koeland he must depend largely upon his own special senses.

They strung out the extra mounts on leads, Weymarc volunteering to manage them, while their four pack ponies snorted and whinnied in usual complaint under burdens that had been most carefully divided among them.

Having splashed across at an upper ford, they angled due south. Mainly because, now very easy to see, stood the dark stronghold of the Wizard Kyark apart from Greyhawk's walls, a place all men with their wits about them knew well to avoid. As long as it was in sight Deav Dyne told his prayer beads with energy and even the elf avoided any glance in that direction.

Not all their company were at ease mounted. Gulth did not croak out any complaint, but Ingrge had had to work his own magic on the steadiest of the mounts before the lizardman could climb on the back of the sweating, fearful horse. Once in the saddle he dropped behind, since the other horses were plainly upset by his close presence. Perhaps that was an advantage, for the ponies crowded head of him, keeping close to the human members of the company.

Milo wondered a little at the past of the scale-skinned fighter. They had all been caught in or by a game. But why had the role of a scale-skinned fighter been chosen by the one who had become Gulth? If Gulth had not been shackled to them by the common factor of the bracelet, Milo would have questioned that he belonged in their party at all.

Naile Fangtooth made no secret of the fact he both loathed and mistrusted the entirely alien fighter. He rode as far from Gulth as he could, pushing up to the fore but a short distance behind Ingrge. None of the other oddly assorted adventurers made any attempt to address the lizardman except when it was absolutely necessary.

Gray-brown grass of the plain grew tall enough to brush their shins as they rode. Milo did not like crossing this open land where there was not even a clump of trees or taller brush to offer shelter. By the Fore-Teeth of Gar—they could be plainly marked from the walls of Greyhawk itself did any with some interest in them stand there now.

Without thinking he said as much aloud.

"I wonder—"

Startled out of his apprehensive thoughts, the swordsman turned his head. Yevele was not looking at him. Rather her gaze slanted back toward the river and the rise of the city beyond it.

"We ride geas-bound," she commented, now meeting his eyes. "What would it profit the wizard if we were picked up before we were even one day on our journey? Look there, swordsman—"

Her fingers were as brown as her face, but the fore one was abnormally long, and that now pointed to the grass a short distance beyond their line of march.

Milo was startled, angry with himself at his own inattention. To go into this land without one's senses always alert was worse than folly and to have betrayed his carelessness shamed him.

For what he saw proved that Yevele might well be right in her opinion that they were not naked to the sight of an enemy. The grass (which was so tough that it stung if one pulled at it) quivered along a narrow line that exactly matched their own line of march.

He did not doubt that quiver marked a slight distortion, only visible to them in this fashion, masking *them* from aught but a counter-spell strong enough to break it.

"It cannot last too long, of course," the battlemaid continued. "I know not how strong a power-worker this Hystaspes may be—but if he can hold our cover so until we gain the tributary of the Vold, the land beyond is less of an open plain."

"You have ridden this way before?" Milo asked. If the girl knew these southwest lands why had she not said so? Here, they depended upon Ingrge as a guide when the elf had admitted he used instinct alone.

She did not answer him directly, only asked a question of her own.

"You have heard of the Rieving of Keo the Less?"

For a moment he sought a way into his memory which had so many strange things hidden in it. Then he drew a deep breath. The answer to the name she spoke—it was something out of the darkness that ever lurked menacingly at the heels of any who swore by Law. It was treachery so black that it blotted the dark pages of Chaos's own accounting—death so hideous a man might retch out his guts if he thought too long upon it.

"But that—"

"Lies years behind us, yes." Her voice was as even and controlled as Ingrge's ever was. "And why should such as I think upon that horror? I am one born to the sword way, you know the practice of the Northern Bands. Those who ride under the Unicorn have a choice after their thirtieth year—they may then wish a union, to become a mother, if the High Horned Lady favors an enlargement of her followers. Then the child, being always a girl, is trained from birth in the ways of the One Clan of her heritage.

"My mother, having put aside the Unicorn and followed her will of union, became swordmistress and teacher. But our clan fell into hard days and there were three harvests that were too thin to support any but the old and the very young. Therefore, those who were still hearty of arm, who could ride and fight— and my mother was a Valkyrie"—Yevele's head lifted proudly—

"took council together. They were, by custom, unable to join the companies again, but they had such skills as were valuable in the open market wherein sword and spear may be lawfully sold. My clan—there were twenty-five who swore leadership to my mother. They came then to Greyhawk to bargain—settling for their pay in advance so that they might send back to the clan hold enough to keep life in the bodies of those they cherished. Then, under my mother's command, they took service with Regor of Var—

Milo's memory flinched away from what that name summoned.

"Those who were lucky died," Yevele continued dispassionately. "My mother was not lucky. When they were through with her. . . . But no matter. I have settled two debts for that and the settlement hangs at the Moon shrine of the clan. I took blood oath when I took the sword of a full clan sister. That is why I do not ride with any Band, but am a Seeker."

"And why you came to Greyhawk," he said slowly. "But you are not—not Yevele—remember? We are entrapped in others . . ."

She shook her head slowly. "I am Yevele—who I might have been in that other time and place which the wizard summoned for us to look upon does not matter. Do you not feel this also, swordsman?" For the first time she turned to look squarely into his eyes. "I am Yevele, and all that Yevele is and was is now in command. Unless this Hystaspes plays some tricks with us again, that is how it will remain. He has laid a geas on us and that I cannot break. But when this venture lies behind us—if it ever will—then my blood oath will bind me once more. Two of-

ferings I have made to the Horned Lady—there are two more to
follow—if I live."

He was chilled. That about her which had attracted his notice had been but a veil hiding an iced inner part at which no
man could ever warm himself. His wonder at their first entrap-
ment grew. Was it some quirk of their own original characters
that had determined the roles they now assumed?

Desperately he tried now to remember the Game. Only it
was so blank in his mind that he wondered, for a moment of
chill, if all Hystaspes's story had been illusion and lies. But the
band on his wrist remained: that encirclement of jewel-pointed
dice was proof in part of the wizard's story.

They spoke no more. In fact, there was very little sound from
the whole party, merely the thud of hooves and, now and then,
a sneeze or cough as some of the chaff from the crushed, dead
grass arose to tickle nose or throat.

The sky was filled with a sullen haze to veil the sun. When
they were well out on the plains Milo called a halt. They fed
their animals from handsful of grain but did not let them graze,
watering each from liquid poured into their helmets, before
they ate the tough bread of which a man must chew a mouthful
a long time before he swallowed. Gulth brought out of a pouch
of his own, some small, hard-dried fish and ground them into
swallowable powder with his formidable array of fangs.

Milo noted that those lines in the grass had halted with
them, even joined before and behind the massing of their company, as if to enclose them in a wall. He pointed them out. Both
the elf and Deav Dyne nodded.

"Illusion," Ingrge said indifferently.

But the cleric had another term. "Magic. Which means we cannot tell how long it will provide us with cover." He repeated Yevele's warning.

"The river has some cover." The girl brushed crumbs of bread carefully into one palm, cupping them there preparatory to finishing off her meal. "There are rocks there—"

Ingrge turned his head sharply, his slanted eyes searching her face, as if he demanded access to her thought. Yevele licked up the crumbs, got to her feet. Her expression was as stolid and remote as Ingrge's own.

"No, comrade elf," she said, answering the question he had not asked, "this road has not been mine before. But I have good reason to know it. My kin died in the Rieving of Keo the Less."

Ingrge's narrow, long-fingered hand moved in a swift gesture. The heads of the other three men turned quickly in her direction. It was Naile who spoke. "That was a vile business."

Deav Dyne muttered over his beads and Wymarc nodded emphatic agreement to the berserker's comment. If Gulth knew of what they spoke he gave no sign, his reptilian eyes were nearly closed. However, a moment later his croaking voice jerked them all out of terrible memory.

"The spell fades." He waved a clawed forefinger at those lines.

Ingrge agreed. "There is always a time and distance limit on such. We had better ride on—I do not like this open land." Nor would he, for those of his race preferred woods and heights.

Gulth was right. That line in the grass was different. Now it flickered in and out, being sometimes clearly visible, sometimes so faint Milo thought it vanished altogether. They mounted in some speed and headed on.

The drabness of the sky overhead, the faded grass underfoot, mingled into a single hue. None spoke, though they stepped up their pace, since to reach water by nightfall was important. There were flattened water skins on one of the pack ponies. They had thought it better not to fill them in Greyhawk. Such action would have informed any watcher that they headed into the plains. They depended upon the fact that Keoland did have three tributaries of size feeding the main stream, which finally angled north to become a mighty river.

As they went now Milo kept an eye on the line of distortion. When it at last winked out he felt far more naked and uneasy than he had in the streets of Greyhawk itself.

Ingrge reined in.

"There is water, not too far ahead. They can smell it even as I—" He indicated the horses and ponies that were pushing forward eagerly. "But water in such a barren land is a lodestone for all life. Advance slowly while I scout ahead."

There was some difficulty in restraining the animals. However, they slowed as best they could as Ingrge loosed his own mount in a gallop.

The elf knew very well what he was about. He found them shelter snug against detection. Visual detection, that was, for one could never be sure if someone of the Power were screening or casting about to pick up intimations of life. It was beyond the skill of all save a near adept to hide from such discovery.

Rocks by the river had been something of an understatement. Here the stream, shrunken in this season before the coming of the late fall rains, had its bed some distance below the surface of the plain. There was a lot of tough brush and small trees to mark its length, and, at the point where Ingrge had led them, something else. Water running, wild, in some previous season, had bitten out a large section of the bank below a projection of rock, forming a cave, open-ended to be sure, but piling up brush would suffice to mask that.

In such a place they might dare a fire. The thought of that normal and satisfying heat and light somehow was soothing to the uneasiness Milo was sure they all shared, though they had not discussed it. They watered the animals, after stripping them of their saddles and packs, and put them on picket ropes, to graze the scanty grass along the shrunken lip of the stream.

Milo, Naile, Yevele, and Wymarc used their swords to chop brush, bringing the larger pieces to form a wall against the night, shorter lengths to provide them with some bedding, though the soil and sand beneath that overhang were not too unyielding.

Deav Dyne busied himself with arranging the armloads they dragged in, while Ingrge had prowled off on foot, heading along the water, both his nose and his eyes alert. He had found them this temporary camp, but his instincts to prepare against surprise must be satisfied.

Gulth squatted in the water, prying up small stones, his talons stabbing downward now and then to transfer a wriggling catch to his mouth. Milo, watching, schooled himself against revulsion. If the lizardman could so feed himself, it would mean that there would be lesser inroads on the provisions later. But he wanted no closer glimpse of what the other was catching.

They did have their fire, a small one, fed by dried drift, near smokeless. Though the lizardman appeared to have little liking for it, (or perhaps for closer company with these of human and elfin kind) the rest sat in a half-circle near it.

They would have a night guard, but as yet it was only twilight and they need not set up such a patrol. Milo stretched out his hands to the flames. It was not that he was really chilled in body—it was the strangeness of this all that gnawed upon him now. Though Milo Jagon had camped in a like manner many times before, the vestiges of that other memory returned to haunt him.

"Swordsman!"

He was startled out of his thoughts by the urgency of that voice—so much so his hand went to his sword hilt as he quickly glanced up, expecting to see some enemy that had crept past the elf by some trick.

Only it was not Ingrge who had spoken. Rather Deav Dyne leaned forward, his attention centered on Milo's hands.

"Swordsman—those rings . . ."

Rings? Milo once again extended his hands into the firelight. His attention had been so centered on the bracelet and what power it might have over him (or how he might possibly bend it to his will) that he had forgotten the massive thumb rings. Apparently they were so much a part of the man he had become that he was not even aware of their weight.

One oval and cloudy, one oblong green veined with red, neither seemed to be any gem of sure price, while the settings of both were only plain bands of a very pale gold.

"What of them?" he asked.

"Where did you get them?" Deav Dyne demanded, a kind of hunger in his face. He pushed past Yevele as if he did not see her and, before Milo could move, he squatted down and seized both the swordsman's wrists in a tight grasp, raising those captive hands closer to his eyes, peering avidly first at one of the stones and then the other.

"Where did you get them?" he demanded the second time.

"I do not know—"

"Not know? How can you not know?" The cleric sounded angry.

"Do you forget who we are?" Yevele moved closer. "He is Milo Jagon, swordsman—just as you are Deav Dyne, cleric. But our memories are not complete—"

"*You* tell me what they are!" Milo's own voice rang out. "What value do they have? Is *your* memory clear on that?" He did not struggle to free himself of the cleric's grip. The rings were queer, and if they carried with them something either helpful or harmful, and this recorder and treasurer of strange knowledge knew it, the quicker he himself learned, too, the better.

"They are things of power." Deav Dyne never glanced up from his continued scrutiny of the two stones. "That much I know—even with my halved memory. This one"—he drew the hand with the green stone a fraction closer to the firelight—"do you not see something about it to remind you of another thing?"

Now Milo himself studied the stone. All he could pick out was a meaningless wandering of thread-thin lines with a pinpoint dot, near too small to distinguish with the naked eye, here and there.

"What do you see then?" He did not want to confess his own ignorance, but rather pry out what the cleric found so unusual.

"It is a map!" There was such certainty in that answer that Milo knew Deav Dyne was convinced.

"A map." Now Naile and Ingrge moved closer.

"It is too small, too confused." The berserker shook his head. But the elf, inspecting the ring closely, reached for a small stick of the drift they had piled up to feed the fire and with his other hand smoothed a patch of the earth in the best light those flames afforded. "Hold still!" he commanded. "Now, let us see—"

Looking from stone to ground and back again he put the point of his stick to the earth and there inscribed a squiggle of line or a dot. The pattern he produced showed nothing that made sense as far as Milo was concerned, but the cleric studied the drawing with deep interest.

"Yes, yes, that is it!" he cried triumphantly as Ingrge added a last dot and sat back on his heels to survey his own handiwork critically. However, nothing in that drawing awoke any spark of memory in Milo. If it had been of some value to the swordsman part of him, that particular memory was too deeply buried now.

"Nothing I've ever seen." Naile delivered his verdict first.

It was the bard who laughed.

"And, judging by the expression on our comrade's face," he nodded to Milo, "he is as baffled as you, berserker, even though he seems to be in full possession. Well, will your prayers"—now he turned to Deav Dyne—"or your scout eye," he addressed Ingrge, "provide us with an answer? As a bard I am a far wanderer, but these lines mean naught to me. Or can the battlemaiden find us an answer?"

There was a moment of silence and then all answered at once, denying any recognition. Milo twisted free from Deav Dyne's hold.

"It would seem that this is a mystery past our solving—"

"But why do you wear it?" persisted the cleric. "It is my belief that you would have neither of those on you"—he pointed to the rings—"unless there is a reason. You are a swordsman, your trade lies with weapons, perhaps one or two simple spells. But these are things of true Power—"

"Which Power?" Yevele broke in.

"Not that of Chaos." Deav Dyne made prompt answer. "Were that so, Ingrge and I, and even the skald, would sense that much."

"Well, if we have in this a map which leads nowhere," Milo shook his right thumb, "then what lies within the other?" He stuck out the other thumb with the dull and lifeless stone.

Deav Dyne shook his head. "I cannot even begin to guess. But there is one thing, swordsman. If you are willing, I can try a small prayer spell and see if thus we can learn what you carry. Things of Power are never to be disregarded. Men must go armed against them for, if they are used by the ignorant, then dire may be the result."

Milo hesitated. Maybe if he took the rings off—he had no desire to be wearing them while Deav Dyne experimented. Only, when he endeavored to slip either from its resting place he found they were as firmly fixed as the bracelet. The cleric, witnessing his efforts, did not seem surprised.

"It is even as I have thought—they are set upon you, just as the geas was set upon us all."

"Then what do I do?" Milo stared at the bands. Suddenly they had changed into visible threats. He shrank from Things of Power, which he did not in the least understand, and which, as Deav Dyne had pointed out, might even choose somehow to act, or make *him* act, by another's control.

"Do you wish me to try a Seeing?"

Milo frowned. He did not want to be the focus of any magic. But, on the other hand, if these held any danger, he needed to know as soon as possible.

"All right—" he replied with the greatest reluctance.

6

Those Who Follow—

TWILIGHT DIM DREW A DARK CURTAIN WITHOUT. NOW GULTH heaved up from his place a little behind the rest of the company. His claws settled his belt, the only clothing that he wore, more firmly about him. From it hung a sword, not of steel, which in the dankness of his homeland might speedily rust away, but a weapon far more wicked looking—a length of heavy bone into the sides of which had been inserted ripping teeth of glinting, opaline spikes. He had also a dagger nearly as long as his own forearm, more slender than the sword, sheathed in scaled skin. But his own natural armament of fang and claw were enough to make any foeman walk warily.

Now he hissed out in the common speech, "I guard."

Naile half heaved himself up as if to protest the lizardman's calm assumption of that duty. His scowl was as quick as it always was whenever he chanced to glance at Gulth. Wymarc had risen, too, his shoulder so forming a barrier before the berserker. Even though the bard was by far the slighter man, yet the move was so deftly done that Gulth had become one with the twilight before Naile could intercept him.

"Snake-skin?" Naile spat out. "He has no right to ride with real men!"

Afreeta wreathed about the berserker's throat, where her head had been tucked comfortably under his chin, swung out her snout, opened slits of eyes, and hissed. Straightway, Naile's big hand arose to scratch, with a gentleness foreign to his thick, calloused fingers, the silvery underpart of her tiny jaw.

"Gulth wears the bracelet," Milo pointed out. "It could well be also that he likes us and our company as little as you appear to care for him."

"Care for him!" exploded Naile. "Tarred with the filth of Chaos they are, most of his kind. My shield brother was dragged down and torn to pieces by such half a year gone when we ventured into the Troilan Swamps. That was a bad business and I am like never to forget the stink of it! What if he does wear the bracelet—the lizardfolk claim to be neutral, but it is well known they incline to Chaos rather than the Law."

"Perhaps," Yevele said, "they find their species do not get an open-handed reception from us. However, Milo is right—Gulth wears the bracelet. Through that he is one with us. Also the geas holds him."

"I do not like that—or him," Naile grumbled. Wymarc laughed.

"As you have made quite plain, berserker. Yet you are not wholly adverse to all of the scaled kind or you would not have Afreeta with you."

Naile's big hand covered part of the small flying reptile as if the bard had threatened her in some manner.

"That is different. Afreeta—you do not yet know how well she can be eyes, yes, and ears for any man."

"Then, if you trust her, but not Gulth," Milo suggested, "why not set her also to watch? Let the guard have a guard."

Wymarc's laugh was hearty. "Common logic well stated, comrade. I would suggest we cease to exercise our smaller fears and suspicions and let Deav Dyne get on with what he would do—the learning of what kind of force our comrade here has wedded to his hands."

Milo felt that Naile wanted to refuse. Reluctantly the berserker held out his hand and Afreeta released her hold about his throat to step upon his flattened palm, her wings already spreading and a-flutter. She took a small leap into the air, soared nearly to the roof of the rock over their heads, then was gone after Gulth.

The cleric had paid no attention to them. Instead he knelt by that same patch of earth on which Ingrge had drawn the map and was now busy emptying out the contents of the overlarge belt pouch that he wore.

He did not erase the crude markings the elf had made, but around them, using a slender wand about the length of palm and outstretched midfinger, he began to sketch runes. Though Milo found stirring in his mind knowledge of at least two written scripts, these resembled neither.

As he worked, Deav Dyne, using the dry and authoritative tone of a master trying to beat some small elements of knowledge into the heads of rather stupid and inattentive pupils, explained what he did.

"The Word of Him Who Knows—this set about an unknown, draws His attention to it. If He chooses to enlighten our ignorance, then such enlightenment is His choice alone. Now—at least this is not of Chaos, or the Word could not contain it intact, the markings would be wiped away. So—let the rings now approach the Word, swordsman!"

His command was so sharply uttered Milo obeyed without question.

He held his two thumbs in the air above those scrawls on the earth, feeling slightly foolish, yet apprehensive. Deav Dyne was certainly not a wizard, but it was well known that those who did serve their chosen gods with an undivided heart and mind could control Power, different of course from that which Hystaspes and the rest of the adepts and wizards tapped, but no less because of that difference.

Running his prayer beads through his fingers, the cleric began to chant. Like the symbols he had drawn which were without meaning to Milo, so were the words Milo was able to distinguish, slurred and affected as they were by the intonation Deav Dyne gave them. But then the ritual the cleric used might be so old that even those who recited such words to heighten their own trained power of projection and understanding did not know the original meaning either.

Having made the complete circuit of the beads on his chain, Deav Dyne slipped it back over his wrist, and picked up from where it lay by his knee the same rod with which he had drawn the patterns. Leaning forward, he touched the tip of it to the map ring.

Milo heard Yevele give a gasp. The rod took on a life of its own, spinning in Deav Dyne's hold until he nearly lost it.

Quickly he withdrew. There were drops of sweat beading his high forehead, rising on the shaven crown of his head from which his cowl had fallen.

Mastering quickly whatever emotion had struck at him, he advanced the rod a second time to touch the oval. The response this time was less startling, though the rod did quiver and jerk. Milo had expected some backlash to himself but none came. Whatever power the cleric had tapped by his ritual had reacted on him alone.

Now Deav Dyne settled back, returning the rod to his bag. Then he caught up a branch, using it to wipe away the drawing.

"Well?" Milo asked. "What do I wear then?"

There was a glazed look in Deav Dyne's eyes. "I—do—not—know—" His words came as if he spoke with great effort and only because he must force himself to utter them. "But—these are old, old. Walk with care, swordsman, while you wear them. There is nothing of evil in them—nor do they incline to the Law as I know and practice it."

"Another gift from our bracelet-bestowing friend perhaps?" Wymarc asked.

"No. If Hystaspes spoke true (and by my instincts he did) that which has brought us here is alien. These rings are of this space, but not this time. Knowledge is discovered, lost through centuries, found again. What do we know of those who built the Five Cities in the Great Kingdom? Or who worshipped once in the Fane of Wings? Do not men ever search for the treasures of these forgotten peoples? It would seem, swordsman, that this Milo Jagon, who is now you, was successful in some such questing. The ill part is that you do not know the use of what you wear. But be careful of them, I pray you."

"I would be better, I think," Milo returned, "to shed them into this fire, were I only able to get them off. But that freedom seems to be denied me." Once more he had pulled at the bands but they were as tight fixed as if they were indeed a part of his flesh.

Wymarc laughed for the third time. "Comrade, look upon the face of our friend here and see what blasphemy you have mouthed! Do you not know that to one of his calling the seeking out of ancient knowledge is necessary to maintain his very life, lest he fade away like a leaf in winter, having nothing to sharpen his wits upon? Such a puzzle is his meat and drink—"

"And what is yours, bard?" snapped Deav Dyne waspishly. "The playing with words mated to the strumming of that harp of yours? Do you claim that of any great moment in adding to the knowledge of men?"

Wymarc lost none of his easy smile. "Do not disdain the art of any man, cleric, until you are sure what it may be. But, in turn, I have another puzzle for you. What do you see in the flames, Deav Dyne?"

Milo guessed that was no idle question, rather it carried import unknown to him. The irritation that had tightened the cleric's mouth for an instant or two vanished. He turned his head, his hand once more swinging the chain of his prayer beads. Now he was staring into the fire. Ingrge, who had drawn a little apart during their delving into the mystery of the rings, came closer. It was to him that Naile addressed another question.

"What of it, ranger? You have certain powers also—this shaven addresser of gods is not alone in that."

"I do not rule fire. It is a destroyer of all that my kind holds dearest. For those of your kin, were, can flee when such destruction eats upon their homes and trails. Trees escape not . . ." He stared also at the leaping of the flames, as if they were enemies against which he had no power of arrow shot or chanted spell.

Deav Dyne continued to stare at the flames as intent as he had been moments earlier when he had attempted to use his knowledge of wand and rune.

"What—?" began Milo, at a loss. Wymarc raised a finger to his lips in warning to be silent.

"They come." Deav Dyne's tone was hardly above a mutter.

"How many?" Wymarc subdued his own voice. His smile vanished, there was an alertness about him, no kin to his usual lazy acceptance of life.

"Three—two only who can be read, for they have with them a worker of power. Him I perceive only as a blankness."

"They are of Chaos?" Wymarc asked.

A shadow of impatience crept back into the cleric's voice.

"They are of those who can be either. But I do not see any familiar dark cloaking them."

"How far behind?" Milo tried to keep his voice as low and toneless as Wymarc's. His body was tense. Their mounts along the river—Gulth—Was the lizardman a good guard?

"A day—maybe a little less—to measure the march between us. They travel light—no extra mounts."

Milo's first thought was to break camp, ride on at the best pace they could make in the dark. Then better judgment took command. Ahead lay another stretch of plain, perhaps a day's journey, if they pushed. Then came a tributary flowing north. There was a second dry march after that, before the third stream, which was the one they sought, leading as it did into the mountains, enough below Geofp so that they might avoid any brush with the fighting there.

That particular stream was born of a lake in the mountains which cupped the Sea of Dust itself. They had decided earlier that it would be their guide in among the peaks where they might or might not be able to discover Lichis's legendary lair.

But the marches from one river to the next, those were the problem. Deav Dyne blinked, passed his hand across his sweating forehead and moved away from the fire. He reached for his bottle of water newly filled from the river, took a long swallow. When he looked up again his face was gaunt and drawn.

"Once only—"

"Once only what?" Milo wanted to know.

"Once only can he scry so for us," Wymarc explained. "Perhaps it was foolish to waste . . . No, I do not believe it is wasted! Our protecting wall of illusion is exhausted. Now we know that there are those who sniff behind us, we can well take precautions."

"Three of them—seven of us," Naille stretched. "I see no problem. We have but to wait and lay a trap—"

"One of them possesses true power," the cleric reminded them. "Enough to mask himself completely. Perhaps enough to provide them all with just a screen as has encompassed us through this day."

"But he cannot draw upon that forever." Yevele spoke for the first time. "There is a limit to all but what a true adept can accomplish. Is he an adept?"

"Had he been an adept," Deav Dyne returned, "they would not need to cover the ground physically at all. And yes, the constant maintenance of any spell (especially if the worker has not all his tools close to hand, as did the wizard who drew us into this misbegotten venture) is not possible. But he will be gifted enough to smell out any ambush."

"Unless," the girl pressed on, "it takes all his concentration and strength to hold the spell of an illusion."

For the first time Naile looked at her as if he really saw her. Though he had showed antagonism toward Gulth, he had refused to notice Yevele at all. Perhaps the near-giant berserker held also a dislike for Amazon clan forces.

"How much truth in that?" he now rumbled, speaking at large as if he did not quite know to whom of their party he should best address his demand.

"It could be so," acknowledged the cleric. "To maintain a blockage illusion is a steady drain on any spell caster."

"With our illusion in turn broken, we should be easy meat," Milo pointed out, "not only for an open attack, but for some spell cast. The way before us is open country. Therefore, we must make some move to halt pursuit. Let Ingrge in the morning lead on with Deav Dyne, Wymarc, Gulth—"

"And we of the sword wait?" Yevele nodded. "There are excellent places hereabouts to set an ambush."

Milo's protest against her being a part of it was on his lips, but died away before he betrayed himself. Yevele might be a girl but she was a trained warrior, even as were he and the berserker. Though he did not deny that the other four of their party each had their own skills, he was uncertain as to how much those would matter in a business that was a well-known part of the battles he had been bred and trained to.

"Good enough," Naile responded heartily. "Tonight we shall divide the watch. I go now to relieve snake-skin—"

Milo would have objected, but the berserker had already left their improvised shelter. Ingrge raised his head as the swordsman moved to follow Naile.

"Words do not mean acts, comrade," the elf said. "There is no love for Gulth in him—but neither will he raise hand against him."

Wymarc nodded in turn. Deav Dyne seemed to have sunk into a half-exhausted sleep, huddled beyond the fire.

"We are bound." The bard tapped the bracelet on his arm. "So bound that each of us is but a part of a whole. That much I believe. That being so, we have each a strength or skill that will prove to be useful. We—"

He did not finish, for Naile had returned to the fire, his lips snarling so that the teeth which had given him his name were exposed nearly to their roots.

"The snake is gone!" His voice was a grunting roar. "He has gone to join *them!*"

"And your Afreeta?" Milo asked in return.

The berserker started. Then, holding out his hand and half turning toward the dark without, he whistled, a single, ear-piercing sound. Out of the night came the pseudo-dragon like a bolt from a crossbow. She was able to stop in midair, drop to the palm Naile extended. Her small dragon head was held high as she hissed, her tongue flickering in and out. Naile listened to that hissing. Slowly his face relaxed from a stiff mask of pure fury.

"Well?" Wymarc stooped to throw more wood on the fire, looking up over one shoulder.

He was answered, not by the berserker, but rather by a second figure coming out of the night. Gulth himself stood there. His scaled skin glistened in the firelight, and water dripped from his snout.

"In the river." Naile did not look at Gulth. "Lying in the river as if it was a bed, just his eyes above level!"

Once more Milo's memory stirred and produced a fact he was not aware a moment before he had known.

"But they have to—water—they have to have water!" The swordsman swung to the lizardman. "He rode all day in the dry. It must have been near torture for him!" He thought of the miles ahead with two more long dry patches to cover. They must think of some way of helping Gulth through that. Even as he struggled with the problem, Ingrge made a suggestion.

"We can change the line of march by this much—upriver to the main stream. We shall have Yerocunby and Faraaz facing us at the border. But the river then will lead us straight into the mountains. And it will provide us with a sure guide as well as the protection of more broken ground."

"Yerocunby, Faraaz—what frontier guards do they post?" Naile placed Afreeta back to coil about his throat.

Their united memories produced some facts or rumors, but they gained very little real information.

They decided to take Ingrge's advice and use the river for a guide as long as possible. Naile tramped out again to take the watch. Milo, wrapped in his cloak, settled for a little rest before he should take his turn at guard.

Though they had all agreed to change the direct line of their march in the morning, they had also planned to set the ambush, or at least a watch on their backtrail. To learn the nature and strength of those trailers was of the utmost importance.

Milo was aware of the aches of his body, the fact that he had been twenty-four hours, or near that, without much sleep. He shut his eyes on the fire, but could he shut his mind to all the doubts, surmises, and attempts to plan without sure authority or control? It seemed that he could—for he did not remember any more until a hand shook his shoulder lightly and he roused to find Naile on his knees beside him.

"All is well—so far," the berserker reported.

Milo got up stiffly. He had certainly not slept away all the aches. Beyond the fire to which Naile must have added fuel, for the others slept, the night looked very dark.

He pushed past Wymarc, who lay with his head half-pillowed on his bagged harp, and went out. It took some moments for the swordsman's eyes to adjust to the very dim light of a waning moon. Their mounts and the pack animals were strung out along their picket ropes a little farther north. Naile must have changed their grazing grounds so that they could obtain all the forage this small pocket in the river land could offer.

A wind whispered through the grass loud enough to reach Milo's ears. He took off his helmet and looked up into the night sky. The moon was dim, the stars visible. But he found that he could trace no constellation that he knew. Where *was* this world in relation to his own? Was the barrier between them forged of space, time, or dimension?

As he paced along the lines of the animals, trying to keep fully alert to any change in the sounds of the night itself, Milo was for the first time entirely alone. He felt a strong temptation to summon up fragments of that other memory. Perhaps that would only muddy the impressions belonging to Milo Jagon, and it was the swordsman who stood here and now and whose experience meant anything at all.

So he began to work on that Milo memory, shifting, reaching back. It was like being handed a part of a picture, the rest of it in small meaningless scraps that must be fitted into their proper places.

Milo Jagon—what was his earliest memory? If he searched the past with full concentration, could he come up with the answer to the riddle of the rings? Since Deav Dyne's discovery, he had moments of acute awareness of them, as if they weighed down his hands, sought to cripple him. But that was nonsense. Only there were so many holes in that fabric of memory that to strive to close them with anything but the vaguest of fleeting pictures was more than he could do. More than he should do, he decided at last.

Live in the present—until they had come to the end of the quest. He accepted that all Hystaspes had told them was correct. But, there again, how much *had* the wizard influenced their minds? One could not tell—not under a geas. Milo shook his head as if he could shake such thoughts out of it. To doubt so much was to weaken his own small powers as a fighting man, he knew, powers that were not founded on temple learning or on wizardry, but on the basis of his own self-confidence. That he must not do.

So, instead of trying to search out any past beyond that of his calling, he strove now to summon all he knew of the details of his craft. Since there was none here save the grazing animals to see or question, he drew both sword and dagger, exercised a drill of attack and defense which his muscles seemed to know with greater detail than his mind. He began to believe that he was a fighter of no little ability. While that did not altogether banish the uneasiness, it added to the confidence that had ebbed from the affair of the rings.

Dawn came, and with it Wymarc, to send Milo in to eat, while the bard kept a last few fleeting moments of watch. As they settled the packs and made ready to move out, Deav Dyne busied himself at the now blank ground where last night he had worked his magic. He lit a bunch of twigs that he had bound into a small faggot, and with that he beat the ground, intoning aloud as he so flailed the earth.

Wymarc returned, bearing with him newly filled saddle bottles. With a lift of eyebrow he circled about the cleric.

"May take more than that to waft away the scent of magic if they have a man of power with them," he commented dryly. "But if it is the best we can do—then do it."

The three who were to play rear guard chose their mounts— the choice being limited for Naile because of his greater bulk. He could not hope for any great burst of speed from his, only the endurance to carry his weight. Were they not pushed for time by the geas he would better have gone afoot, Milo knew, for the were-kind preferred to travel so.

As the line of march moved out, he, Yevele, and Naile waited for them to pass, moving at a much slower pace and searching with well-trained eyes for a proper setting where they might go into hiding.

7

Ambush

THEY HAD RIDDEN ON FOR AN HOUR BEFORE THEY FOUND WHAT Milo's second and stronger memory hailed as a proper place to set their trap—a place where the river banks sank and there was a thicket of trees, stunted by the plain's winds, but still barrier enough to cover them. Seven rode into the fringe of that thicket and four, with the pack train, rode out again, Ingrge in the lead.

Naile, Milo, and Yevele picketed their mounts under the roof of the trees and gave each a small ration of dried corn to keep them from striving to graze on the autumn-killed grass. The berserker waded through the season-shrunken flood to the opposite bank where there was a further edging of the growth and disappeared so well into that screen that Milo, for all his search, could not mark the other's hiding place. He and the battle-maiden picked their own points of vantage.

Waiting plucked at the nerves of a man, Milo knew that. Also, it could well be that they were engaged in a fruitless task. He did not doubt Deav Dyne's Seeing of the night before. But those who sought their party could have ventured on straightway and not upstream. Until, of course, they came across no further evidence of trail. Then they would cast back—action that would take time.

Here in the brush he and Yevele were not under the wind which carried a chilling bite. It blew from the north promising worse to come. However, there was a pale showing of sun to defy the gray clouding.

"Two men, plus one worker of some magic," Milo spoke more to himself than to the girl. In fact she, too, had withdrawn so well into the brush he had only a general idea of where she now rested.

The men would be easy enough to handle, it was the worker of magic that bothered Milo. Naile, as were and berserker, had certain spells of his own. Whether these could, even in part, counteract that dark blot Deav Dyne had read in the flames was another and graver matter. The longer they waited the more he hoped that their turn north upstream had indeed thrown the followers off their trail.

He saw a flicker of color in the air, speeding downstream. Afreeta—Naile had released the pseudo-dragon. Milo silently raged at the rash action of the beserker. Any worker of magic had only to sight the creature—or even sense it—and they would be revealed! He knew that the berserkers, because of their very nature, were impetuous, given to sudden wild attacks, and sometime unable to contain the rage they unconsciously generated. Perhaps Naile had reached that point and was delib- erately baiting the trailers into action.

Then—Milo looked down at the bracelet on his wrist. There was a warmth there, a beginning stir of dice. He tried to shut out of his mind all else but what the wizard had impressed upon them—that concentration could change the arbitrary roll of the dice. Concentrate he did. Dice spun, slowed. Milo concentrated—another turn, another—so much he did achieve, he was certain, by his efforts.

Moving with the utmost caution, the swordsman arose, drew his blade, brought his shield into place. Now he could hear sounds, clicking of hooves against the stones and gravel of the shrunken river.

Two men rode into view. They bore weapons but neither swords nor long daggers were at the ready, nor was the cross-bow, strapped to the saddle of the second, under his hand. It would seem that they had no suspicion of any danger ahead.

Two men. Where was the third—the magic worker?

Milo hoped that Naile would not attack until they learned that. However, it was Yevele who moved out. Instead of drawn steel she held in her hands a hoop woven of grass. This she raised to her mouth, blowing through it. He saw her lips shape a distinct puff. There came a shrill whistling out of the air over-head, seemingly directly above the two riders.

They halted, nor did the leader, who had been bending for-ward to mark the signs of any trail, straighten up. It was as if both men and mounts had been suddenly frozen in the same position they held at the beginning of that sound.

Milo recognized the second rider—Helagret, the beast dealer they had met in the market place in Greyhawk. His companion wore half-armor—mainly mail. His head was covered by one of those caps ending in a dangling streamer at the back, which might be speedily drawn forward and looped about the throat and lower part of the face. This suggested that his employment was not that of a fighter but rather a skulker, perhaps even a thief. The crossbow was not his only armament. At his belt hung a weapon that was neither dagger nor sword in length but between those two. That he used it skillfully Milo had no doubt.

There was a limit to the spell Yevele had pronounced, Milo knew. But though they had so immobilized two of the enemy (which was an improvement on an outright ambush), there was still that third.

Milo waited, tense and ready, for *his* answer to Yevele's action.

Afreeta was heard before she was seen—her hissing magnified. Now, with a beat of wings so fast that they could hardly be distinguished, save as a troubling of the air, she came into sight, hung so for a moment, and was gone again downstream. Milo made a quick decision. If the spell vanished, surely Naile and Yevele could between them handle the two men in plain sight. It was evident that the pseudo-dragon had located the third member of the party and was urging that she be followed to that one's hiding place.

The swordsman stepped out of concealment, saw the eyes of the two captives fasten on him, though even their expressions could not change, nor could they turn their heads to watch him. On the other side of the stream Naile appeared, his axe swinging negligently in one hand, his boar-topped helm crammed so low on his head that its shadow masked his face. He lifted a hand to Milo and then pointed downstream. Apparently the same thought had crossed his mind.

As Milo twisted and turned among the rocks and bushes, so did the berserker keep pace with him on the other side of the flood, leaving Yevele to guard the prisoners. Seemingly Naile had no doubts about her ability to do so. Had her spell-casting answered to concentration on her bracelet, thus giving it added force? Milo hoped fervently that was so.

Naile's hand went up to signal a halt. That the were possessed senses he could not himself hope to draw upon, Milo well knew. He drew back into the shadow of one of the wind-tortured trees, watching Naile, for all his bulk, melt into a pile of rocks and drift.

There was no sound of hooves this time to herald the coming of that third rider. But he was now in plain sight, almost as if he had materialized out of sand and rock. His horse was long-legged, raw-boned as if it had never had forage enough to fill its lean belly. In the skull-like head it carried droopingly downward, its eyes burned yellow in a way unlike that of any normal beast. Nor did he who rode it guide it with any reins or bit.

Seemingly it strode onward without any direction from the one crouching on its bony back.

The rider? The rusty robe of a druid, frayed to thread fringes at the hem, covered his hunched body. Even the cowl was drawn so far over the forward-poking head as to completely hide the face. Milo waited to catch the hint of corruption that no thing of the Chaos passing this close could conceal from one vowed to the Law. But the frosty air carried no stench.

Still, this was not one of Law either. Now his beast halted without raising its head, and the cowl-shadowed face turned neither right nor left. The druid's hands were hidden within the folds of the long sleeves of his shabby robe. What he might be doing with them, what spells he could so summon or control by concealed gesture alone, the swordsman could not guess. The stranger was not immobilized, save by his own will—that much

Milo knew. And he was a greater danger than any man in full armor, helpless and weaponless though he now looked.

Afreeta came into view with one of those sudden darts. Her jaws split open to their widest extent then closed upon a fold of the cowl that she ripped back and off the head of the druid, leaving his brownish, bare scalp uncovered. His face writhed into a mask of malice but he never looked upward at the now hovering pseudo-dragon, or made any move to re-cover his head.

Like all druids he seemed lost in years, flesh hanging in thin wattles on his neck, his eyes shrunken beneath tangled brows that were twice as visible on his otherwise hairless skin. His nose was oddly flattened, with wide-spaced nostrils spreading above a small mouth expressing anger in its puckered folds.

To Milo the man's utter silence and stillness was more of a menace than if he had shouted aloud some runic damnation. The swordsman was more wary than ever of what those hands might be doing beneath the wrinkles of the sleeves.

Afreeta flew in a circle about the druid's head, hissing vigorously, darting in so close now and then it would seem she planned to score that yellow-brown flesh or sink her fangs into nose or ear. Yet the fellow continued to stare downward. Nor did Milo see the least hint of change in either the direction of the eyes or the expression of the face. Such intensity could only mean that he was indeed engaged in some magic.

The pseudo-dragon apparently had no fear for herself. Perhaps she shared with her great kin their contempt for humankind. But that she harassed the druid with purpose Milo did not doubt. Perhaps, though the man showed no mark of it, his concentration on what he would do was hindered by the gadfly tactics of the small flyer.

Out of the rocks Naile arose. All one could see of the berserker's face was his square jaw and mouth. The lips of that mouth were drawn well back to expose the fangs. When he spoke there was a grunting tone to his voice, as if he hovered near that change which would take him out of the realm of humankind, into that of the four-footed werefolk.

"Carlvols. When did you crawl forth from that harpies' den you were so proud of? Or did the Mage pry you out as a man pries a mussel forth from its shell? It would seem, by the look of you, that you have lost more than your snug hole during the years since our last meeting."

Those unblinking eyes continued to hold their forward stare, but for the first time the druid moved. His head turned on his shoulder, slowly, almost as if bone and flesh were rusted and firmly set, so that to break the hold was a very difficult thing. Now, with his head turned far to the left, he bent that stare on Naile. However, he made no answer.

Naile grunted. "Lost your tongue also, dabbler in spells? It never served you too well, if I rightly remember."

Now—while his attention was fixed on Naile!

Milo leaped. He had sheathed his sword slowly, so as to make no sound. What he was about to do might well mean his life. But something within him urged his action—as if some fate worse than just death might follow if he did not try.

He gained the side of the bony horse in that one leap. His mail-mittened hand arose, almost without his actually willing it, to catch at the nearer arm of the druid. It was like clasping an iron bar as he swung his full weight to pull the arm toward him. By a surge of strength he did not know he could produce, Milo dragged apart those hidden hands, though the druid did not lose his position on the horse.

"Ahhhhh!" Now the head had swiveled about, the eyes tried to catch the swordsman's. The other hand came into view, the sleeve falling back and away. It clawed with fingers that were nearer to long-nailed talons, swooped at Milo's face, his eyes—

Between him and that awful gaze swept Afreeta. The pseudo-dragon snapped at the descending hand with a faster movement than Milo could have made. A gash appeared in the flesh, dark blood followed the line of it.

The arm Milo still held jerked and fought against him. It was as if he strove to imprison something as strong as a north-forged sword governed by a relentless will. Afreeta dove again at the other hand. For the first time the druid flinched. Not from the swordsman, but from the pseudo-dragon's attack. It was as if his will now locked on his other and smaller opponent.

In Milo's grasp the right arm went limp, so suddenly he near lost his own balance. His hands slid down the arm which was no longer crooked against the body but hung straight, sleeve-hidden hand pointing to the gravel. From that hand fell an object.

Milo set his foot on what the druid had dropped. That it was the other's weapon he had no doubt at all.

"Milo, let go!"

Just in time he caught the berserker's cry and loosed his hold. There was a kind of dark shimmer, so close that he felt the terrible chill in the air which must have been born from it. Afreeta shrieked and tumbled, to catch her foreclaws in Milo's cloak and cling to him. He stumbled back.

Where the druid and his horse had been there was, for one long moment, a patch of utter darkness, deeper than any a lightless dungeon or a moonless night could show—then nothing.

Naile splashed back across the river. Afreeta, gathering herself together, flew straight for him. Milo, recovering his senses, had gone down on one knee and was examining the ground. Had the druid pulled with him into that black nothingness what he had dropped? Or was it still to be found?

"What's to do?" The berserker loomed over Milo.

"He dropped something—here." Milo's hand darted forward at the sight of something black, dark enough in the gravel to be easily seen when he looked closely enough. Then caution intervened. He did not touch it. Who knew what power of evil magic (for it had been plainly meant to be used against them) was caught up in this thing.

The force of his foot pressure had driven it deep into the sand and fine gravel. Now he grabbed at a fragment of driftwood nearby and gingerly began to clear it. Two sweeps of the stick were enough.

It was a carving, perhaps as long as his palm had width. The thing was wrought as a stylized representation of a creature that was not demonic as far as he could judge, and yet held in it much of menace. There was a slender body, a long neck and a head no larger—almost the likeness of a snake which was more mammalian than reptile. The thing's jaws gaped as wide as could Afreeta's upon need, and small needlelike teeth appeared set within them. The eyes were mere dots, but the whole carving carried a suggestion of ferocity and fury.

"The urghaunt!" Naile's voice had lost some of its grunt. "So that was what that son of a thousand demons would bring upon us."

His axe swung down, slicing the carved thing into two pieces. As he broke it so, a puff of evil stench arose to make Milo cough. That carving had been hollow, holding within it rotting corruption.

Once again the axe fell, this time flatside, so that the two pieces broke into a scatter of black splinters, shifting down into the sand, lost except for a shred or two in the gravel.

"What is it?" Milo got to his feet. He felt unclean since first that stench had entered his nostrils. Though he drew deep breaths, he could not seem to clear his nose of its assault.

"One of Carlvols's toys." Though he had made a complete wreckage of the carving, Naile now stamped hard upon the ground where it had lain as if to hide the very last of the splinters forever.

"You knew him—"

"Well," growled the berserker. "When I was with the Mage Wogan we marched against the Pinnacle of the Toad. That was," he hesitated as if trying to recall something out of the past, "some time ago. Time does not hold steady in my mind any more. This Carlvols was not of the Fellowship of the Toad. In fact he had reason to fear them, since he had poached on their territory. He came crawling to Wogan and offered his services. His services—mind you—to an adept! Like a lacefly offering to keep company with a fire wasp!" Naile grinned sourly.

"He had not pledged himself to Chaos, but he would have to save his own dirty skin. We all knew it. We also knew what he had in his mind—the Toad Kind had their secrets and he wanted a chance to steal a few. Wogan ordered him out of our camp and he went like a hound well beaten. He dared not stand up against one so far above him in learning.

"We took the Pinnacle—that was a tricky business. Wogan saw what lay within it destroyed—giving Chaos one less stronghold in the north. What Carlvols may have scrabbled out of the ruins. . . . Anyway, this is beast magic. He summoned, or was summoning, death on four legs with that thing."

Milo was already on the back trail. They had found and somehow, between them, confounded the druid. But what if he had joined the two Yevele held. That fear sent the swordsman plunging along, no longer cautiously but running openly. He heard the pound of Naile's feet behind him. The berserker must have been struck by the same thought.

They came around a slight curve in the river to see the two prisoners still frozen on their mounts. Yevele leaned against a tall rock, her eyes fast upon the men. There was a bared sword, not a spell hoop, now in her hand. Milo thudded on. He needed only to note the tenseness of her body to realize that the spell must be about to fade.

Breathing fast he came up to the right of the mounted men, while Naile moved in from the left. Would Carlvols suddenly also wink into view, even as he had vanished, to add to the odds?

One of the frozen mounts bobbed his head and whinnied. Milo, just as he had sprung for the druid, caught at Helagret. Exerting strength, he pulled the man from his horse, dumping him to the ground, his sword out, to point at the beast tamer's throat in threat. He heard a second crashing thump and knew that Naile was dealing similarly with the other.

Helagret's eyes were still afire with the fury they had shown when he was ensorceled. Now, however, his mouth writhed into a sly parody of a smile and he made no move.

Yevele came to them, her own sword ready. "The other one?" she asked.

"For the nonce gone," Milo replied shortly. "Now, fellow, give me one reason why I should not blood this point."

Helagret's smile grew a fraction wider. "Because you cannot kill without cause, swordsman. And I have yet to give you cause."

"You've tracked us—"

"Yes," the other admitted promptly. "But for no harm. Do you smell aught of the dark forces about me or Knyshaw here? We were bound to the service of him who follows us—or did follow us. Mind bonds were laid upon us. Since mine, at least, seem to have vanished, perhaps he is tired of this play. Look at me, swordsman. My weapons are not bared. I was pressed into service since I know somewhat of this country. Knyshaw has other talents. Not magic, of course, that was only the learning of the druid."

Milo backed a step or two. "Throw your weapon," he ordered. "Throw it yonder!"

Helagret obeyed promptly enough, sitting up to do so. But Yevele was at his back, her steel near scratching his neck as he moved.

A moment later the weapon of Naile's captive also clattered out on the gravel. In spite of the cruel strength one could read in his face he apparently was willing enough to prove his helplessness.

"Why do you follow us?" Milo demanded.

The beast tamer shrugged. "Ask no such question of me. As I told you, I know something of this land. When I refused to be recruited as guide by that shave pate, he laid a journey spell on me. Already he had Kynshaw bound to him in the same manner. But he did not share with either of us the reason for our journey. We were to be used; we were no comrades of his."

Plausible enough and, Milo was sure, at least half a lie. The glare faded from Helagret's eyes. It was plain he was putting much effort into his attempt to establish innocence.

"A likely story," snorted Naile. "It will be easy to ring the truth out of you—"

"Not," Yevele spoke for the first time, "if they are indeed geas bound."

Naile peered at her from under the edge of his heavy helm.

"An excuse, battlemaid, which can cover many lies."

"Yet—" she was beginning when, out of the brush behind them, arose a neighing that held in it stark and mindless terror. The two mounts of their captives shrilled in answer, wheeled and pounded in a mad stampede across the river, running wildly as the neighs from the woods rose in a terrible crescendo of sound.

Helagret's face twisted in a terror almost as great as that of the animal.

"Give me my sword!" he demanded in a voice that rose like a matching shriek. "For the sake of the Lords of Law, give me my sword!"

Naile's head swung around. He grunted loudly and then his body itself changed. Axe fell to the ground, helm and mail imprisoned, for a moment only, another form. Then distinct in sight, a huge boar, near equalling in height the heavy horse

Naile had earlier ridden, stood pawing the gravel, shaking its head from side to side, the red eyes holding now nothing of the human in them, only a devouring rage and hate.

Milo jumped toward the woods. From the frenzied screaming of their horses, he knew whatever menace came was a threat of death. The horses must be saved. To be set afoot in this country could mean death.

He had not quite reached the line of twisted trees when the first of the attackers burst into the open. It was plainly an animal, near eight feet long, four-footed. Body, neck, and head were nearly of the same size. The black thing that he and Naile had destroyed was here in the flesh far worse than even that nasty carving had suggested.

The creature reared up on stumpy hindlegs, its head darting back and forth as might that of a snake. The were-boar charged as the thing opened a mouth that extended near the full length of its head and showed greenish fangs.

Milo caught up his shield. His patchy memory did not recognize this creature. He was dimly aware that Yevele moved in beside him, her steel as ready as his own. Their two captives had to be forgotten as a second serpentlike length of dull fur slithered out to front them.

The things were quick, and, whether or no they had any intelligence, it was plain that they were killing machines. As the were-boar charged, the first flung itself forward in a blur of movement almost too quick for the eye to register. But the boar was as fast. It avoided that spring by a quick dart to the left. One of its great tusks opened a gash along a stumpy foreleg.

Then there was no watching of that duel, for the second creature leaped, leaving the ground entirely, and landed in a shower of sand and gravel, its head shooting out toward Milo and the girl.

The thud of its strike against his shield nearly sent Milo off his feet. He choked at its fetid odor.

"Horrrue!" The battle cry of the women clans cut across the hissing of the creature. Milo thrust at that weaving head. He scored a cut across its neck, but only, he knew, by chance. He saw that Yevele was lashing out at its feet and legs as it spun and darted. The swordsman strove to land a second blow on the neck, but the thing moved so fast he dared not try, for anything now but the bigger target of the body. Then there came a warning cry. He looked around just as a third black head pushed through the thicket to his right.

"Back to back!" he managed to gasp out. Yevele, who had shouted that warning, leaped to join him. So standing they each faced one of the nightmare furies.

8

Black Death Defied

MILO SMASHED HIS SHIELD INTO THE GAPING, LONG-FANGED mask of beast fury, at the same time thrusting with his sword. Then, out of nowhere Afreeta spiraled, darting at the bleeding head as she had when harassing the druid. The urghaunt drew back on its haunches, its head swung up to watch the pseudo-dragon for an instant. Milo took advantage of that slight second or two of distraction, as he had during their struggle with the master of these things. He launched a full-armed swing at the creature's column of neck.

The steel bit, sheared halfway through flesh and bone. With a shriek the urghaunt, paying no attention to its fearful wound, launched itself again at Milo. Though the swordsman brought up his shield swiftly, the force of its body striking against his bore him back. He felt Yevele stumble as his weight slammed against her. Claws raked around the edge of the shield, caught and tore the mail covering his sword arm, pierced the leather shirt beneath, bit into his flesh with a hot agony.

But he did not lose grip of his sword. Nor had the fury of that attack wiped away the practiced tactics his body seemed to know better than his mind. Milo thrust the shield once more against that half-severed head, with strength enough to rock the creature.

In spite of pain, which at this moment seemed hardly a real part of him, he brought up his sword, cutting down at the narrow skull. The steel jarred against bone but did not stop at that barrier. He was a little amazed in one part of his mind at his success as the besmeared steel cut deeper.

Despite wounds that would have finished any beast Milo knew, the urghaunt was near to charging again. Now the swordsman's hand was slippery with blood until he feared the hilt would turn in his grip. Shield up, and down, he beat at the maimed head with crushing blows.

The body twisted. Broken-headed, blind, the thing still fought to reach him. It might not be dead but it was nearly out of the fight. Milo swung around. It had taken his full strength to play out that encounter—strength that until this very moment he had never realized he possessed. Yevele—weaponwise as she was—how could she fare?

To his surprise the battlemaid stood looking down at a second heaving body. Implanted in its elongated throat was her sword. One forepaw had been severed. From the stump sputtered dark blood to puddle in the gravel. Milo drew a deep breath of wonder. That they had won—almost he could not believe that. The raw fury radiated still by the dying creatures struck against him, as if they could still use fang and claw. He heard a heavy grunting and glanced beyond. The giant boar, its sides showing at least two blood-welling slits made by claws, nosed a pile of ripped skin.

The urghaunt Yevele had downed snapped viciously as the battlemaid cooly drew her steel free of its body. She avoided a small lunge, which sent the blood pumping faster from the wounds, and used the edge of her weapon, striking full upon the narrow head with two quick blows.

But even then the thing did not die. Nor was Milo's own opponent finished. Only the torn body the were-boar had shredded lay still. The boar trotted to the water's edge. For the first time Milo remembered their captives.

Neither man was in sight, and their weapons were gone from where they had thrown them. He swung around to look into the fringe of trees. The crossbow had vanished, still strapped to the saddle of the horse that had fled, so they need not fear any silent bolt out of cover to cut them down.

"Ware!" Milo turned swiftly at that warning.

Naile Fangtooth, not the boar, stood there once more, his axe in his hand. But his warning had been needed. The mangled thing Milo had thought in the throes of death—which *should* have been dead—was gathering its body for another spring. Axe ready, upraised, the berserker advanced a couple of strides. His weapon rose and fell twice, shearing both heads from the bodies.

As the last flew a foot or so away from the fury of that blow, Naile gave an exclamation and one hand went to his side, while Milo was aware that his sword arm now burned as if a portion of it had been held in the flames of an open fire.

"Marked you, too?" The berserker gazed at Milo's mittened hand. Blood showed in a rusty rim about the edge of that mitten. "These beasts," he kicked the head he had just parted from the body away from him, "may have some poison in them. So they are gone, eh?"

He had apparently noted the absence of their prisoners also. Yevele answered him. "To be set afoot here is no fate I would wish on any—even of Chaos."

Milo remembered the screaming of their own hidden horses which had alerted them to the attack. The three might now be faced by an ambush in the net of trees, but it would be well to find their mounts and ride.

Afreeta had been dipping and wheeling out over the water, her hissing sounding like self-congratulation at her own part in their battle. Now she came to Naile. He winced again as he raised his fist for her to perch upon, holding her near the level of his eyes. Though Milo caught no rumble of voice from the berserker he was sure the other was in communication with his small companion.

The pseudo-dragon launched from his fist, whirled upward in a spiral, and then shot off under the trees.

"If those skulking cowards plan to play some game," Naile remarked, "Afreeta will let us know. But let us now make sure that *we* are not also afoot."

Milo wiped his sword on a bush and sheathed it with his left hand. It hurt to stoop and pick up his battered shield on which most of the painted symbols had now been scratched and defaced. The fire in his arm did not abate, and he found that his fingers were numb. He worked his right hand into the front of his belt to keep the arm as immobile as he could, for the slightest movement made the flame-pain worse.

Grimly he set his thought on something else, using a trick he had learned when he had marched with the Adepts of Nem, that pain could be set aside by a man concentrating on other things. How much they could depend upon the pseudo-dragon's scouting he was not sure. But Naile's complete confidence, and what he himself had seen this day when she had flown with intelligence and shrewdness to aid in their battles, was reassuring.

They cut through the trees to where they had left their mounts, only to face what Milo had feared from the first moment he had heard those screams. A sick taste rose in his mouth as he saw the mangled bodies. The urghaunts had not lingered at killing, but the mauling of unfortunate horses had been coldly complete. Not even their gear could be sorted out of that mess.

The fate Yevele had not wished even on a sworn enemy was now theirs also. They were afoot in territory where there was no refuge, and how far ahead their comrades rode they could not even guess. Yevele gave one level-eyed glance at what lay there. There was a pinched line about her mouth and she turned her head quickly.

But Naile approached more closely, while Milo leaned against the trunk of a tree and fought his battle against admitting pain into his mind. The berserker gave a snort of disgust.

"Nothing of the supplies left," he commented. "We are lucky there is the river. Now we had best be on the move. There are scavengers who can scent such feasts."

Milo only half heard him. Along the river, yes. It was to be the guide of their party north and at least they would not go without water. Water! For a moment the fire in his arm seemed to touch his throat. He wanted—needed—water.

"What if"—he forced the words out—"there were more than three of those things?"

"If there had been we would already know it," returned Naile. He ran his fingertips, with an odd gesture as if he feared to really touch, down his side. "They do not hunt singly. And, since the druid's summoner is ground to dust, he cannot call them down upon us again."

Milo stood away from his tree. "Back to the river then." He tried to get the right note of purpose into his voice, but it was a struggle. Naile's suggestion that the claws of those black devils might be poisoned ate into his mind. He had taken wounds in plenty—with scars on his body to prove it—but he could not recall any pain as steady and consuming as this before. Perhaps washing the gash out with cold water would give some relief.

Twice he stumbled and might have fallen. Then a hand slipped under his arm, took his shield and tossed it to Naile who caught it in one fist as if it weighed nothing. Yevele drew Milo's arm across her own mailed shoulder, withstanding his short struggle to free himself. His sight grew hazy with each faltering step and in the end he yielded to her will.

He did not remember reaching the river, though he must have done so on his own two feet. Cold, fighting the heat of his wound, made him aware that his mail, his leather, and his linen undershirt, had been stripped away and Yevele was dripping water on a gash along his arm from which the blood oozed in congealing drops. So small a gash—yet this pain, the lightness of his head. Poison?

Did Milo say that word aloud? He did not know. Yevele leaned down, raised his arm, held it firm while she sucked along that slash and spat, her smeared lips shaping no distaste for what she did. Then Naile, his great hairy body bare to the waist, gashes longer than that which broke Milo's skin visible near his ribs, loomed into the swordman's limited field of vision.

The berserker held his hands before him, cupped, water

dripping from the fingers. Kneeling beside the girl he offered what he so held. With no outward sign of aversion, she plucked out of the berserker's hold a wriggling yellow thing, hardly thicker than a bow cord. This she brought to Milo's arm, holding it steady until it gripped tight upon the bleeding wound. Three more such she applied before settling the arm and the things that sucked the dark blood by his side. Then she set about doing the same for Naile, though it looked as if his skin was not so deeply cut after all, for there were only two or three patches of drying blood. Perhaps the boar's hide that Naile had worn during his change was even better than man-fashioned mail for defense.

Milo lay still and tried not to look upon his arm, or what fed there, draining his blood, their slimy lengths of bodies growing thicker. There was a shimmer in the air and Afreeta hung once more above them, planing down to settle her claws in the thick mat of hair that extended even upon the berserker's shoulder. Her long beaked head dipped and lifted as she hissed like a pot on the boil.

"They are fools—" Milo heard Naile's words from a kind of dream. "Not all men make their own choices. It may be that their master will have some use for them again, enough to see them out of the wilderness. But to take to the plain without food or water—" Naile shook his head and then spoke to Yevele. "Enough, girl. Those draw-mouths are a-plenty to do the work."

He had five of the yellow things mouth-clamped to his wounds. Turning to the stream he tossed those he still held in his hands back into the water. Then he approached Milo and leaned over, watching closely the wrigglers the swordsman did not dare to look upon lest he disgrace himself by spewing forth whatever remained in his stomach.

"Ah—" Naile sat back on his heels. "See you that now?" he demanded of Yevele.

Milo was unable to resist the impulse to look, too.

The bodies of the wrigglers had thickened to double their original size. But one suddenly loosed its mouth hold and fell to the gravel where it moved feebly. It was joined moments later by a second that also went inert after a space of three or four breaths. The other two remained feeding.

Naile watched and then gave an order. "Use your snap-light, comrade. They would suck a man dry were they left. But their brethren have taken the poison, the wound is clean."

Yevele brought from her belt pouch a small metal rod and snapped down a lever on its side. The small spark of flame which answered touched the suckers one by one. They loosed, fell, and shriveled. Naile examined his own busy feeders.

Three followed the example of the drinkers of Milo's poison and fell away. At the berserker's orders, the battlemaid disposed of the rest.

Milo became aware that, though he felt weak and tired, the burning he had tried so hard to combat was gone. Yevele slit his shirt and bound it over the wound, having first crushed some leaves she went into the edge of the wood to find, soaking them before placing them directly on the skin.

"Deav Dyne will have a healing spell," she commented. "With that you will forget within a day that you have been hurt."

Deav Dyne was not here, Milo wanted to comment, though he found himself somehow unable to fit the words together, he was so tired. They were without mounts, perhaps lost in this land. Now. . . . Then the questions slid out of his mind, or into such deep pockets they could be forgotten, and he himself was in a darkness where nothing at all mattered.

He awoke out of the remnants of a dream that bothered him, for it seemed that there was a trace of some message which still impressed a shadow on his mind. Yet it drifted from him even as he tried vainly to remember. He heard a whinny—and awoke fully. The horses! But he had seen those slain. . . .

A face hung above him—familiar. He strove to put a name to it.

"Wymarc?"

"Just so. Drink this, comrade."

Milo's head was lifted, a pannikin held to his lips. He swallowed. The liquid was hot, near as hot as had been the torment in his arm. But, as its warmth spread through him, Milo felt his strength fast returning. He sat up, away from the supporting arm of the bard.

There were horses right enough—he could see them over Wymarc's shoulder—fastened to the fringe trees.

"How—" He was willing to lick the interior of the pannikin to gather the last of that reviving brew.

"Deav Dyne did another seeing having been able to renew his energy. I came back with mounts." Wymarc did not even wait for him to finish his question. "He sent the elixer too. Comrade, it is well that now we mount and ride."

Though most of his shirt was now bandaged about his wound (his arm stiff and sore but with none of the burning pain he had earlier felt), Milo was able with the bard's help to pull on once again the leather undergarment, even take the weight of mail. They were alone and Milo, seeing that his sword was once more in sheath, his battered shield ready to be hung from the saddle, looked to Wymarc for enlightenment.

"Yevele—Naile?" He still had odd spells of detachment, almost drowsiness, as if he could not or had not completely thrown off the effects of the poison.

"Have gone on—we shall catch up. The old boar," Wymarc's face crinkled in what might be an admiring grin, "is stouter than we, comrade. He rode as if hot for another fight. But the river is a sure guide and we must hurry for there lies a choice ahead."

Milo was ashamed of his own weakness, determined that the bard need not nurse him along. Once mounted he found that his head did clear, even though he was haunted by the vague impression of something of importance he had forgotten.

"What choice?" he asked as they trotted along the riverbank.

"There are watchers on the frontier. It would seem that Yerocunby and perhaps even Faraaz is astir. Though who they watch for—" Wymarc shrugged. "Yet it is not wise to let ourselves be seen."

Milo could accept that. The disappearance of the druid came to him in vivid recall. Magic could meddle with the minds of unshielded men—make friends or the innocent into enemies to be repulsed.

"Ingrge urges we go back to the plains to the north. Deav Dyne has rigged a protection for the scaled one—a cloak wet down with water—so he can stand the dryness of such traveling. We have filled the drinking sacks also. Ingrge leaves certain guide marks to take us west while once more he scouts ahead. He swears that once among the mountains we shall be safer. But then there will be forests, and to the elven kind forests are what stout defense walls are to us."

They caught up with Yevele and Naile before night and took shelter in the fringe forest. The battlemaid came to Milo, examined his arm where the claw slash had already closed, and rewound the bandage saying, "There is no sign of the poison. Tomorrow you should be able to use it better. We have indeed been favored by the Horned Lady thus far."

She sat cross-legged, looking down now at the bracelet on her wrist.

"In a way, the wizard's suggestion works. When I laid the spell upon those skulkers, I thought on these." She touched the dice with the tip of that overlong forefinger. "And it is true—of that I am sure—they moved farther by my will. Thus the spell held the longer."

"You cannot use that one again," Milo reminded her.

"Yes, it is a pity—that was a good spell. But I am no follower of magic, nor a priestess of the Horned Lady, that more of the Great Art be mine. I do not like," she now looked at him and there was a frown line between her wide-set eyes, "this druid who can vanish in a puff of smoke. There was nothing of the art in the two I held—only their own cunning strength. But he whom you fronted is a greater danger than near a hundred of their kind could be. Still Naile says he was not of Chaos, when he knew him of old, rather one of those who went from side to side in battle, striving to choose the stronger lord to favor. What lord has he found, if it be not one of the Dark?"

"Perhaps that—or the one we seek," Milo returned as he laced up his leather jerkin once again.

He saw her shiver, and she moved a little closer to their small fire. Though he did not believe what chilled her came from the outside, but rather lay within.

"I have ridden with the Free Companies," she said. "And you know what quest I followed alone when this wizard swept us up to do his will. No one can lose fear, but it must be mastered and controlled as one controls a horse with bit and bridle. I have heard the clan victory chants—and know"—her face was somber and set—"of their defeats. We have gone up, sword out, arrow to bowstring, against many of the creatures of Chaos. But this is something else."

Now she pulled her riding cloak closer about her, as if the chill grew. "What do you think we shall find at the end of this blind riding, swordsman? Hystaspes said it was not of Chaos. I believe he thought it could master even Chaos—the Black Adepts and all who are bound to their service. This being true, how can we prevail?"

"Perhaps because in a manner we are linked to this alien thing," Milo answered slowly. His fingers ran along the smooth band of the bracelet. "We may be this stranger's tools, even as the wizard said."

The girl shook her head. "I am under only one geas—that set by Hystaspes. We would know if another weighted upon us."

"—Up by dawn—" Naile came close to the fire with his heavy tread. Once more Afreeta lay, a necklet, about his throat, only her eyes showing she was a living thing. Wymarc had come with him to open a bag of provisions. They shared out a portion of its contents, then drew lots for the night watch.

Once more Milo paced and looked up at stars he did not know. He tried not to think, only to loosen his senses, to pick up from the world about him any hint that they were spied upon, or perhaps about to be beleaguered by the unknown. That they had defeated the druid and that which he had summoned once was no promise that they could be successful a second time.

Dawn skies were still gray when they rode on at a steady trot. It was close to noon when Wymarc halted, pointing to a rock leaning against another on the far side of the river.

"We ford here. There is the first of the guides as Ingrge promised us."

There had been little talk among them that morning; perhaps each in his or her own mind, thought Milo, was weighing all that had happened to them, trying to foresee what might lie ahead. The compulsion of the geas set upon them never lessened.

Another day they rode with only intervals of rest for their horses. Milo learned fast to watch for the twist of grass knotted together which pointed their way onward. One of them at each such find dismounted to loose the knot, smoothing out as best they could the marking of their way.

On the third day, close to evening, even though they had not dared to push their horses too much, they came to the second tributary of the border river. A camp awaited them there, where the cleric and Gulth had pulled brush to make a half shelter. The clouds had broken earlier in the afternoon to let down a steady drizzle of rain, penetrating in its cold, but there was no fire for them.

Gulth lay in the open, moisture streaming from his skin. He watched as they rode up and picketed their horses, but he gave not so much as a grunt of welcome as they pressed past him into the shelter.

Deav Dyne sat cross-legged there, his hands busy with his prayer beads, his eyes closed in concentration. Respecting that

concentration they did not break silence even among themselves.

Milo had drawn his sword during their day's ride and used
his arm over and over again, determined that he would be able
to fight and soon. The wound still was bandaged, and there was
an angry red scar as if indeed fire had burnt his flesh. But he
was content that his muscles obeyed him, and the soreness his
actions left could be easily ignored.

They had settled down, sharing out food, when Deav Dyne
opened his eyes. He gave them no formal welcome.

"The elf has gone on. He seeks the mountains as a man dying
of thirst would seek water. But his trail we can follow. It is in his
mind that he can find some clue to the dwelling of Lichis." His
voice kept to a level tone as if he gave a report. "He has gone—
but—"

For a long moment he was silent. Something made Milo look
away from him to the opening through which they had crawled.
Gulth shouldered his way in. But it was not the lizardman the
swordsman was looking for. Milo did not know what he
sought—still there was something.

"We light no more fires. That feeds *them*," the cleric continued. "They must have a measure of light to manifest themselves. We must deny them that."

"Who are 'they'?" growled Naile. He, too, slewed around to
look without.

"The shadows," returned Deav Dyne promptly. "Only they
are more than shadows, though even my prayers for enlightenment and my scrying cannot tell me what manner of manifestation they really are. If there is no light they are hardly to be seen

and, I believe, so weak they cannot work any harm. They came yesterday after Ingrge had ridden forward. But they are no elven work, nor have I any knowledge of such beings. Now they gather with the dark—and wait."

9

Harp Magic

THEY WATCHED, NOW ALERTED, AS THE TWILIGHT FADED. MILO noted patches of dark that were certainly not born from any tree or bush, but lay in pools, as if ready to entrap a man. Always, if you stared directly at them, they rested quiescent. But if you turned your head you caught, from the corner of an eye, stealthy movement, or so it would seem.

"These are of Chaos," Deav Dyne continued. "But since they take shape in no real substance—as yet—perhaps they are but spies. However, the stench of evil lies in them." His nostrils expanded. Now Milo caught, too, that smell of faint corruption which those who gave allegiance to the Dark always emitted.

The cleric arose. From the bosom of his robe he brought forth a small vial carved of stone, overlaid with runes in high relief. He went to the mounts Wymarc and Milo had ridden, and taking the stopper from the bottle, he wet the tip of his right forefinger with what it contained.

With this wetted finger he drew invisible runes on the horses' foreheads and haunches. When he returned he sprinkled a few drops across the entrance to their cramped camp.

"Holy water—from the Great Shrine." He gave explanation. "Such as those may spy upon us. But we need not fear their attempting more—not while they are out there and we are here."

Naile grunted. "These are your spells, priest, and you have confidence in them. But I have no liking for what I cannot turn axe or tusk against."

Deav Dyne shrugged. "The shadows have no weight. If you could put axe against them—then they would be something else. Now, tell me how you fared—more of this druid who set a calling spell . . ."

He held his hands cupped about his prayer string, not looking at any of them, remaining tense and listening as each in turn told his or her part of the story. When they had done, he made no comment. In fact they had brought out supplies and were eating when he, not noting the share Yevele had laid near his knee, spoke. "A tamer of beasts, an adventurer who may be of the Thieves Guild, and one who can summon—You know this druid?" It was too dark now to see much, but they knew he asked that in the direction of Naile.

"I know of him. He lurked about when the Mage Wogan led us to the finding of the Toad's Pinnacle. Wogan would have no dealings with him, and he sniveled like a white-blooded coward when the mage sent him out of our camp. Since then he seems to have gained some courage—or else his magics are the greater."

"Never underestimate one who has the summoning power," commented the cleric.

"We destroyed what he used to bring the urghaunts upon us," Milo pointed out. "Is it not true that a spell once used, unless it can be fed from another source, will not answer again?"

"So we have believed," Deav Dyne assented. "But now we deal with a thing—or a personality—that is alien. What tricks its servants may be trained in we cannot tell."

They set no watch that night, for the cleric assured them that, with the holy water sign upon them, their mounts would not wander, nor could anything come upon them without a warning that would alert him.

There were no shadows in the morning. However, as the day lengthened into afternoon, all of the party were aware that the flitting, near-invisible things again both trailed and walled them in. By twilight they reached the next tributary of the northern river. In the half-light they could see a mountain range silhouetted against the western horizon.

"Running water." Deav Dyne looked down at the stream. "Now we shall see what manner of thing these splotches of dark may be. We shall cross—"

The girl interrupted him. "You mean because some evils cannot cross running water? I have heard that said, but is it the truth?"

"It is the truth. Now let us push to the other side and test it on our followers."

Ingrge had left a stone marker by what must be the shallow part. The pack ponies had to be driven on and the water came well up their shaggy legs. Their own mounts picked a way cautiously, advancing as if they mistrusted the footing. Once they were across, Deav Dyne swung around, and the others followed his example, to look back at the shore they had just quitted.

There were distinct blots of murk there right enough, no clean shadows, but something of the Dark able to mimic such. These separate parts flowed together, pooling on the sand. And then—it flapped up!

Milo heard the battlemaid's breath hiss between her lips. That hiss was answered with far more strength by Afreeta. Their horses snorted, fought for freedom.

The black thing flapped as might a banner in a heavy wind—save there was no wind. It was well off the ground now, rising vertically. Once aloft, it made to dart after them, spreading an even stronger stench of evil.

But though it stretched out over the sand and gravel that bordered the water, it could not thrust the long tongue it now formed far enough to reach them. That tongue flailed the air, beat against an unseeable wall.

"It cannot pass water," Deav Dyne observed with quiet satisfaction. "Therefore it is but a very inferior servant."

"Maybe it can't pass water," Wymarc broke in. "But what of that?"

He pointed north. Milo's horse was rearing and plunging. For a moment or two his attention was all to controlling the frightened animal. Then he had a chance to glance in the direction the bard had indicated.

A twin to that which still strove to reach them befouled the air, flapping along. But apparently that way of progress was difficult for it to maintain. Even as the swordsman caught sight of it, the mass ceased its flying and settled groundward.

It broke apart the instant it touched the earth, small patches seeping away like filthy water from an overturned, rotting tub. The light was good enough for them to watch this dispersal of the creature—if it were a single creature able to loose itself into parts. Though the shadow bits moved, they did not turn toward their party, as Milo fully expected. Rather, like flattened slugs, they set a path parallel to the line of march but some distance away.

Naile spat at the ground beyond his horse's shoulder. "It goes its own way." he commented. "Perhaps it is rightly wary." He looked to the cleric. "What say you, priest? Do we hunt it?"

Deav Dyne had been leaning forward in his light saddle watching the flopping of the new set of shadows as they strung out.

"It is bold—"

Milo caught the inference of that. "What does such boldness mean?"

The cleric shook his head. "What can I say about any of Chaos's servants? If a man does not guard well against even the most simple appearing of such, he is three times a fool."

"Let us test it then." Before Deav Dyne could protest the berserker launched into the air the pseudo-dragon, who circled his head and then shot with the speed of a well-loosed arrow toward the nearest of the moving blobs. Having reached a position above it, Afreeta hovered, her supple neck arching downward, her jaws open as if she meant to dive straight into the thing and do battle.

The blob of darkness on the ground puddled, halting its advance. Toward it hastened another to join with it, then a third. From the center of that uniting there arose a tendril of darkness like the tentacles of a sea monster. But Afreeta was not to be so caught. She spiraled upward, keeping just above that arm of black. Other parts of the shadow-creature poured toward the site. As they watched, these, too, joined with the first and the reaching whip grew longer, higher.

"So," commented Naile, "it would do battle."

Deav Dyne, who had kept his attention on the scene, his eyes narrowed with speculation, now swung his bead string in his hand. Milo, suddenly thinking that perhaps they did have something to give them warning of possible attack, glanced downward at the bracelet about his wrist. He was somehow certain that if this dark thing meant them harm, the bracelet would come to life. Yet it had not.

The cleric slid his beads back, cupping them in his hand. "Call back Afreeta, warrior. This thing is a spy and not a fighter. But whether it can summon that which *will* do battle, I cannot tell."

"Let it watch us, since it would seem we have no real choice in the matter," cut in the bard. "But let us also seek the mountains and speedily. Ingrge has knowledge of safe places thereabouts where there are defenses against Chaos—very old but known to his own people."

So they rode on, while the shadow bits kept pace with them. Their hands were ever close to their weapons, and Naile kept Afreeta loose and flying. Now and again she fluttered down to ride upon the berserker's shoulder for a short distance, hissing into his ear as if reporting. But if she had anything of importance to say, Naile did not share it with the others.

Milo kept closing and unclosing his hand that had been so weak after the wound. His fingers could grip now with all their old vigor on the sword hilt when he put them to the test. There was a small ache beginning in his shoulders, as his tenseness grew, and he continually searched the ground ahead for signs of danger. That these shadows which spied on them could summon some greater menace was only plain logic.

The pack ponies were no longer reluctant, dragging back on their lead ropes. Rather they crowded up until they trotted along between the riders, sometimes snorting uneasily, although they never swung their heads to watch the shadows. Perhaps it was the stench of ancient evil, which a rising wind brought, that spurred them so.

Again the riders found the trail markings the elf had set. To-day they made no attempt to erase them. It was enough that they were companied by these representatives of Chaos. There was no longer reason to hope they might conceal their passing.

Twice they halted to water and rest the horses and to eat. The moisture of Gulth's cloak, dried out in the wind, had to be renewed from one of the water bags. As usual the lizardman made no comment. He rode ungracefully, for his kind did not take to any mounts except some scaled things one found in the Seven Swamps, which could not be used far away from those mudholes. His eyes, set so high above his snouted lower face, never even turned toward the shadow, Milo noted. It was as if the amphiban alien was concentrating all his strength of will and mind upon another matter.

The land began to rise. Now the grass thinned, the ground was broken here and there by shrubs and standing stones that were like pillars and seemed unnatural, as if they had been set so for some reason, save that their setting followed no pattern.

Milo, studying how they dotted the way before them, was mindful of something else. He did not need to see the shadows suddenly surge forward to understand what might menace their party here.

"'Ware the stones!"

"Yes," Deav Dyne made answer. "They are shadow bait. See—"

The shadows slipped ahead and dropped out of sight, though the pools they formed now must lie hidden about those pillars. Naile, who had taken the lead, plainly refusing to ride close to Gulth, did not even nod in reply. Rather he wove a zigzag way for them, keeping as far from each of the stones and the things that might lurk about them as he could. It was not easy to choose a way keeping them on their general course and yet avoiding close proximity to the standing stones.

So, as twilight began once more to close in, thus rendering more dangerous the route before them, they needs must slow from a steady trot to a walk. The animals of their company resisted and sullenly fought that curbing. Trees showed ahead, not the twisted stunted ones that had formed the thickets along the rivers, but tall standing ones. They too might give shelter to the enemy. Milo had not seen any movement of shadows since they had disappeared among the stones. He glanced now and then at his wrist. The bracelet showed no life. Was it true that it could warn?

Wymarc broke the silence.

"We are losing our guard."

"How do you—" the swordsman began sharply, his tense weariness riding his voice.

"Use your nose, man," returned Wymarc. "Or has it held the smell of evil so long that it reports falsely?"

Milo drew a deep breath. At first he could not be sure, then he was certain. The wind still blew in the same direction, from the north. But the taint it had carried earlier was indeed less strong. Instead there came a trace of the clean mountain air, the scent of pine.

The cleric faced his mount around.

"Be ready!" he warned.

They had nearly reached the end of the place of standing stones. The pack ponies, breathing laboredly, trotted on. Gulth, for the first time in many hours, cried aloud, in croaking words they did not know.

Milo edged his own mount around, the horse fighting his control.

From behind some of the stones stepped figures as solidly black as the shadows, but now standing tall. They were man-shaped if you counted the limbs that raised their bodies from the ground, the two arm appendages that each held high and wide, as if they were about to rush to embrace the travelers.

On Milo's wrist the bracelet came to life. Feverishly he fought to control the spin. But the shadow men were so alien to all he had known that what he saw interfered with his concentration. He knew without any words from his companions that this was the attack toward which the dark unknown had been building.

The shadow men glided toward them, even as their former substance had flowed across the earth. Milo did not reach for his sword. He knew within himself that against such as these the sharpest steel, even an enchanted blade, could not deliver any telling blow.

There came a trilling of sound. At first Milo thought it issued from the enemy, yet there was something in the sound that strengthened his courage, instead of increasing his doubts.

Wymarc had unbagged his harp. Now, as he swept his fingers back and forth across the strings, their mounts stood rock still. Music—against *those*?

The freshness of the air was once more overlaid with the stench of evil. Shadow men drew close—and before them spread not only the rotten scent, but also a cold, deep enough to strike a man as might the full breath of a blizzard.

Wymarc's chords rose higher and higher on the scale. It seemed to Milo that the shadows slowed. This music hurt his ears, rang in his head. He wanted to shut it out with his hands, but that terrible cold held him in thrall.

He could no longer really hear—yet Wymarc still swept the strings of the harp. Yevele cried out, swayed in her saddle. There was no sound, only pain within Milo's head, cutting out all else.

The swordsman's eyes blurred. Was this attack the work of the shadows, or what Wymarc wrought with his harp? For the bard continued to go through the motions of playing, even though there was nothing now to be heard.

Shudders ran through Milo's body in a rhythm matching the sweep of fingers across the strings. The shadows had halted—stood facing the riders only a little more than a sword length from Wymarc. The bard's hand moved faster and faster—or did it only seem so? Milo was sure of nothing save the pain beating in his head, passing downward through his body.

Then—

The shadows shivered—visibly. He was sure he saw that. They wavered back as their bodies shimmered, began to lose the man form, dripped groundward bit by bit as might melting candles near the heat of an open fire. They stumbled on stumps of feet, trailing lines of oozing matter behind them as they strove to reach again the shelter of the stones. Wymarc played on.

Now there were no manlike bodies, only once more dark pools that heaved in a losing battle against what the bard had launched. Those pools flowed, joined. A single manifestation half arose. It formed no quasi-human body—rather suggested some monstrous shape. A toad head lifted for a moment, but could not hold, dissolving back into the mass. Yet the shadow thing continued to struggle, bringing forth a tentacle here—a taloned foot there. Then the heaving ceased. The pool of dark lay quiescent.

Wymarc lifted his hand from the harp strings. The pulsation of pain eased in his listeners. Milo heard Naile's voice.

"Well done, songsmith! And how long will *that* spell hold? Or is the thing dead?"

"Do not grant me too much power, comrade. Like any spell, this has its limitations. We had better ride." He was slipping the harp into its bag. Once more their horses stirred.

Without having to rein their mounts, they turned toward the ridge beyond and began to move up it. There was a track to follow here, faint, as if it had been some seasons since it had been in use. One of Ingrge's markers pointed them into it. Up and up they went, the clean air washing from them the last of malaise brought on by the confrontation with the shadows.

As they had reached the top of the ridge, Ingrge appeared. He had rounded up the pack ponies who had gone before. Now he said to Wymarc, "You have been busy, bard. 'The Song of Herckon' is not for playing by just any hand."

"To each his own magic, ranger. This is my kind." There was a halting in Wymarc's reply, as if what he had done had drawn out of him much of his energy.

"I have found an Old Place," Ingrge said. "In it our magic is still firm. Nothing of Chaos—or, even, of Law—dare enter there unless made free to it by one of elven blood. You can all lie snug tonight without watch or warder."

He led the party along the ridge to a second and steeper climb beyond. Here the trees stood taller, closed in. How long they rode Milo could not tell. He only knew that weariness rode pillion behind him, gripping him tightly.

Once more stones arose, not grim and gray, like age-darkened bones as the others lingered in his memory. These were set edge to edge, forming a wall that opened from the path. They were cloaked in the green velvet of moss, a moss that was patterned here and there by outcrops of small red cups, or brilliant, orange-headed, pin-sized growths.

As they passed between those rocks—which stretched out on either hand to form a continuous wall—there came a lift of spirit for the riders. The sound of the horses' shoes was muffled by another carpet of moss, and straight beyond them, was what Milo took first to be a mound overgrown with small bushes. Then he saw that it was a single tree whose leafed branches (the leaves as green and full as if the season were spring and not the beginning of autumn) grew downward to touch the ground.

Ingrge swept aside a mass of trailing vine, which formed the door cover, and ushered them in, leaving them to explore while he went to loose the ponies from their loads, their horses from the saddles.

In the center stood a mighty trunk of such girth as two men

might well conceal themselves behind. Hanging from the underside of the drooping branches that formed the inner shell of this forest house were globes shaped like fruit, but which glowed to give light.

Moss again was the carpet, a very soft and thick one. Around the limb wall were wide ledges, also moss grown, each long enough to provide a bed. Most and best of all was the feeling of peace that seeped into one's weary body, Milo thought. He had spent nights in many places. But never had he been greeted by such a lifting of the heart and soothing of the spirit as wrapped about him in this elven stronghold. Weariness flowed away, yet he was content to seek one of those ledges, settle himself upon it, put off his helm, and let the forest life sink into him, renewing strength and spirit.

They had eaten and were lounging drowsy and content when Ingrge spoke to Wymarc.

"You have shown us one magic, bard. But I do not think that is the limit of what you carry. Can you play 'The Song of Far Wings'?"

Wymarc's hand went out to touch the harp bag which he kept ever within reach.

"I can. But to what purpose, ranger?"

"When we climb to the West Pass," Ingrge returned, "we must have a guide beyond if we seek Lichis. He has the will and power to hide himself from both men and elf; we cannot find him without some aid. It has been many years since any have hunted him. But he will feel our thoughts and strengthen his guard-spell unless we come to him by some way he has left unmarked, a way the feathered ones know. Then, once discovering the way"—the elf turned now to Naile—"it would be well for you, berserker, to loose that small one." He pointed to Afreeta. "Of the same blood she is, and she can carry our plea to Lichis. He is old, and long ago he swore he would have no more of any of us. But he might be interested enough to allow us to him—if we have an advocate of his species."

"Well enough," Naile agreed. Afreeta, as if she understood all the elf had said and approved of her own role to come, bobbed her head twice, then turned to hiss gently into Naile's ear—his boar-helm being laid aside, leaving in view for the first time thick braids of hair coiled and pinned to add protection for his skull.

10

The Domain of Lichis

THEY STOOD IN A SHARP CUT OF A PASS. HERE THE AIR WAS THIN, very cold. Snow had drifted down to cloak the heights that walled them in. The edge of frost in the air that flowed about them was so cutting that they had tied over their faces any manner of scarf or strip torn from extra clothing to keep out what they could of the cold.

Horses drooped, feet spraddled, their limbs shivering from the effort of the last part of the climb. The mountain had been nearly like a ladder, so they had come up it at a crawling pace—dismounted riders leading the animals.

Frost gathered upon their improvised wind masks, streaked their cloaks. For the last of the upward effort Milo had wondered if Gulth would survive. The lizardman had grown more and more sluggish in his movements, though he had never voiced any complaint. In fact his silence made Milo sometimes speculate as to what thoughts passed through that alien mind. Now Gulth squatted against a small fall of rock, his ice encrusted cloak about him, his head huddled down under the hood until only the tip of his snout protruded.

Ingrge turned to Wymarc, laying his mittened hand upon the arm of the bard, gesturing with the other to the harp in its bag. It was plain what he wanted of Wymarc. But in this wind and cold—surely the bard dare not expose his fingers to summon up his own brand of magic.

Yet it would seem that Wymarc was agreeing. He caught the end of his furred mitten between his teeth to yank it off his hand. The bared fingers he inserted under the edge of the binding about his chin and mouth, perhaps to warm them with the scanty breath these heights left in a man's lungs.

With the other hand he worried off the bag protecting his skald's harp. Then he settled down on the same fall of rock behind which Gulth crowded. Milo moved forward as quickly as he could, taking up a position to shield the harper with his body as much as he might. Seeing what he would do Deav Dyne, Yevele and Naile speedily came to aid in making that windbreak. Only the elf stood alone, staring out into the swirl of clouds that screened what lay on the western side of the pass.

For several long moments Wymarc's face mask heaved and twisted. Then he brought out his hand to the strings of the harp. Milo saw him flinch and guessed that in this cold he faced a pain as immediate and severe as if the strings were molten metal.

Touching the harp steadied Wymarc. He began to weave a spell of sound. Wind screamed and moaned, but through that clamor arose his first notes, as clear and well defined as any temple gong. They echoed and re-echoed from the rocky walls, until it seemed that more than one harper plied his art.

No pain from this playing attacked his listeners. The notes Wymarc repeated over and over again rang through and then out-called the wind, like a summons. Four times the bard swept the harp strings to play the same questing call. Then, once more, he thrust his stiffening fingers beneath the mouth scarf to blow upon them.

"AYYYYYYY!" Ingrge's shout could well bring down an avalanche should there be any dangerous overhang of snow and rock, Milo thought apprehensively.

The elf had cupped his hands to form a trumpet and once more voiced that upsurging shout. Through the grayish roofing of the upper clouds descended a great winged thing. Murky as the pass was, it did not hide those widespread wings. Memory once more moved in Milo's mind, opening grudgingly another door.

It was a gar-eagle—the greatest of all winged creatures (save, of course, a dragon) that his world knew. The very beating of those wings churned up snow as the bird descended. And when it came to perch at last on a rock a little farther ahead, closed its fifteen-foot wings, and twisted its head downward toward the elf—over whom it would have towered another head's length had they been meeting on level ground—even Naile pushed back a fraction.

The curved beak was brilliant scarlet—the hue of new-spilled blood—and the fierce eyes, which raked them all contemptuously in a single survey, were the gold of flames. But for the rest there was nothing but the white of the purest snow.

Ingrge held up his mittened hands, palm outward and at the level of his own heart in a ceremonial gesture of greeting. The head of the huge bird dipped again, dropping lower so that they were indeed now eye to eye. Milo did not hear any sound save that of the wind which once more howled since the magic of the music no longer battled with it. Their communication must be in the "silent speech," mind to mind, as the elven folk were able to do not only among themselves but with all the sons and daughters of nature who wore feathers, scales, or fur—or even leaves—for it was rumored that to the elves trees were also comrades, teachers, and kin-friends.

The gar-eagle's hooked beak, formed to rend and tear, opened and the bird screeched ear-piercingly. Ingrge moved back to allow it room as it spread once more those near unbelievable wings, rising up into the clouds.

When their visitor had entirely disappeared, Ingrge returned. "We can move on." A wave of his hand gestured ahead. "The great one will track us when he has word. And we dare not linger here lest the cold finish us."

Luckily the slope downward from the pass was less difficult than the climb. However, they did not try to ride, but stumbled along, stumping on feet numbed by cold. Milo chose to play rear guard, mainly because he feared that Gulth might drop behind and not be noticed. While he had no particular friendship for lizardmen in general, this one was part of their company and deserved an equal chance.

He had guessed right that the saurian was near the end of his strength, for Milo was not yet out of the pass cleft when Gulth fell forward into the snow, making no effort to rise.

"Wymarc!" Milo raised his voice. The bard, half-hidden in cloud mist, faced around, returning as quickly as he could. Together they bundled Gulth across his horse and went on, Milo leading the mount, the bard hovering beside to steady the limp body of the lizardman if he showed any sign of sliding off.

Mist hid the rest of the party ahead, but once they were out of the pass itself the wind ceased to buffet them and Milo welcomed that small encouragement. Luckily there was only one possible path to take. It curved to the right where trampled snow, fast being covered, was their guide. The swordsman longed to speed up, but he was breathing in short gasps, and he could guess their footing was treacherous. Though it was a less exacting a road, it was still steep enough to call forth caution. Soon it became a series of ledges, each a fraction wider than the one above.

They were below the cloudline now so Milo looked ahead eagerly for their party. Hooves and boots had beaten down the snow—but he could see nothing of those who had made that trail. Confused, he halted, while the horse moved up a step, nudging at him.

"What's the matter?" Wymarc asked.

"They're gone!" Milo's first wild thought was of some snare of spell that had netted the rest in spite of Ingrge's talent at scenting such.

"Gone?" The bard loosed his hold on Gulth and crowded forward to look over the swordsman's shoulder.

Milo examined ledges with greater care. The three immediately below and beyond where they had paused were trail-marked. But only half of the fourth one showed disturbed snow, as if the rest of their company had been snatched up at that point and—

Before he could share such a suspicion with Wymarc, Ingrge

appeared straight out of the mountain wall. The bard's laugh made Milo flush at his own stupidity. Perhaps the cold had slowed his wits and let his imagination take over.

"Cave!" Wymarc gave the answer Milo should have known. "Let us get there with all speed. If our friend here still has a spark of life in his body we had better be tending it."

Ingrge joined them before they were along a third of the next ledge. The elf's aid made the rest of their descent the easier. Both horses and men trusted him and did not have to pick such a careful path.

They pushed through a slit in the stone to enter a cave. Despite the narrow entrance, it widened beyond into a space large enough for both men and animals. Nor was that all. A fire blazed on a flat stone, marked with the scorching of earlier flames, and about it sat the others, holding out their hands to the blaze, crowding in upon the small glow of heat.

With Ingrge's help Milo and Wymarc carried Gulth to the source of heat. Deav Dyne arose hurriedly. As they pulled away the ice-stiffened cloak, he leaned solicitously over the scaled body. Milo himself could distinguish no sign of life. But the healing spells of priests were well known to be able to save one very close to death.

Beads in hand, Deav Dyne drew his other palm in long soothing strokes from the lizardman's domed head to his scaled and taloned feet, then down each arm in turn. The cleric's voice muttered a chant. Now the elf knelt on the other side of Gulth, joining his long-fingered hands to Deav Dyne's in the stroking.

On the opposite of the fire, feeding it from time to time from a pile of sticks heaped between two outflung spurs of rock, squatted Naile. And almost nosing into the meager flames was

Afreeta, low upon her belly, her wings outspread as if she would take into her body all the warmth she could. Wymarc rubbed the hand he had bared to the wind in the pass, alternately blowing upon the fingers and holding them to the fire. Yevele had pulled open one of their supply bags to bring out a roll of the most strength-providing food they carried—dried fruit beaten into a thick pulp and then crumbled to be combined with coarsely ground dried meat.

For a time the mere fact that they were out of the breath of the mountain wind, under cover and in shelter, was enough for Milo. He watched the labor of the elf and the cleric apathetically, wondering if their efforts were not already in vain.

Neither Ingrge nor Deav Dyne were willing to concede such a defeat. In the end, their efforts were rewarded. There was a hiss of pain from the lizardman. His horn-lidded eyes opened slowly, and now Milo could see the rise and fall of his arched chest. Deav Dyne stopped his stroking, searched again within his robe and brought out a small curved horn stoppered with a metal cap.

With infinite care he loosed the stopper while Ingrge raised the heavy saurian head upon his own knee, working his fingers between the fearsome fangs of Gulth's jaws to open the half-conscious alien's mouth. Onto the purplish tongue thus exposed, Deav Dyne dropped four small measures of the liquid the horn contained, then made haste to shut the container before he turned back to his patient.

Gulth blinked slowly. His head settled a little to one side in Ingrge's hold. Then his eyes closed. The cleric sat back on his heels.

"Cloaks!" he demanded without looking at the rest of them. "All covering you can spare!"

Only when his patient was wrapped in a layer of cloaks, with even the horse blankets heaped over him, did Deav Dyne relax. He spoke to the elf. "If he stays in the mountain cold we cannot answer for his life. His people are of the steaming swamps—not conditioned to such trails as these."

"Then let him return whence he came," broke in Naile. "I know of old these snake-skins. They are as full of treachery as a drinking horn of ale in an indifferent inn. We should have been the better, priest, had his spirit departed from him!"

"You forget," the battlemaid answered him. "Is not the same fetter on him as the ones we must wear?" She thrust her arm farther into the firelight, where the flames awoke to glinting life the reddish gleam of the bracelet. "I do not know by what method we were chosen, but it is plain that he was meant to be one of our company."

Naile snorted. "Yes—to betray us, perhaps. I tell you, that one I shall watch, and should he in any way raise doubts of his actions he will answer to me." His lips flattened against his tusk-fangs.

Milo stirred—this was no time for the berserker to allow his change-making rage to take control of his human part. He inched forward and dared to lay hand on the massive arm within his reach. "There is more wisdom in what she says than in your doubts, warrior."

Naile's head swung in his direction. The berserker's small eyes already held a warning light. "I say—"

"Say—say—say—" Wymarc repeated. But he made of that

single word a singsong of notes. His uncovered harp rested on his knee, and now he fingered one string and then another, not as if he chose to use his song magic, but rather as if he tried each in turn to make sure of its strength, even as a warrior before battle looks to the state of his weaponry. Yet even such a seemingly idle plucking carried with it sounds that echoed softly through the cave.

Milo, who had been about to tighten his grip on Naile's arm in perhaps a futile attempt to bring the berserker to his senses, found his hold broken. His hand fell away to rest on his own knee. Just as the warmth of the fire sank into his chilled body, so did those random notes warm his mind, bringing a release from tension, a gentle dreaminess from which all that might harm or threaten was barred.

The swordsman chewed away at the bit of rolled journey-food Yevele had handed him, content with the warmth and that ease of mind, though an instinct buried deep inside him still was wary enough to cry out that this easement was of magic and would not long hold.

Outside the cave, darkness gathered. Only Ingrge arose now and then to feed the fire, but no longer with wood. Rather he brought lumps of coal from some inner bay to be set with skill among the brands so that in turn those kindled, giving new life and strength to the flames. Now and then one of the horses or ponies, tethered farther in, stamped or snorted, but those by the fire were sunk in the silence born of their own thoughts or dreams.

Once Milo roused enough to mention the need for a sentry, but Naile, his voice a whispering rumble, pointed to Afreeta, saying, "She will give voice in warning. Her senses are better than ours for such service."

The pseudo-dragon had waddled so close to the fire that Milo wondered if it would not singe her. Her long neck uncoiled, her head darted forth and her jaws clamped upon a bit of glowing coal. She crunched it, as if it were some dainty to be relished, and pounced upon a second. What Milo knew of her kind, even of the greater, true dragons, was very little. He had always supposed that their legendary fire-eating was just that—a legend with no truthful foundation. But it would seem that it was true.

Naile made no attempt to prevent her epicure feast, even though there was a faint puffing of smoke trails from her throat.

"Eat well, my beauty," the berserker half whispered. "You will need such fire within you if we stay long in this land."

To stare into the fire brought drowsiness. Naile might believe that his winged companion was adequate protection for their camp, but the tested soldier within Milo could not quite accept that. Finally he got up and went to the mouth of the cave.

In doing so he seemed to pass through an actual wall. The heat that hung so comfortingly around the fire was lost instantly. He shivered and drew closer his cloak, as he peered out into a night so dark and starless that he had to depend upon his ears rather than his eyes to guess what was beyond.

The sound of the wind among the peaks made a threatening cry, like that of a hunting beast prowling the mountains. It shrieked and puffed fine snow into his face, which stung his flesh like needles of ice.

By all the sounds he could identify, a storm had closed in upon the high country. Perhaps only the cave shelter had saved their lives. Even magic could not withstand such raging of nature. Milo stepped back. The others, even Ingrge, slept, but the swordsman found himself shaken out of the charmed contentment Wymarc's harping had produced.

Though he settled down once more by the fire he could not drowse. Rather he tried to order his thoughts, looking from one to another of his strangely assorted company. Each represented certain abilities and strengths (also, probably, weaknesses), which differed. Even though he, Naile, and Yevele were fighters, they were far from being alike. The cleric, the bard, and the elf commanded other talents and gifts. The lizardman—like Naile, Milo wondered why the alien had been added to their motley company. It was true that the saurian-ancestored ones were swamp dwellers, needing both water and turgid heat about them to function best. Yet Gulth, uncomplaining, had ridden into the near waterless plains and climbed as long as he could into what must be for him a hell of cold.

The lizardfolk in their own lands, and with their own weapons, were warriors of high standing. Therefore, there must be some reason why Gulth should ride with them now, not just because he also wore the bracelet which was the badge of their slavery to some unknown menace. As he gazed into the fire Milo was once more plagued by fleeting memories of that other world. He stirred uneasily. Those—he must seal them away for his own sake. To be divided in mind when danger stalked (and when did it not here?) was to be weakened.

He slept at last. This time he dreamed vividly. A dark stone wall loomed large. About the base of the wall grew greenery, a greenery that was not natural—that was too bright—that shuddered and shook, as if the plants themselves strove to drag their roots from out the soil and charge at him.

Gray wall, green that had a life he could not understand and—

There was a piercing shriek. Milo roused. For a moment he was so completely bewildered at the breaking of his dream that he only stared bewilderedly at a fire. Gray walls—fire. . . . No, the walls had not been composed of flames, but rather of solid stone.

Again that shriek. Now Ingrge moved lightly toward the outer entrance. The others stirred, sat up. Naile's hand gripped his axe and Afreeta perched on his shoulder. Though her mouth was open and her tongue darted in and out she did not hiss. Milo, hand about sword hilt, moved out behind the elf.

There was no dark ahead now, rather the gray of an overcast day. But their view of the dull sky was nearly hidden by the vast form of the gar-eagle who had settled on the ledge without, its head lowered so that it might look into the cave.

Once more the bird loosed its mighty scream. Ingrge fronted it eye to eye in the same form of silent communication they had earlier held. Milo fidgeted at his side, not for the first time wishing that some of the talents of the elven kind were also shared by men.

That confrontation of elf and bird continued for what seemed a long space. Then Ingrge stepped within the overhang of the cave as huge wings fanned the air. Up into the thin atmosphere of the heights sped the gar-eagle, while the elf returned to the company now roused and waiting by the fire.

"Lichis lies to the south in a place he has made his own," Ingrge reported shortly. "It remains to be seen if he will accept our company. Your little one"—now he spoke to Naile—"it is she who must speak for us in the end."

The berserker nodded. "Afreeta knows. But how far is this dragon dwelling? We have not the wings of your messenger. Nor can Afreeta take the way such a mighty one follows. A single blast from the wind in these reaches would beat her far off course."

"She need not try her wings, not until we reach the boundaries Lichis has established to protect himself," returned the elf. "As to how far away—" He shrugged. "That I cannot measure in our distance upon land—for Reec"—he waved to the outer world, plainly naming the gar-eagle—"does not reckon distance as do we who are wingless. He has set the way in a pattern for my mind only—as he looked down upon it from afar. However, we can descend to the lower lands and move from one valley to another, sheltering in part from the cold."

Even Gulth aroused enough to sit one of the mounts, still wrapped as well as they could manage against the chill of the heights, making no complaint as Deav Dyne led his horse once more out into the blasts that had nearly killed the lizardman. Thus they followed the path of the ledges down, until scrub trees, finally forest giants, closed about them in a dark green silence through which Ingrge took a twisting route with the same confidence as one treads a well-marked road.

11

Lichis the Golden

THE SILENCE ABIDING IN THE FOREST WAS DAUNTING. MILO FOUND himself glancing over his shoulder now and then, not because he heard any sound, but rather because he heard nothing. This was the same feeling that had gripped him in the inn at the start of this whole wide adventure, that he was under covert observation.

Perhaps some distant kin of Ingrge patroled these ways, keeping out of sight. But it was strange that no bird called within the dark green fastness, that the party caught no sight, heard no sound of any beast.

There was no way of telling the hours, and so zigzag was the path the elf followed that Milo could not be sure whether they still headed south or west. They did mount rises separating one valley from another. From these ridges all he could see was the loom of the cloud-veiled mountains behind, with other dark and dreary-looking peaks massing ahead.

At length they emerged from the trees into a section where the rough terrain was of congealed lava, long hardened, yet retaining sharp edges. This brought their progress to a crawl, making it necessary to constantly watch for the safety of their own footing and that of their animals.

Above them, at last, was the break in the mountainside through which, ages ago, this once molten flood had found a path. Ingrge waved to that opening in the rock wall and spoke to Naile. "It is time to loose Afreeta. We stand at the outer edge of Lichis's own domain. Beyond this point we do not dare to go without invitation."

"So?" The berserker raised his hand to the pseudo-dragon nested within the upturned collar of his hide cloak. "Well enough."

Afreeta uncoiled, crawled out upon his palm, her wings shimmering in the air as she exercised them. This time she seemed too eager to even look at the man she had chosen to companion; rather she took off in a glide. Then her wings whirred swiftly as she beat her way up toward that break in the mountainside. So swiftly did she go that she vanished as if blown afar by some act of magic.

"We wait." Ingrge moved out among their ponies, unfastening the feed bags. Milo and Wymarc joined him, measuring out handsful of corn which the small beasts greeted with eager whinnies. The horses munched the grain and were watered from bags not nearly as plump as they had been earlier. The riders rationed themselves to a small portion of water, well below the rim of a cup Ingrge filled and passed from hand to hand.

Gulth slumped in the saddle of his mount. Milo guessed that had the lizardman dismounted it could well be that he could not have won aloft again. His cowled head hung forward so that his snout nearly touched his breast. But, as usual, he uttered no complaint.

Naile strode back and forth. It was never easy for one of his mixed nature to wait patiently. As he paced, he turned his head ever upward, seeking a glimpse of Afreeta returning.

Deav Dyne set his back to a jutting rock. He began to pass his prayer beads through the fingers of one hand, while the other rested on the breast of his robe, guarding what secrets he carried there in the inner pockets.

A man, raised and trained in the precincts of one of the great temple-abbeys, would find consorting with the dragonfolk hard. Those of the scaled and winged kind owned no gods—or demons either. Their own judgment of right or wrong was not that of mankind, and their actions could not be either foreseen or measured by those whom they considered lesser beings.

The Golden Dragon himself was known to have always favored the road of Law. Lesser beings of his race consorted openly with Chaos, giving aid capriciously to Dark adepts. The stories concerning Lichis all stated that, when he withdrew from the world, he had, finally, fiercely bade men go their own heedless ways and expect no more commerce with him. That he would break with his word now, even though they had indeed come to his private nest place—how dared they count on any favorable reception?

Milo fingered the bracelet that bound him to both a mad and seemingly endless quest, finding little good in such thoughts.

"If this be indeed Lichis's nest," Yevele's voice was thoughtful as she came to stand beside the swordsman, "why should he harken to *us*?"

"That same question I have been asking myself," Milo answered. He surveyed the jagged, broken top of the heights. Unlike the mountain of the pass, here was no cloud to conceal any part of those forbidding pinnacles cutting into the dull sky. In the west, behind the peaks, a sullen, dire, blood-red band across the heavens proclaimed the hour of sundown.

The girl raised her arm, her attention for the band about her wrist.

"If we play a game, swordsman, then it is a doom-darkened one. This wizard-talk of things not of our world using the very fact of our existence to weave some spell . . ." She shook her head slowly. "Though there are always new things, both good and ill, waiting to be learned—"

What she might have added was cut off by a harsh cry from Naile. The berserker came to a halt, facing up slope, his thick muscled arm flung out in greeting and to serve as a perch for Afreeta. The pseudo-dragon settled, her claws clicking on his mail as she climbed to his shoulder and there fell to hissing, her head bobbing almost as fast as her wings moved in the air.

Naile's eyes gleamed bright beneath the overhang of his helm.

"We can go on," he reported. Ingrge nodded and set about, with the others' help, to get their train in order. Only this time Naile took the lead, Afreeta, plainly excited to a high pitch, sometimes sitting on his shoulder, sometimes whirring aloft for short flights, impatient at the careful plodding of those who must walk on two feet or four.

The lava flow formed the most tricky of roads. All but Gulth dismounted, sometimes needing to turn back and lead a second or a third of their beasts across some very broken strip. As they made that very slow climb the light faded more and more from the sky. Dusk closed in too rapidly.

True twilight had fallen when they reached at last the lip of the break through which the then molten lava had flowed. Here they halted, looking down into the domain of Lichis.

A crater formed an irregular cup, but the fires that had burst loose from the earth's core at this point had long since died. There was the gleam of water in the deepest part of the center and around that a rank growth of shrub and grass, not autumn browned but still sullenly green.

Water birds, looking hardly larger than Afreeta from this distance, wheeled above that small lake, settled on it, took off again as whim directed. Save for them, no other life could be sighted. Once more Afreeta cried and leaped into the air, circling Naile's head, then winging out, not toward the downward descent that ended at the lakeside, but rather along the rim of the crater to the left.

Deav Dyne fumbled in his robe, to produce a ball of dull silver about which he ringed the prayer bead string. The dullness of the globe vanished, rays of light which rivaled beams of a full moon sped forth. He pushed by Naile and went slowly, holding his strange torch closer to the ground so that, by its pale, steady light, they could see any obstacle.

Their pace now became little more than a crawl. All at once Deav Dyne halted. What his improvised torch showed them was another cleft in the rock. And, as he threw himself belly down, lowering the globe by a coil of his bead string, they could sight below a level of path angling over the ridge, down into the now-shadowed crater.

Ingrge swung over, went down on one knee, peering at that

path. When the elf's white face was lifted into the stronger glow of the globe, he was already speaking. "This is a game trail of sorts. I would say that if we loose the animals they will drift down for feed and water. There they will abide unstraying." Now he spoke once more directly to Naile, about whose head Afreeta was buzzing and darting impatiently. "What we seek is here above?"

"Yes," rumbled the berserker.

Even the globe could not continue to aid them through the steadily growing dark. To force their mounts and the ponies farther on such a rough way could well mean a broken leg, a snapped hoof, or injuries even Deav Dyne, with all his skill, could not heal.

So they followed Ingrge's suggestion, stripping the weary mounts and the pack ponies, urging them carefully down into the cut and giving them their heads. Straightway, horses whinnied, ponies nickered as they trotted free to where water and grazing waited. Piling most of their gear among the rocks, the party made ready to forge ahead.

Gulth, perhaps because he had ridden through most of their day's travel, seemed able to keep his feet. But Wymarc, without a word, moved up close enough to the lizardman to lend a hand if aid should become necessary.

Even though they did not now have to seek the best way for the breasts, their advance was slow. But at last they came to a narrow seam turning inward along the crater wall. Down this they crept step by cautious step, their left hands gripping whatever hold they could find. Then Deav Dyne moved out upon a ledge and stood, globe held high, to light them down.

Even as a ledge backed by the cave had been their refuge in

the mountains, so did this one also furnish a threshold for a great arch of rock. It might have been that their arrival before that dark hole was a signal. The restricted light of Deav Dyne's torch was swallowed up in a blaze of radiance, feverishly red, dyeing all their faces. Out of that crimson flood came not a voice but a thought which pierced minds with the same clarity as a shout might have reached their ears, a thought so strong that to receive and understand it brought a feeling of pain.

"Man and elf—were and small kin—aye, and scaled one of the water, come you in. You who have dared disturb my quiet."

Go in they did. Milo was sure they could not have withstood the will behind that mind-voice even had they so wished. About them washed scarlet light, forming mist through which they could move, yet could not see.

Out of habit and instinct Milo's mittened hand rested on his sword. He unconsciously brought up his battered shield. The dragonkind were legend, had been legend for generations. Deep in him there was awe born of those same legends.

The red mist swirled, puffed, arose as one would draw upward a curtain. Under their boots was no longer gray rock, rather a patterned flooring of glinting crystals, perhaps even of gems, set in incomprehensible designs. Red—all shades of red—and yellows and the white of ice were those bits of brilliance. But only for a moment did Milo see and wonder at them.

For now the mist moved high to disclose the master of this nest. Confronting them was another ledge, this one with a rim to hold back what it contained, though here and there some of that shifting substance had cascaded to the floor, sent spinning by movements of great limbs. What formed that bedding (if bedding it might be termed) was lumps and pieces of gold, some of it coins so old that their inscriptions were long since worn away.

Bright and gleaming as that metal was, the creature who used it as the softest of beds was more resplendent. Afreeta was indeed a miniature copy of this huge and ancient kinsman, but, like the gar-eagle of the heights, Lichis's size was such as to reduce all facing him to the insignificance of small children. His body scales were larger than Naile's hand, and over the basic gold of their coloring gem lights rippled steadily, as the water of a pool might be stirred by a summer breeze. Mighty wings were folded and the snouted head was high held in a curious, near-human way by the resting of the fanged jaw on a taloned paw folded in upon itself like a fist, the "elbow" of that huge limb supported in turn by the rim of the gold-filled nest.

The great eyes were still half-lidded, as if their arrival had disturbed its slumber. No man could read any expression on that face. Then the mighty tail stirred, sending a fresh shower of gold thudding out onto the gem-set floor.

"I am Lichis." There was a supreme confidence in that thought which overbore all defenses, struck straight into their minds. "Why come you here to trouble me in the peace I have chosen?"

He regarded them drowsily and then, though Milo had expected that one of the others—the cleric who dealt in magic, the elf whose blood was akin to the land itself, or even Naile who companioned with Afreeta—would be set to answer that half-challenge, it was at the swordsman that question had been aimed.

"We lie under a geas," Milo verbalized because that was more

natural for him. "We seek. . . ." Then he fell silent for it seemed
to him that some invisible projection from Lichis reached deep
into his mind, seeking, sorting, and he could raise no defense
against that invasion, try as he might.

Milo was not even aware that his shield had clanged to the
floor, that his hands pressed against his forehead. This was a
frightening thing—part of it a sickening revulsion, a feeling of
rape within the very core of his mind.

"So—" Invasion ceased, withdrew. Lichis reared his head
higher, his eyes fully opened now so that their slitted pupils
were visible.

That clawed paw on which he had rested his jaw made a gesture. About them the whole of the cave nest trembled. The
mountain wall itself quivered in answer to Lichis's thought demand, though Milo sensed force, aimed not at him but elsewhere, thrusting into dimensions beyond the comprehension of
those who knew not the talent.

A ball of scarlet haze rolled from overhead, began to spin.
Though it made him increasingly sick and dizzy to watch its gy-
rations, Milo found that he could not turn his eyes from it. As it
spun, its substance thickened and then flattened. The ball became a flat surface, steadying vertically above the floor at Milo's
shoulder height.

On that disk arose configurations. The red faded to the gray
of the mountain lands. Lapping the wall of rock was now an expanse of yellow-gray, without any features, just a billowing surface.

"The Sea of Dust," Ingrge said. Lichis did not glance in the
direction of the elf. Rather he leaned his great head forward,

staring intently at the miniature landscape which ever changed, grew more distinct. Mountains lay to the right—the Sea stretched on over three-quarters of the rest of the disk.

Now, at the extreme left, within the dust land, there arose a dark shadow, irregular—like a blot of ink dropped from the pen of a scribe to spread across a yet unlettered parchment. The stain became fixed on the very edge of the disk.

Lichis's head drooped still more, until his great snout nearly touched that blot. Milo thought that he saw the dragon's wide nostrils expand a little as if he were sniffing.

Then once more the thought voice reached out for the swordsman.

"Stretch forth your right hand, man."

Obediently he swung his palm up and out, not allowing his flesh to touch the miniature landscape. On his thumb the oblong of the ring began to glow. The minute red lines and dots on it awoke into a life of their own.

"You carry your own guide," Lichis announced. "Loosen your hand, man—now!"

So emphatic was that order that Milo obeyed. He tried to allow his hand to go limp where it hung above the miniature mountains walling the pictured sea. His flesh met and rested upon some invisible support in the air. Then, by no will of his, it moved from right to left, slowly, inexorably, while on the ring the lines and dots waved and waned. Toward the blot on the left his hand swung. The compulsion that held him, tugged him into taking one step forward and then another. His index finger, close to the thumb, clung tightly, one length of flesh near-wedded to the other. Now that finger pointed straight to the blot.

"There is your goal." Lichis sank back to his former indolent position. Below Milo's outstretched hand the disk spun furiously, bits of the mist from which it had been fashioned breaking off, the clear-cut picture of the land disappearing.

"The Sea of Dust," Ingrge mused. "No man—or elf—has dared that and returned—"

"You have seen where lies that which you would find." Lichis's thought conveyed no emotion. "What you do with this knowledge is your own affair."

Perhaps because the Golden Dragon had used him to point out their path and he was beginning to be irked at being another's tool, Milo dared to raise another question. "How far must we go, Dragon Lord? And—"

Lichis shifted on his bed of gold. There was a rippling of color across his scales. From him, to catch in their minds, flowed a warning spark of the ancient lord's irritation.

"Man—and such other of you as walk on two feet, ride upon four—measure your own distances. To the end of your strengths your road will stretch. I have seen in your memories what this wizard would have you do. To his small mind the logic is correct. But he has his boundaries in all those scraps of the old learning he clutches to him and seeks to store in his limited memory. This I believe: what you seek now lies at the core of the Sea of Dust. It is alien, and even I cannot fathom what it hides, though the blood-kin of my species have, in their time, passed from world to world in dreams or waking—when they were foolishly young, nearly still damp from the egg and filled with the impetuosity of unlearned spawn.

"You will dare the Sea—and what haunts it. In it are the younger brothers such as Rockna, who in the past went a-hunting there."

"The Brass Dragon!" Naile broke out, and Afreeta hissed, thrusting her head into hiding beneath the collar of his cloak.

Something close to amusement—of a distant and alien kind—could be sensed in Lichis's answer.

"So that one is still making trouble? It has been many span of years since he played games with men and answered, when he so willed, the calling of the Lords of Chaos. I think none now live who would dare so to call now. But once he made the Sea of Dust his own. Now"—Lichis settled down farther in his strange bed, burrowing his limbs into the loose gold—"I weary of you, men, elf, and all the rest. There is nothing new in your species to amuse me. Since I have answered your questions I bid you go."

Milo found himself turning, without willing that action, saw that the others were also doing so. Already the red mist fell in thick rolls, to curtain off their reluctant host. As the swordsman drew away he looked back over his shoulder. Not only had the mist now completely veiled Lichis but it was fading into shadows; as they came out on the ledge above the crater valley, there was nothing left behind them but impenetrable dark.

They descended, burdening themselves with the packs and gear they had stripped from the horses, to where their animals grazed about the lake. The tall walls of the crater cut off those mountain winds that had lashed them and it was actually warmer than it had been at any time since they had set forth from Greyhawk. They did not need the fire this night for ease of temperature, yet they crowded to it as a symbol of a world they understood, an anchorage against danger, though Lichis's domain held no threat of Chaos. The dangers of the Outer Dark could not venture so close to one who had been ever triumphant over the magic of evil.

"The Sea of Dust." Naile had eaten his portion of their journey-food and now sat, his back against a boulder, his heavy legs outspread. Afreeta perched upon one of his knees so that now and then he drew a caressing finger down her spiked backbone. "I have heard many tales of it—but all third and fourth hand or even still further removed. Do any of you know more?"

Ingrge threw a twist of tough grass to feed the fire. Sparks flew upward.

"I have seen it," he stated flatly.

Their attention centered upon the elf. When he did not continue, Naile prompted impatiently:

"You have seen it. Well, then what manner of country is it?"

"It is," the elf replied somberly, "exactly what men call it. As the seas better known to us are filled with water which is never quiet, pulled hither and yon by tides, driven by storm winds, breaking in ceaseless waves to eat away at the land, so exists the Sea of Dust. It may not have its tides, but it has its winds to encase a traveler in clouds of grit, until he is totally lost. He sinks into it, to be swallowed up as water may swallow a man who cannot swim. How deep its layers are no one knows.

"There was once a race who made it their own. They built strange ships—not like those that go upon the oceans, but flat of bottom, with runners extending some distance fore and aft, wide and webbed to hold them on the surface. They raised sails to the ever-blowing winds and coasted thus. Now after a heavy storm it is said that sometimes a wreck of one of their ancient ships may be seen jutting out of the wind-driven dust. What became of *them*, no man of our age knows. But to venture out into those quicksands afoot is to sink—"

Naile hunched forward a little, his hands made into fists resting upon his knees.

"You speak of webbed runners to support a ship," he mused. "And you warn of men sinking straightway into this treacherous stuff. But what if men who would try such a journey could also use foot webs, spreading as it were the weight of their bodies over a wider expanse? In the frozen lands men walk so upon the surface of soft snow in winter, where without such support they would flounder into drifts."

"Snowshoes!" Milo's other memory quirked into life for an instant. He looked at the elf. "Could such work, do you think?"

Ingrge shrugged. "We can but try." He sounded none too sure. "I have not heard of such before. But I see no way we can venture, without some aid, into that shifting, unsolid country. We cannot take the beasts with us. Only what we ourselves can carry will provide our sustenance there."

Milo thought of the map Lichis had created. How far away was the center? The Golden Dragon had refused even to guess the distance. As he rolled himself into his cloak it was with a dampened spirit. What a man could do he was ready and willing to try—but there comes a time when even strength and will can be challenged, wrung to the uttermost, with failure the final sum of all.

12

The Sea of Dust

THEY CHOSE TO CAMP SHELTERED BY SCRUB TREES. THERE THEY slumped wearily for a space to nurse aching feet, shoulders galled by packs. However, at this end of the day's laborious march they did at last look out upon that feared trap, the sea of restless dust. It was no more level than the wind-disturbed ocean. Where ocean waves roll, here dunes mounded and gave off a haze of grit from their rounded crests at the slightest breath of breeze. Farther out, whirling pillars of dust devils danced, rose and fell, skittered across a rippling surface, demons of the waste.

Looking out into and over that desolation, Milo longed to turn his back upon it. A man could fight against upraised weapons. He might even summon up reserves of courage to front demonic threat or alien, monstrous enemies produced from a sorcerous nightmare. But this land itself was against human kind.

Yet there was no easing of the geas compulsion that had drawn them hither. Whether or no, they were committed to the penetration of what lay ahead, with no sure knowledge of any trail (for how could one mark a trail when there was a constant shifting of dunes, the haze of driven dust?) or how long they must fight for survival before they reached their goal.

With the next day's dawning they began to fashion their only hope for going farther. Ingrge chose the material, and he did it as though he loathed the task. As with all the elven kind, any destruction, even of these crooked and spindling scrub trees that grew on the lip of the sea, was a thing against his innermost nature. They selected with care the most pliable of lengths he gave them, soaking them in a pool of water that was murky with dust puffed from the south, giving the turgid water a yellow velvet surface.

Once they were thoroughly soaked, Naile used his strength to bend the chosen pieces and hold them while they were lashed together. The berserker also sacrificed a goodly portion of his leather cloak to be slit into narrow thongs to lace across the resulting egg-shaped "sand shoes." Then, into that netting, the rest interwove roots, twisting in this material until the whole took on a solid appearance.

Edging his boots carefully into thongs, Milo was the first to try the clumsy looking footgear, venturing out into the drear yellow-brown waste of dust. The surface gave under his weight, and some of the particles oozed over the edges of his footgear. But, though he had to proceed with a spraddle-legged walk, he sank no farther. In the end, they decided they had found the answer to one of the perils of the sea.

They discarded all the gear that they dared, taking only their weapons, a measure of their journey supplies, and a water-skin for each. Once they had filled those from the pool, filtering the contents through a cloth Yevele provided, Gulth waded into the water, which washed no higher than his waist, and squatted down in the liquid until only his snout could be seen. He had taken his cloak with him, letting it sop up in its tough fabric as much of the liquid as possible. Alone of the company he refused to be fitted with the sand shoes. His own webbed feet, he insisted, would accommodate him on the treacherous surface as they did in the ooze of his home swamps.

Last night they had completed those shoes and now it was morning once more. For the first time, and when they wished it the least, the clouds that had hung over them for much of their journey cleared. Sun arose, to glare down upon the shifting surface of the gray-brown sea. Like Gulth, they went cloaked, even with hoods pulled over their helmets to shield them from dust powder and grit. Their progress was very slow as they waddled awkwardly on, fighting to balance on the clumsy web shoes.

Gulth quickly became a stumbling pillar of dust as it clung to his wet cloak. But he had been right in that his own webbed feet proved better able to walk here than on the hard stone of the mountain's bones.

Milo took the lead. He held his thumb stretched out so that he could see the ring that Lichis had told them was a guide. Though the lines and dots upon it meant no more to him than they had ever done, he saw, for the first time, that there was a glow at the base of the stones. As they advanced that glow crept slowly up the green surface.

It had begun near the end of one of the lines and Milo, wanting to test the efficiency of this strange and, to him, improbable guide, angled a little away from a straightforward line. The glow dimmed.

He was right! As he swung back again, the glow deepened, fastened upon the line directly. The swordsman remembered tales of the voyagers who had dared this waste with wind-driven, dust-skimming ships. Could the lines mark the paths their ships had taken? Since he could do no better, he kept to what he read in the ring, seeking, each time the glow wavered, to move right or left back to the line.

At the fifth such change in the line of march, Naile demanded angrily what he was trying to do—wear out their strength moving hither and thither like some mindless earth beetle? But on Milo's pointing out the direction of the ring lines, the berserker subsided with a grunt. Ingrge and Deav Dyne gave assent with nods. The elf added that the line Milo had chosen, mainly by chance, did indeed run toward that portion of the sea where Lichis's map had produced in miniature the seat of the evil they sought.

Their pace continued necessarily slow. The effort required to raise a foot from the sucking embrace of the dust and to place it ahead tried muscles that ordinary walking did not use. While the sun's glare centered heat on them, Milo called halts closer and closer together and was glad to see that none of them, even Gulth, took more than a sip or two from their supply of water.

The question that lay at the back of all their minds was how long a trail might stretch before them. Added to that was the uncertainty of their finding more water even at the end, though if their enemy had his—or its—headquarters there, Milo reasoned, there must exist some source of food and water.

He called a longer halt at midday for he noticed that Gulth, though as usual the lizardman offered no protest, was wavering. The heat had long since sucked all moisture from his dust-

burdened cloak. Now it must be drying his skin in turn. Yet if
they gave him freely from their own containers of water it might
mean death for them all. Two high-heaped dunes quite close together provided a measure of protection from the air that was
filled with powder and dust. It found a way into their mouths,
clogged their nostrils, irritated their eyes. Creeping between the
hillocks, Milo and Wymarc shed their cloaks and battened them
down with handsful of grit to form a roof under which the party
lay close together, striving to shut out the misery of the day,
their shoes under them to support their bodies. To have attempted this journey by day, Milo decided, was folly. They
should have started at night when at least the sun would have
been eliminated from their list of torments.

Deav Dyne roused him some time later. The cleric's face was
a smear of dust making a grotesque mask. But the trouble in his
eyes was plain to read.

"Gulth—he will die," he stated bluntly, pointing to where the
lizardman lay a little apart from the others, as he always did.
Yevele now knelt beside him, only partly visible in the dusk, for
it was close to night. The thick cloak had been pulled aside
from the scaled body while the battlemaid wiped the arch of the
alien's chest with a cloth. When she uptipped one of the water
bags and wet the cloth, Milo would have protested, but his
words were never uttered. Instead he crept over to her side.

Gulth's eyes were shut, his snouted mouth hung open a fraction, dark tongue tip exposed. Yevele dribbled a little of the water into his mouth, then set aside the bag, to once more rub the
lizardman's chest with her dampened cloth. She glanced up at
Milo.

"This does little good." Her voice sounded harsh as if the

dust had gotten into her throat to coat her words. "He is dying—"

"So he dies." Naile sat up. He did not even turn his head to view the girl's efforts at rousing the lizardman. "The world will be the sweeter with one less snake-skin in it!"

"One expects nothing from the boar but blind rage and little thought." She spat, as if to clear her mouth of both the words and the dust. "But think of this, boar warrior." Yevele lifted Gulth's limp wrist exposing the bracelet. "Seven of us bear this. Do you not speculate that if we are so tied, the fate of one is in the end entwined with the fate of the rest? I know not what magic has bound us on this wheel of companioned adventure, but I should not care to take the chance of losing any one of you. Not because we are truly sworn companions or shield mates, but because together we may be mightier than we are separately. Look about you, berserker. Is this not seemingly an ill-assorted company?

"We have an elf, and the elven-kin are mighty fighters, to be sure. No one within this world will gainsay that they have proven that many times over. But they have other gifts that the rest of us do not possess. Behind you is a bard—a skald—and *his* weapon is not first that sword he wears, rather the power he draws from that harp of his. Can any other of us touch its strings to such purpose?

"Deav Dyne—no warrior, but a healer, a worker of spells, one who can draw upon potent powers which or who would not answer to any other's voice. And you, yourself, Naile Fangtooth— all know the gifts of the were-kind, both their powers and what trouble may follow the use of them. I am what I am. I have the spell that I used and perhaps one or two others I can summon.

However, I am no true daughter of such learning, rather one schooled to war. Yet again, I may have what each of the others of you lack. While you," she looked last to Milo, "are a swordsman, a rank that marks you as a seasoned fighting man. Still, it is what you wear upon your thumb that guides us through this desert.

"So, each of us having our own talent to offer, can we say that Gulth does not also have his?"

"Being what?" demanded Naile. "So far we have had to coddle him as if he were a babe. Would you now dowse him with all our water so he may stumble on, say, another day—or night's—journey? What then? Having used up our supplies—he is no better and we are the worse. I tell you, girl, battlemaid or no, such an action is a foolishness that only the greenest of country lads who has never borne the weight of a shield might decide upon—"

"However, she is right!" Milo slewed around to front the berserker, knowing well that perhaps he might also face a disastrous flare-up of the big man's murderous temper. What Yevele had just said was logical good sense. Their very mixed party differed from any questing company he could remember—so diversified that there must be some reason for its assembly. Certainly Gulth had contributed nothing so far but the weight of a burden. But he did wear the bracelet, so it followed he had his place in the venture.

For a moment, the swordsman thought that Naile would vent his anger. Milo was sure that he could never stand up to a berserker's attack. Then—

There came a ripple of notes. Milo, his own blood pounding heavily in his ears, was confused. A bird—here in this death wilderness?

He saw the flush subside in Naile's face, felt his own hand fall away from his sword hilt. Then he realized that Wymarc was smiling. His fingers on the harp strings made them sing once more.

Naile looked at the bard. "You play with magic, songsmith, and sometime you may find those fingers of yours burned." But there was no real threat behind his warning. It was as if the music had drawn the poison of anger out of him as speedily as a sword could let the life out of any man.

"My magic, berserker," returned Wymarc. "We may not be blood comrades, but the battlemaid has the right of it. Deserve it or not, we are bound fast together in this ploy. Therefore, I have one small suggestion to offer. This Afreeta of yours, if she is like all her kind, she can smell out both food and drink. Suppose you loose her, berserker. In the meantime, if our scaled fellow here needs water to keep life within that long body of his, I say give him of my share. I have often tramped roads where wells lay far apart."

Deav Dyne looked up from his beads. "Give of mine also, daughter." He pushed the skin he had borne closer to her.

The elf said nothing, only brought his skin, while Milo tugged at the stopper on his. For a long moment Naile hesitated.

"A snake-skin," he growled, "struck my shield mate's head from his shoulders. On that day I took oath, as I laid Karl under his stones of honor, that I would have vengeance for his blood price. That was three seasons ago and in a far part of the world. But if you all agree to this folly, I shall not be lessened by you. As for Afreeta—" He raised his hand to his throat and the pseudo-dragon crawled out, to sit upon it. "I think she will find us nothing beyond what we see here and now. But I cannot answer for her. She shall do that for herself." He loosed his small flyer into the night.

Deav Dyne, the girl, and Milo worked together, laving the skin of Gulth, until the lizardman coughed. His eyes, dull and nearly covered by the extra inner lid, opened.

They could not wet down his cloak again, that would have taken all the water of a small pond, Milo imagined. Perhaps though, with it about him the moisture on his skin would not evaporate so soon. At least the burning sun was gone. As they freed the cloaks they had used to roof their day shelter, the swordsman looked to his ring. To his great surprise fortune at last favored them a little, for, even in the dark, a spark of light shone there on what they hoped was their path.

Deav Dyne stepped up beside Gulth, pulling one of the lizardman's dangling arms about his own shoulders, lending him part of his own strength. The rest shrugged on their packs, Naile, without a word, slinging the cleric's along with his own. There were a few stars, high and cold, very remote, but tonight no moon. Still, the dust itself seemed oddly visible though Milo could discern no real radiance out of it—merely that it stretched as a pallid field ahead.

They wobbled and fought for balance until their aching muscles perforce adjusted to a gait necessary to maintain them afoot. At least the blowing of dust powder, which had accompanied them during their half-day's travel, appeared to have died away. Their surroundings were clear enough of the punishing haze for them to breathe more easily and see to a greater distance.

Milo moved out, his attention ever divided between the ring

and the way ahead, for they had to detour from time to time to avoid the rise of dunes. They had halted twice for rests before Afreeta's hissing call brought them to a quick third pause.

The pseudo-dragon sped directly to Naile, hooked claws in the folded back hood of his cloak, and pressed her snout as close to his helm-concealed ear as she could get.

"That way—" Naile gestured with his hand to the right. "She has made a find."

He stepped out of the line of their advance, apparently quite confident of Afreeta's report. Because the others had some hope in that confidence, they fell in behind him. Weaving a way through a miniature range of dust hills, they came out into a wide open expanse. From its nearly flat surface jutted upward two tall, thin columns, starkly dark against the pallid sand. Afreeta took wing once more, hissing loudly. She reached the nearest of those pillars and clung with taloned feet, her head pointing downward to the smooth dust. Her hissing became a squawk of excitement.

Milo and Naile floundered on until the berserker set hand to the pillar below the perch of his winged companion.

"Wood! Wood!" Now he pounded on it. "You know what this is? I have seen service aboard the free ships of Parth—this is a mast! There is a ship below it!"

He dropped to his knees scooping away dust with his cupped hands, sending its powder flying over his shoulder as a hound might dig at the burrow of prey gone to earth.

"But"—Milo moved away from the flying dust that swirled out from the berserker's exertions—"a buried ship—what might that still hold after all these years?"

"Anything." Ingrge's voice was calm, yet it would appear he

was infected with the madness that had gripped the berserker only with a little more logic in his action. For, before he squatted down a short distance away, he had drawn off one of his dust shoes and was using it as a shovel, doing greater good with that than Naile had been able to accomplish with his hands.

Milo was certain some madness born of this alien and threatening world (perhaps, even an outreaching of that which they sought and which must have defenses they could not conceive) had gripped both of them. Then Wymarc moved closer and deliberately knelt to unfasten his own webbed foot gear. He glanced up at Milo, his dust-begrimed face showing that lazy smile.

"Do not think they have taken leave of all senses, swordsman. Any ship that breasted such a sea as this must have gone well provisioned. And do not underrate our winged friend there. If she was told to seek water—that was what she quested for, nor would she make a mistake. It seems that perhaps miracles may yet be with us, even in these unregenerate and decadent days." With that, he, too, began to dig.

Though Milo could not really accept that they would find anything, he discovered he could not keep apart from their labor. So, save for Gulth, who lay on the dust well away from the scene of their efforts, they united to seek a ship that might have lain cradled in the dust since before even one stone of Greyhawk's wall had been set upon another.

It was a back-killing and disheartening task, for the dust shifted continually through their improvised shovels. And, though they mounded it as far away from where they dug as they could, streams of dust continually trickled down the sides of the hole to be lifted out again. They tried to steady these walls with the fabric of their cloaks, but Milo believed they were wasting their strength in folly. Then Naile gave a shout mighty enough to move the dunes themselves.

"Decking!"

Long ago Deav Dyne had produced his light-giving globe to aid their sight, and now he swung it below. It was true enough—what Milo had never really expected to see was firm under the berserker's boots—a stretch of planking. Afreeta fluttered down from her perch on the mast and landed on a ridge of yet uncleared dust. There she began to scrabble with her feet, again uttering her high squawk.

Naile pursed his lips, hissed in turn. The pseudo-dragon fluttered up, keeping her wings awhirr while he scooped vigorously at the site she had indicated. Within moments his sweeps had uncovered what could only be the edge of a hatch.

At the same moment, Milo looked down at his wrist. His bracelet had come to life.

"'Ware the dice!" he cried out, as he strove to concentrate with all the energy his tired body could summon on the beginning whirr of those warnings of danger. He did not even know if his warning had reached the others.

Heat warmed the metal as the points of light glinted. On, his mind urged. On—give me—give me—

The dice stopped, allowing their pattern to blaze just for a moment before they were dead, metal and gem together again. Milo snatched up the shield he had been using to carry off the up-thrown dust from the edge of the pit they were digging. His sword was already drawn as he swung slowly about, searching for an enemy he was sure must exist. He saw Gulth throw off the heavy cloak, pull himself to his knees, his hand fumbling weakly at the hilt of his own quartz-studded weapon.

Yevele, dumping a burden of dust from her own shield, scrambled to her feet and sank calf-deep in the loose ground. For the first time Milo thought of this impediment to any battle. To fight on their dust shoes would make even the most dexterous of swordsmen unsteady, unable to use even a fraction of his skill. To discard the webbing might plunge them instantly into a trap, keeping them fast-pinned at the pleasure of the foe.

Where *was* the enemy?

The pale stretch of the dust above the pit and the hillocks of powdery stuff they had dumped at a distance were clearly vacant of any save themselves. Ingrge crawled up, made for his bow and the arrow quiver that he had left beside the depleted water skins. The elf's head swung from side to side, and, though in this half-light Milo could not be sure, the swordsman believed Ingrge's nostrils expanded and contracted, testing the air for a scent human senses were too dulled to discover.

Deav Dyne was the next to crawl into sight. He must have left his light globe below in the pit, though his prayer beads swung from his left wrist. Now he stooped a foot or so away from the edge of their pit to gather up a fistful of dust. Chanting, he tossed this into the air, pivoted slowly, throwing similar handsful to each point of the compass as he used one of the archaic tongues of the temple-trained.

What he strove to do, Milo could not guess. But as far as he himself could gauge it, the spell achieved nothing.

"Heave, man, I have the lashing cut." Naile's bellow sounded from below. Had the berserker not heard the warning or taken heed of his own bracelet? Milo, reluctant to leave his post above, shouted back.

" 'Ware, Naile—"

"Take watch yourself!" roared the other. "I have seen the dice spin. But what we must face lies—"

There was a crash. Dust rose out of the pit in a great billowing cloud to blind their eyes, fill their mouths and noses, render them for a long moment helpless.

Then came another shout, fast upon that the warning grunt of a battle-mad boar many times louder than any true boar could utter. Without clear thought of what might happen, Milo, still wiping at his watering eyes with the back of his left hand swung around to wade toward the lip of the pit. For there was no mistaking the sounds now. Battle was in progress there.

13

The Liche Ship

THE DUST ITSELF CHURNED AND MOVED, UPSETTING MILO AS A wave might sweep the feet from under a man. He heard cries through the murk, fought to keep his feet, instinctively threw up his shield arm to give him a small breathing space between the billow of rising grit and his body which the dust threatened to bury.

Already the swordsman was held thigh deep in the outward spreading flood of gray-brown powder. More than half-blinded, gasping for breath, Milo reeled and fought against the powder that entrapped him. For all he could tell he was alone, the others might have been swallowed up, buried by this eruption. Yet he could still hear faintly that infernal grunting, even what might be the clash of steel against steel.

Firm in the shifting clouds of dust was a dark mass. There was a great upheaval where the ship lay. The craft might itself now be answering to some spell once laid upon it. Milo, his eyes smarting and watering to rid themselves of the fine grit, moved toward it, only to be brought up (unable to judge distance, against what seemed a solid wall, with force enough to drive the shield back against his chest and shoulder.

The waves of dust sent surging by the rise of this barrier were subsiding, the air clearing. Now the sound of battle came far more strong. Milo slung his shield to his back, forced the blade of his sword between his teeth in his dust-coated mouth and swept his hands along the wall for some method of climbing.

To the left his gropings caught the dangling skeleton of a ladder. With a mighty effort he pulled himself toward that, wondering if the stiff rope of its sides, the wood of its doles might crumble under his weight. He knew that, strange and unnatural as it might be and surely born of some form of unnatural magic, this was no wall that had risen so summarily from the depths of the Dust Sea. Rather it must be the long-buried ship.

He gripped the ladder and fought to raise himself out of the dust, kicking it to loosen its hold on him, drawing himself up with all the strength he could muster in his straining arms. The sea sucked at him avidly, but he won on to the next handhold and the next.

His feet came free, found purchase on the ladder, so he pulled himself aloft haunted by a horror of falling back into the dry sea, there to perhaps lie entombed forever.

Somehow Milo won to the deck, out into air that he could breathe, where the mist of dust had fallen away. Wymarc stood with his back against the butt of one of the masts. The bard's harp lay at his feet while in his hand his sword made swift play, as controlled as fingers had been on the strings of his instrument, keeping at bay three attackers.

Naile, in were form, plowed fearlessly into others emerging from the hatch he had broached, his heavy boar's head flashing with a speed seemingly unnatural to such an animal, his tusks catching and ripping up ancient mail as if age had pared it to the thinnest parchment.

While the enemy. . . .

Milo did not need the faint, musty smell of corruption that wafted towards them from that crew to know that these were liches, the Undead. Their body armor was the same color as the dust that had been their outward tomb for so long. They even wore masks of metal, having but holes for eyes and nostrils, which hung from their helmets, covering their faces.

The masks had been wrought in the form of fierce scowls, and tufts of metal, spun as fine as hairs, bearded their chins to fan outward over their mail corselets. They poured up from the hold, swords in hand—strange swords curved as to blade— which they swung with a will. And the Undead could not die.

Milo, as he reached the surface of the deck, saw Naile-boar savage one of the Undead with his tusks, breaking armor as brittle as the shell of a long-dead beetle, in fact breaking the liche almost in two. But its feet continued to stand and the torso, as it fell, still aimed a blow at its attacker.

"ALL-LL-VAR!" Without being aware that he had given voice to the battle cry of his youth, Milo charged at the liches that ringed Wymarc at the mast. His shield slammed into the back of one. Both armor and the dried body beneath broke. The swordsman stamped hard on an arm rising from the planking to sweep at his legs with one of the curved swords, brought down his own weapon on an angle between head and shoulder of another of the enemy advancing on Wymarc's left, while two of his fellows kept the bard busy.

Steel clanged against the breastplate edge, sheered a spread of metal thread beard, then took the helmed head from the thing's narrow shoulders. Yet Milo must strike again and again before, with a blow from his shield, he could send the dried body blundering out of his path.

Dimly he heard shouts from the others, though Wymarc held his breath to conserve energy for the fight. Milo leaped forward to engage a second of the Undead coming up behind the mast, its curved sword held at an angle well calculated to hamstring the bard. This liche was half crouched and the swordsman slammed his shield with all his power against its bowed shoulders. Tripping over the severed arm of one of those Wymarc had earlier accounted for (an arm that still heaved with the horrible Undead power), he fell, bearing under him the liche.

He was hardly aware of a curved sword striking the planking only inches away from his head. Milo rolled away from the liche. Without waiting to rise farther than his knees, he used his shield as a battering weapon for a second, striking the thing's head and shoulders. Then looking around he saw one that had been striving to free its weapon from the nearly fossilized wood lose both arm and half the shoulder from a blow aimed by Yevele, her sword used two handed and brought down with all the force she could deliver.

Ingrge, his green-brown forest garb standing out here as a bright color, waded into the mélé beyond. No arrow, not even one poisoned by the secret potions of the western hunters, could bring death to those already dead. So the elf had dropped his bow and was using his sword. Above all other sound, arose ever the terrible battle cry of Naile who charged again and again, blood dripping now from his thickly bristled shoulders, shreds of dried skin, bits of time-eaten metal and brittle bone falling from his tusks as he stamped and gored.

Something caught at Milo's heel. A head, or the travesty of a head sheared from a body, freed of the grotesque mask, lips long since completely dried away, snapped its teeth in open menace. The swordsman kicked out, sickened. Under the force of his blow that disembodied head spun around, was gone. Milo's shield was already up to meet another rush from the two that had been the last to climb into the air.

"Ayy-yy-yy-yy-yy-yy!" The were-boar turned in a circle, striving to free himself from the weight of one of the Undead. The thing had either lost or discarded its concealing helm. Its jaws were set in Naile's hind leg and there it gnawed with mindless ferocity at the tough flesh. Then, down through the air swept a sword serrated with wicked points of quartz, smashing the bodiless head into a shattered ruin. Gulth staggered on a step or two. Naile, with a last furious shake of his leg, wheeled away from the lizardman to hunt fresh prey. He charged again, and again, not at new attackers now, but stamping and lowering his great head to catch and toss aloft fragments of the Undead. Though there was still movement among the fallen, arms that strove to raise aloft swords, mouths that snapped, legs fighting to rise only to continually fall back again, none of those that had been imprisoned in the ship stood whole or ready to move against the adventurers.

Wymarc's arm hung limply against his side, blood dribbling sluggishly from ripped mail near his shoulder. Ingrge knelt well away from the mass Naile still stamped, using the blade of his sword to force apart jaws that had closed upon his ankle, with better luck than those that had earlier threatened Milo. Gulth leaned against the second mast. His snouted head was sunk upon his breast and he kept on his feet only by his hold on the mast and the fact that his sword, point down on the deck, gave him support.

The were-boar, having reduced to shreds and shards all the fallen, shimmered. Naile Fangtooth stood there in human form, breathing hard, some of the beast's red glare still in his eyes, wincing, as he moved, from a wound on his flank.

He drew a couple of deep breaths, but it was Wymarc, nursing his slashed arm against him, who spoke first.

"There are never guardians without that which they must guard. What is it, I wonder, that these were set here to protect?"

Yevele had withdrawn to the edge of the deck, wiping her sword blade over and over with a corner of her cloak, then deliberately cutting off the portion of the cloth that had touched the steel and discarding it among the mass of broken bodies and armor.

"They were near the end of the spell that bound them so," she said, not looking at what lay there. "Else they would have given us a far greater battle—"

"Or, perhaps"—Milo looked to the bracelet—"we have indeed learned a little of what Hystaspes told us could be done. Did you also will the aid of fortune in this?"

There was a murmur from the rest—mutual agreement. It would seem that they had perhaps changed in a little by their concentrated wills the roll of those dice which marked their ability to continue to exist.

Up from the open hatch spiraled Afreeta. She wheeled around Naile, uttering small cries into which imagination might read some measure of distress as she hovered on the level of his leg wound. The berserker gave a gruff sound which might almost have been a laugh.

"Now, then, my lady. I have taken worse. Yes, many times over. Also"—his laugh grew—"do we not have a healer-of-wounds with us?" He waved a hand to the bulwarks of the raised ship where Deav Dyne once more cradled his beads, the cleric's lips moving with inaudible, but none the less, meant-to-be-potent prayer. "However, what have we uncovered here, besides the spells of some wizard? As the bard has said, guardians do not guard without good reason." Limping, the berserker made his way to the edge of the hatch that had been pushed back to allow the exit of the liche defenders.

Milo glanced at Deav Dyne, the one among them best trained to pick up any emanation of Chaos, or perhaps of some other evil even older than men now living could guess. But the cleric's eyes were fast closed, he must be concentrating upon his own petitions. The swordsman went after the berserker. Even Yevele had picked a way to that opening, avoiding the noisome litter on the deck.

The faint stench of corruption was stronger here. Ingrge snapped his firestone and caught up a bit of ancient rag to bind about an arrow shaft. He did not use his bow, but rather sent the small flame down as a hand-thrown dart. It stuck into a chest, burning brightly enough to let them see that nothing now moved there.

What they looked into was a well, over which reached, fore and aft, a walkway. On either side of it were wedged great stoppered jars, plus a few chests piled one upon the other. Afreeta fluttered down to perch on the sealed lid of one of those man-tall jars, pecking away at it between intervals of hissing. For the third time Naile laughed.

"She has found us what we asked of her. Down there lies something drinkable."

Milo could hardly believe that countless centuries might have left any water unevaporated. He swung over and down, making his way cautiously toward the jar Afreeta indicated, alert to any sound from out of the dark which might signal that all the liches had not yet come forth to fight. Reluctantly he sheathed his sword, used his dagger to pick at the black sealing stuff on the jar which was near iron-hard. At last, using the blade as a chisel and the pommel of his sword as a hammer, he broke loose a first small chunk. Once that was free the rest flaked into a dust Milo could brush away.

He levered up the lid.

"What have we then?" Naile demanded as the swordsman leaned over to sniff at the contents. "Wine of the gods?"

The smell was faint but the jar was full to within two fingers' breadth of the top. Milo wiped a finger on his breeches and lowered it. Wet and thin—not like something that had begun to solidify. He drew forth his finger, holding it close to his nose. The skin was pink, as if flushed by blood. But the smell that came to his nostrils was not unpleasant.

"Not water, but liquid," he reported to those above. Afreeta clung to the lip of the jar and sent her spade-tipped tongue within, to lick and lick again at its contents. An object dangled down to swing within Milo's reach. He recognized one of the smaller bottles that had been fastened to their saddles.

"Give me a sample!" Naile boomed from above.

Obediently the swordsman wiped off the outer skin of the

bottle, pushed it deep enough into the container so that a wave of liquid was sent gurgling into the bottle. Then he allowed it to swing aloft.

Prying loose the burning arrow he trod carefully along the runway of the hold. There were at least fifty of the great jars, all sealed and wedged upright, as if their one-time owners were determined they would not leave their racks before the ship came to harbor once more.

The chests were less well protected against the ravages of time. He threw open two, to expose masses of ill-smelling stuff that might have either been food or material now near rotted into slime. Of the liches or where they had been during their imprisonment here he could see no sign. He had no wish to move far from the promise of escape the open hatch gave.

When Milo swung up, via a helping rope of two capes twisted together, he found Deav Dyne with his healing potions. Wymarc's arm was already bound, and the bard held his hand out before him, flexing his fingers one after the other to test their suppleness. Ingrge and Yevele, portions of material wrapped about their noses and mouths, were using the sweep of their swords and Yevele's shield to push from the deck, over into the dust, the remains of the spectre force.

Gulth squatted by the far mast. His quartz-studded weapon lay across his knees, and he had bowed his head on his folded arms, as if he had withdrawn into some inner misery. Naile lay on the deck, his hairy thigh exposed. Into his wound Deav Dyne was dribbling some of the liquid from the newly opened jar below.

"Ha, swordsman." Naile hailed Milo. "It would seem these dead men had something to fight for after all." He took the flask from the cleric's hand and allowed a goodly portion to pour from its spout into his mouth. Deav Dyne gave one of his narrow, grudging smiles.

"If I be not mistaken, today we have found a treasure here. This is the fabled Wine of Pardos, that which heals the body, sharpens the wits, was the delight of the Emperors of Kalastro in the days before the Southern Mountains breathed forth the plague of fire. But," now Deav Dyne's smile faded, "we have troubled something that may have been a balance in this land and who knows what will come of that?"

Naile took another and larger swallow. "Who cares, priest? I have drunk of the vintages of the Great Kingdom—and twice plundered caravans of the Paynim who fancy themselves the greatest vintners of our age. Naught they could offer goes so smoothly down a man's throat, fuels such a gentle warmth in his belly, or makes him look about him with a brighter eye. Wine of Pardos or not"—he set down the flask and slapped his hand against his chest—"by the Brazen Voice of Ganclang, I am whole and a proper man again!"

Since Deav Dyne had pronounced the bounty from below good they drew upon it freely, filling the skins that had shrunken to empty flaps. Gulth offered no refusal when the cleric washed down once more the lizardman's dust-clogged skin and soaked his cloak in another of the jars; leaving it there to become completely saturated.

They made their camp on board the ship and speculated as to what had brought it boiling out of the dust and set its dead defenders upon them. Perhaps here, too, a geas had been set on ship and defenders which their disturbance of its burial had brought so to fulfillment. Though the elf and the cleric had used their talents to sniff out any form of the Greater Magic that might lie on board, both admitted that they were left with that mystery unresolved. Milo privately believed that the army of the liche had not been set, for what might be a millennium, merely to guard a cargo of wine jars, precious though those might be.

He could not deny that the wine did have powers of recuperation. Wounds bathed in it closed nearly instantly, while it was as refreshing to the taste as the clearest and coldest of spring water could have been. As he took the second part of the night watch, he moved slowly back and forth along the deck wishing they might use this ship to travel onward. But the masts were bare of any sail, and neither he nor the others, though they had discussed the matter wistfully, could see any other form of propulsion. They had not tried to explore the ship farther than the hatch Naile had originally forced open.

At the stern there was the bulk of a cabin, the door of which had resisted even Naile's strength when he had earlier tried it. Milo believed that the berserker was now willing to leave well enough alone. The battle with the liches, a victory though it had been, had left them all shaken. It was one thing to face the living, another to have to batter to pieces things already dead but endowed with the horrible strength and will these had displayed.

Milo made his way to the bow of the ship. As always, in the Sea of Dust, here came a soft whispering from the dunes. Now it seemed to him that he heard more than just the wind-shift of the dust, that the whispering was real. He strained to catch actual words, words uttered in a voice below, just below, the level of his hearing. So vivid was the impression that out there enemy forces were gathering that he glanced now and then to his bracelet, expecting to see it come to life in warning. Milo made his sentry rounds, up one side of the deck, down the other, passing the cloak-wrapped forms of the others, with an ever-growing urgency. He even went to hang over the side railing and stare down to where the debris of the battle had been flung.

But there was nothing of it to be seen—shattered bone, rust-breached armor, all had vanished into the dust as if those they had fought had never existed at all. However, there was something abroad in the night—

The swordsman set a firm rein upon his imagination. There was nothing abroad in the night! He was well aware that his senses were far inferior to those of either Ingrge or Naile—that Afreeta, perhaps, had the keenest ability of them all. Surely the wine they had drunk had not brought any dimming of mind with it—only a renewal of strength.

Then why did he seek what was neither to be seen nor heard?

Still he tramped the deck and watched and waited. For what he could not have said. Ridden by increasing uneasiness, he went to awaken Naile to take the next watch. Yet the swordsman hesitated to speak of his unrest, knowing full well that the berserker would be far more able to detect anything that was wrong.

Milo could not remember having dreamed so vividly before as he did now in the sleep into which he swiftly slid. The dream had the same background as when he had been on watch, possessing such reality he might have been fastened by some spell to the mast, immobile and speechless, to watch what happened.

Naile, limping very little, was making the same round Milo himself had followed during his tour as sentry. When the berserker reached the bow of the ship the second time, he stood still, a certain tenseness in his stance, his head turned to stare southward over the billows of the dust sea.

Then Milo, in the dream, followed Naile's fixed gaze. It was . . . it was like those shadows that had dogged them across the plains, and yet not the same either. He believed that he did not really see, he only caught, through Naile's mind, in some odd, indescribable way, the sensation of seeing. As if one were trying to describe to the blind the sense of sight itself. But there was that out there which Naile did not see and which held the berserker's attention locked fast.

Naile hitched his cloak about him, axe firmly grasped in his hand. He returned to where the ladder hung. Down he climbed, over the rail and into the dust. As he so passed out of Milo's sight, the swordsman fought against the bonds of the dream, for he was now certain, without being told, that Naile Fangtooth was being drawn away, led by what he saw.

Milo's struggles to awaken did not break the dream. He was forced to watch Naile, dust shoes once more bound to his feet, slip and slide away from the ship, his broad back turned on his companions, as if they had been wiped from his memory. There was an eagerness in Naile's going. It was almost as if he saw before him someone or something he had long sought. In spite of the unsteady surface beneath his feet, he ploughed steadily southward, while Milo was forced to watch him vanish, wearing a path among the whispering dunes.

When Naile was swallowed up by the dust sea, Milo himself dropped into a darkness in which there was nothing more to be seen or puzzled over.

"Milo!" A voice roared through the darkness, broke open his cocoon of not caring.

He opened his eyes. On one side knelt Wymarc, the laughter lines about his generous mouth, bracketing his eyes, wiped from his suntanned skin. As Milo shifted his head at a touch upon his shoulder, he saw to his left Yevele, her helmet laid aside, so that the red-brown of her tightly-netted hair was fully visible. In her thin face her eyes narrowed in a strange wariness, measuring him.

"What—?" he began.

"Where is Naile?" The question drew Milo's attention back to the bard.

The swordsman levered himself up on his elbows. Out of the smothering and deadening dark from which they had drawn him came, in a burst of vivid memory, that strange dream. Before he thought of what might be only a vision he spoke aloud.

"He went south." And, at the same moment, he knew that he indeed spoke the truth.

14

Rockna the Brazen

SWIFTLY MILO ADDED TO THAT GUESS (WHICH WAS NO GUESS, HE was certain, but the truth) the description of his dream. Deav Dyne nodded before the swordsman had finished. Head high, the cleric had drawn a little away to the same position in the bow that Naile had first held in Milo's vision. Now he leaned forward, his attention centered afar as the berserker's had been.

Milo scrambled up behind him, one hand clutching at the cleric's shoulder.

"What do *you* see?" he demanded.

His own eyes could pick up nothing but the waves of dust dunes marching on and on until the half-light of early dawn melted one into another.

"I see nothing." Deav Dyne did not turn his head. "But there is that out there which awakes a warning. Sorcery carries its own odor—one which can be tainted even as those dead be-fouled this ship."

The cleric's nostrils were distended, now they quivered a little, as do those of a hound seeking out the trace of a quarry. Ingrge moved up to join them with the noiseless tread of his race.

"Chaos walks." His words were without emotion as he, too, stared into the endless rise and fall of the dust billows. "And yet . . ."

Deav Dyne nodded sharply. "Yes, it is 'and yet,' elf-warrior. Evil—but of a new kind—or perhaps old mingled with the new. Our comrade-in-arms goes to seek it—and not with his mind—"

"What do you mean?" Milo wanted to know.

"That sorcery has laid a finger on him, and mighty must be the power of that finger. For the were-kin possess their own potent magic. I say that Naile Fangtooth does not govern his body in this hour, and perhaps even not his mind," Deav Dyne replied slowly.

The bard and Yevele had drawn closer. Now Wymarc slung his bagged harp over his shoulder.

"That would argue that we may be needed," he said matter-of-factly.

Within himself Milo knew the truth of a decision he had not even been aware of making. Though they were not kin by either blood or choice (he had no strong liking for the were-kind as no fighter did who had not the power of the change) yet at this moment he could walk in no way that did not lead him on the trail of Naile. Tied they were, one to the other, by a bond stronger than choice.

He glanced at the ring that had led them by its thread-map patterning. A film of dust lay across the veined stone. When Milo rubbed at the setting with his other thumb, striving to clear it, he discovered the haze was no dust but an apparent fading of the lines themselves.

South and west Naile had tramped in the swordsman's vision, Alfreeta curled in slumber about his throat. Was it that both the berserker and the pseudo-dragon had been ensnared in a single spell? Across these dust dunes what man could leave a trail to be followed after he himself had disappeared? The rest of them could wander here, lost, until they died from lack of water or were caught in the menace of some trap such as this ship had held. Yet, south and west they must go.

They busied themselves with their packs. Gulth drew about him the cloak which had been left to soak up all that it might of the wine. Then, one by one, they dropped from the deck of the ship, their dust-walking shoes strapped on firmly, to set out in the wake of the berserker.

The elf, as he had on the plain, moved to the fore of their party, walking with steady purpose as if he guessed what they sought lay ahead.

Slowly the sun arose. In this land it had a pallor and was obscured from time to time by wind-driven clouds of grit. Once more they bound those strips cut from their clothing about their mouths, shielding that part of their faces left bare below the outjut of helm, the hood of travel cloak. Milo wondered at the sureness of the elf who led them. In this fog of dust he himself would have been long since lost, might perhaps wander in circles until he died.

He kept close watch upon his map-ring, hoping that it would flare once more into life, provide a compass. That did not happen.

Luckily those gusts of wind that carried the dust in swirls and clouds blew only intermittently. There were periods when the fog of particles was stilled. During one such moment, Ingrge paused, raised one hand in a signal that halted the others, the plodding Gulth, muffled in his now dust-covered cloak, plowing into Milo with force enough to nearly knock the swordsman from his feet.

"What—?" Yevele's voice was hoarse. She had uttered but that one word when the elf made a second emphatic gesture. Wymarc shifted the harp upon his shoulder. His head was upheld, but his face was so covered by the improvised mask that Milo read urgency only in the movements of his body. Whatever had alerted the elf had reached the bard also. Still Milo himself was aware of nothing.

Nothing, until. . . .

The sound was faint—yet he caught it. A hissing scream. Such a cry came from no human throat.

"Big scaled one . . ." The slurring in Gulth's voice nearly matched the hiss of that scream. Though he stood shoulder to shoulder with Milo, the lizardman's words were muffled and hard to catch. A second and a third time that challenge sounded. For it *was* a challenge and such as Milo had once heard with dread. A scrap of memory stirred awake in his mind.

Big scaled one? Dragon! In that moment the bracelet on his wrist gave forth the warmth he both waited and feared. Feverishly he tried to channel his power of thought, not to awaken memory, but to affect the turn of the dice. A dragon in full battle fever. What man—or men—could hope to stand against such? Still, with the rest, he moved toward the source of that cry, his dust shoes shuffling at the fastest pace he could maintain.

Even a were with power of the change could not hope to front a dragon and come forth unscathed—or even living. . . .

They tried to make better time by seeking out a way between the dunes, not up and down the treacherous sliding heights of those mounds. Again they heard the dragon call—which did not yet hold any note of triumph. Somehow, he whom they sought, for Milo never doubted that it was Naile Fangtooth who fronted the scaled menace, managed to keep fighting on.

The hissing of the giant reptile was louder. On their wrists the dice had ceased to live and spin. How successful had they been in raising their power? To fight a dragon—Milo shook his head at his present folly. Still he plowed on, his sword now in his hand, though he could not remember having drawn it.

So they came into a space where the dust dunes had been leveled through some freak of the wind. This miniature plain formed the arena of battle.

The dragon, its wings strangely small as if shriveled to a size that could not raise the bloated body from the earth, beat the air—raising a murk through which its own brazen scales shone with the menace of a raging fire. This creature was smaller than Lichis, but that was no measurement to promise victory. As its head snapped aloft and it opened its fanged jaws for another of those screams, its rolling red eyes caught sight of their party.

With a speed its bulk should have made impossible, that double-horned head darted at them, striking snakelike. Milo could smell the strong acid stench of the pointed tongue which dripped with venom, a poison to fire-eat the flesh from a man's bones in the space of five breaths, for which no sorcery could supply a remedy.

His battered shield had been lifted only a finger's breadth and he had no chance, he knew, against such a lightning swift attack. For it seemed to Milo those blazing red eyes were centered on *him*. Then, out of the air, there came a darting thing, small enough in size to ride upon the spear point of that dripping tongue. But it was not to ride so that the thing made a blurr of attack. Rather she spread small claws to gash and tear at the tongue, fearless of the venom gathered and dripping from the lash of yellow-red flesh.

The tongue whipped and struck from side to side, curling to seize its small attacker and draw into the dragon's maw the glittering body of Afreeta, even as a frog of the marshes strikes and takes into its gaping mouth an unwary fly.

Now the pseudo-dragon twisted and turned in the murk, sometimes hidden, now visible again. Afreeta could not come at the tongue again to strike, but neither did she retreat. Her maneuvers meant that the dragon might not carry forward its attack on the party below.

Out of the dust cloud, which the dragon's fanning wings kept alive, came the boar-shape Milo had seen in action before. But this time Naile Fangtooth was hampered. His were-shape vanished and he was a man for three strides, then a boar, and then a man, a constant change of shape that it seemed, the berserker could not control. The man-body held for longer and longer moments, until, at last, Naile gave up his struggle to go were. Instead, axe in both fists, he fronted the dragon as a man.

The fitful strikes and twists of the scaled body made a blur in cloudy battle. But it was Afreeta's determined assault on the creature's head and tongue that prevailed, though the pseudo-dragon was twice nearly caught in looping coils snapped whip-fast through the air.

Something else pierced the cloud of dust. Milo saw an arrow thud against the heavy brow-ridge of the embattled dragon, fall to the ground. Ingrge was methodically aiming at the most vulnerable part of the creature, its slightly bulbous eyes—only so fast were the dartings of the dragon head that it would seem even one with the fabled skill of the ranger folk could not hope to strike such a target.

The constant fanning of those wings was a distraction, and the grit they brought into the air stung in the eyes, was like to blind those the creature fronted. It screamed and bellowed, striving to use its tongue, the forked barb on the end of that, more deadly than any arrow human or elfkind could fashion.

Milo moved in, discovering that fear and a kind of anger, which the sight of that body awoke in him, made him a battle-field of their own. The emotions remained equally matched, so he did not run from the encounter as half of him wanted, but humped forward, hampered by the dust shoes.

There were other shadows in the deepening rise of the dusk the wings created. He was not alone, still he was—walled in by that fear he could not yet raise enough anger to master. His sword was heavy in his hand as he caught enough sight of that pendulous, scaled belly to give him a target of sorts.

Milo struck with all the speed and skill he could muster. Unlike the fight on the ship, nothing gave or broke under that blow: Rather it was as if he had brought the point of his blade against immovable stone. The hilt was nearly jarred from his hold. Then, close enough so that the stench of it made his head swim for an instant, the looping tongue, with behind it that armory of great, discolored fangs, swept toward him.

There was a speeding dart through the air. Perhaps more from an unusual turn of fortune than an inherent skill, the down-turned spike of that tongue was pierced through by an arrow. The shaft gravitated in a wild dance as the dragon lashed back and forth its most cunning weapon, striving to free its tongue end.

Out of the dust cloud arose a clawed foot, each talon on it being a quarter of Milo's own body length. The foot expanded and contracted those claws, striving to catch at the arrow. In so doing the movements exposed, for instants only, a small, scaled pocket of noisome flesh existing between limb and body. The swordsman threw himself forward, nigh losing his balance because he had forgotten the dust shoes. Though Milo went to one knee, he thrust again with his sword into that crevice between limb and body.

Then he was hurled aside, skidding face downward into the dust, where his fight changed to one for breath alone. He waited for a second slash of that foot to rip him into bloody rags. But the blow did not come. Desperately he squirmed deeper into the dust, one arm protecting his face, hoping in some way to use the stuff that had defeated him to protect him a little now.

One breath-length of time, perhaps a little more, passed. Then there sounded a cry that deafened him. The sound went on, ringing through his head, until the whole world held nothing else but that bellow of fury and agony.

A hand caught at his shoulder, pulled at him. Milo squirmed in the direction that clutch would draw him. Why he had not been seized already by the claws of the dragon he did not know. Each second of freedom he still had he determined to put to escape, vain though any hope of that might be.

Now a second set of fingers was on his other shoulder, and they bit as deep as his mail would allow, new strength in them drawing him on. Behind sounded another screech, and through it the roaring of another voice, human in timber, mouthing words Milo could not understand.

When he was again on his feet, aided by those holds upon him, he saw that it was Deav Dyne and Gulth who had come to his aid. Breathless, his mouth and throat choked with dust until he was near to the point of retching, he swung around.

Naile in human form fronted the dragon. From the right eye of the maddened beast bobbed the feathered end of an arrow, proving that the famed skill of the elfkind was not distorted by report. The axe of the berserker moved with skill—and speed— to strike at the maimed head that darted down at him. Near enough to evoke attack in turn was a slender figure with shield raised as a protection against the venom-dripping tongue, sword held with the readiness and cool skill of a veteran.

Steel arose and held steady. The creature had shaken free of the arrow that had pinned its tongue, but the tonguetip was now split raggedly asunder. Perhaps in its pain the dragon lost what wits it carried into combat, for the tongue flicked at that steadily held sword as if to enmesh the steel and tear it from the warrior's hand. Instead the now ragged flesh came with force against the cutting edge of the blade. There was a shower of venom and dark blood—a length of tongue, wriggling like a serpent, flew through the dusty murk.

Now jaws gaped over the warrior, the head came down—

Naile struck, his axe meeting the descending head with a force that the dragon's attack must have added to. The creature gave another cry—spewing forth blood—and jerked its head aloft. So it dragged from Naile's hands the axe that was embedded in its skull between the eyes. It reared high and Milo cried out—though his warning might be useless even as he gave it.

Naile's arm swept Yevele from her feet, sending her rolling into the embrace of the dust, into which she sank as into a sea of water. Even as the berserker had sent her as well out of danger as he could, Naile himself threw his own body backward, striving to avoid the second descent of that fearsome head.

So loudly did the dragon cry, Milo heard no twang of bowstring. Yet he saw a feathered shaft appear in the left eye, sink into it for most of its length. The creature crashed forward. Though its stumpy wings still fluttered, the force of its fall sent it deep into the dust, just missing Naile who fought his way through it as if he swam.

Up from the embrace of the dust the blinded head of the dragon heaved once, curving back upon the wings, snout and evil mask of the foreface pointing to the sky above them. The roar from the fanged jaws was such that Milo's hands covered his ears, endeavoring to shut out that scream of pain and fruitless rage. Twice more did the creature give voice—and then its head sank, jerked up a little, sank again. The ensuing silence held them all as might a spell.

Milo dropped his hands, stared at the bulk now sinking deeper into the hold of the dust. A dragon—and it was slain! He found his heart beating faster, his breath coming quicker. Fortune indeed had stood at their backs this day!

Naile floundered to his feet, fought the dust to get back to the creature's side. His hands closed upon the haft of his axe and his body tensed with effort as he strove to loosen the blade from the skull. Milo looked to Ingrge.

"Never shall I doubt what is said of the arrow mastery of your people," he said through the dust which still clogged his throat.

"Nor sword and axe skill of yours," returned the elf. "Your own stroke, swordsman, was not one to be despised."

"My stroke?" Milo glanced down at his hands. They were empty. For the first time he thought of shield and sword.

"If you would regain your steel," Deav Dyne said, "you needs must burrow for it before the scaled one is utterly lost in the dust." He gestured to the body of the dragon, now indeed some three-quarters buried—though the wings still twitched feebly now and then, perhaps so keeping clear the scaled back that they could still see through the dispersing fog.

Two forms, so clothed in dust as to seem a part of that same fog, came blundering away from where Naile still fought to free his axe. The larger brushed the clinging grit from the smaller, the hump of harp between his shoulders identifying the bard.

At the cleric's words, he raised his head, his face so masked in dust that he might have walked by blood kin and not been hailed.

"This was such a battle as can make song fodder." He spat dust. "Yes, swordsman, that was a lucky stroke of yours beneath the leg. Even as this valiant battlemaid did sever the poison tongue. Dragon-slayers, all of you! For it took the skill of more than one to bring down Rockna of the Brass."

"Ha!" Naile had his axe free. Now he looked over his shoulder. "Dig it will be for your steel, swordsman." Even as Milo pushed forward, trying vainly to remember the feel of scaled skin parting from his own blow and finding that that second or two of realization eluded him, the berserker began to dig furiously along the body of the dragon, using, as they had on the ship, his dust shoe for a scooping shovel.

Milo hastened to join. The fetid smell of the creature's body was near to overpowering as they worked shoulder to shoulder. Now Wymarc and Deav Dyne came to aid them. A lost sword was enough to threaten them all in this place and time.

Milo coughed, spat, and kept to his scooping. Their combined efforts laid bare the shoulder of the creature and the top of the foreleg. Naile put hand to the leg and heaved, striving to draw it aside, leaving a crevice between body and leg free from the slither of the ever-moving dust. Milo leaned far over, gagging at the stench. There indeed was his sword. He could sight the hilt protruding at an angle from the softer-scaled leg. Lying across the limb of the dragon, he put both hands to the hilt, as Naile had done with the axe, and exerted his full strength.

Though he could not remember planting that steel so, he must have done it with energy enough to bury it deeply. At first there was solid resistance to his struggle, then the length buried within the body of Rockna gave. He sprawled back, the bloodstained blade snapping up and out into the open.

"Hola!"

That cry drew all their attention. Ingrge had, unseen, climbed one of the dunes that ringed this arena in which they had fought. He was looking north and now his arm arose in a gesture Milo could not read. But Deav Dyne started a step or so forward, then came to halt. The dusty face he turned toward the others was grave.

"We go from peril to peril." He fumbled with his beads again.

Naile's head lifted, he growled, his rumble sounding more like the irritated grunt of a bear than either man or boar.

"What hunts us now, priest? Dragon, liche . . . ?"

Wymarc watched the elf who was coming down the dune, setting one foot below the other with careful precision and more speed than Milo knew he himself could give to such action.

"The wind." The elf came up to them. "There is a storm raising the dust and coming toward us."

Dust! Milo's thoughts moved fearfully. A sea of dust—just as a desert was a sea of sand. And he had heard only too much of what happened to those caught in the wild whirl of sandstorms. This dust was finer, would be more easily swept up and carried to bury a man.

Wymarc swung around, looking to the dragon their efforts had partly unburied.

"What was our bane may be our fortune," he observed with some vigor. "The storm is from the north?"

Ingrge gave a single swift nod. He, too, was looking to the dragon's body.

"You mean . . . Yes, a perilous chance indeed, but perhaps our only one now!" Deav Dyne dropped his beads into the front of his robe. "It is such a chance as the Oszarmen take in desert lands when caught in storms." He stooped and loosed one of his dust shoes—then made his way around the half-uncovered dragon and started to dig with the same vigor that Milo and Naile had used moments earlier.

That they could use the body for a barrier against clouds of whirling dust Milo doubted. But perilous though such a chance might be, to find any better escape was now out of the question.

So they dug with a will, heaping the dust they dredged out on the far side of the scaled body. Suddenly Yevele spoke.

"If that were set down"—she pointed to the stuff they raised and tossed beyond—"would it not cake into a greater barrier? See, here the dragon's blood has stiffened this dust into a solid surface. We fight against dust not sand. What we deal with is far lighter and less abrasive."

"It is a thought worth the following." Milo looked to where those skins filled with the ship's wine lay. If one balanced drinkers' needs against such a suggestion—which would give them the best chance for survival?

"A good one!" Wymarc started for the skins. "As you say we do not face sand—for which may the abiding aid of Faltforth the Suncrown be praised!"

They decided that two of the skins might be sacrificed to their scheme. It was Deav Dyne and the bard who, between them, dribbled the wine across the heaped dust beyond the dragon's bulk. Milo took heart at their efforts when he saw that indeed the blood that had seeped from the slain creature had puddled and hardened the fine grit into flat plates which could be lifted and used to reinforce the wine-stiffened dust.

They worked feverishly, moving as fast as they could. Now one could see the dust cloud darkening the sky. Moments later they crouched, their cloaks drawn over their heads to provide pockets of breathable air—air that was air whether it be tainted with the stench of the dragon's body or not. The rough edges of the dead beast's scales bit into their own flesh as they strove to settle themselves to endure attack from this subtle and perhaps more dangerous foe.

15

Singing Shadow

MILO STIRRED. A WEIGHT PINNED HIM TO THE GROUND. SOME-time during the force of the storm he had lost consciousness. Even now his thoughts were sluggish, blurred. Storm? There had been a storm. His shoulder rasped against something solid and his nose was clogged not only with the ever-present dust, but also with a stench so evil that he gagged, spat, and gagged again. To get away from that—yes, that was what he must do.

It was dark, as dark as if the dust had sealed his eyes. He forced his hands into the soft powder under him, strove to find some firm purchase there to enable him to heave himself up, to shake the burden from his back. There was no such solid surface. None but the wall scraping at his shoulder. Now he flung out an arm and used it to push himself up and away.

Dust showered down as he wavered to his feet, steadying himself by holding onto the rough barrier he had found. At least he was upright, looking up and out into night. Night—?

Milo shook his head, sending more powdery stuff flying outward in a mist. It was difficult to marshal coherent thought. Some stealthy wizardry had claimed him—freezing, not his clumsy body, but his mind into immobility.

But. . . .

Milo's head turned. He had heard *that*! He edged around so that, though the barrier against which he had sheltered still half-supported him, it was now at his back. On his wrist there was movement. Still deep in the daze which nullified even his basic sense of danger, he saw the dice flicker alive, begin to turn.

There was something—something he must do when that happened. Only he could not think straight. Not now—for from the waste of dunes came that other sound, sweet, low, utterly beguiling. The song of a harp in the hands of a master? No, rather a voice that shaped no words, only trilled, called, promised.

Milo frowned down at the bracelet. If he could only think what it was he should do here and now! Then his arm fell to his side, for that trilling sound soothed all his wakening anxieties, pulled him. . . .

The swordsman moved forward toward the hidden source of that call. He sank nearly to his knees in the dust drifts, floundered and fought, dust shoes near forgotten until he strove impatiently to lash them on. The need to find this singer who used no words moved him onward as if he were drawn by a chain of bondage.

Fighting against the insidious pull of the dust, he rounded the base of a dune. Moonlight sent strange shadows across his way. The night was bitterly cold. But there was no wind and the dust disturbed by his floundering efforts fell quickly back again.

There was light—not moonlight but a stronger gleam, though

it did not have the warmth of a torch or the steady beam of a lantern. Rather. . . .

Milo came to a stop. She stood with her back to him, her hands upheld to the moon itself. Between those hands swung a disk on a chain—a disk that made a second moon, a miniature of the one above her.

Yevele!

No helmet covered her head now, nor was her hair netted tight. Instead it flowed about her like a cloak. The pallid light of her moon pendant took away the warmth of color that was in her hair by day, gave to all of her a silvery overcast.

She had used the spell of immobility—what other sorcery could she lay tongue and hand to? There were women secrets that even the wizards could not fathom. Milo had heard tell of them. He shook his head as if to loosen a pall of dust from his mind, as he had in part from his body.

Women magic—cold. Moon magic. . . . All men knew that women had a tie with the moon which was knit into their bodies. What she wrought here might be as alien to him as the thoughts and desires of a dragon—or a liche—if the dead-alive had thoughts and not just hungers and the will of Chaos to animate them. Yet Milo could not turn away—for still that trilling enticed, drew him.

Then she spoke, though she did not turn her head to see who stood there. It was as if she had knowledge of him, perhaps because she had sent this sorcery to draw him. That sudden thought, he discovered, held a strange new warmth.

"So you heard me then, Milo?" There was none of the usual crisp note in her voice, rather gentleness—a greeting subtle and compelling as a scent.

Scent? His nostrils expanded. The foul odor of the dead dragon was gone. He might have stood in a spring-greened meadow where flower and herb flourished to give this sweetness to the air.

"I heard." His answer was hardly more than a whisper. There worked in him now emotions he could not understand. Soldier's women he knew, for he had the same appetites as any man. But Yevele—though mail like unto his own weighted upon her, blurred the curves of her body—Yevele was unlike any woman he had stretched out hand to before.

Now his right hand did rise, without any conscious effort on his part, reaching toward Yevele, though she still did not turn to look at him. The cold light caught on the bracelet he wore with a flicker. It might have been that one of the dice had made a turn of which he was not aware. But the thought hardly touched his mind before she spoke again, driving it fully from him.

"We have powers, Milo, we who follow the Horned Lady of the Sword and Shield. It is sent to us from time to time—the forelooking. Now it has come to me. And this forelooking tells me that our lives are being woven into a single cord—both of us being the stronger for that uniting. Also—" Now at last she did move and he saw clearly her features, which were as solemn and set as might be those of a priestess intoning an oracle from a shrine. "Also we have in truth a duty laid upon us."

Her straight gaze caught and held his eyes, and there appeared a dazzle between them. He raised higher the hand he had put out to her, to shade his eyes from that bemusing sparkle of light. But it was gone in an instant. Then he asked dully, "That duty being?"

"We are to be the fore of the company, because we are in

truth meant to be one. Strength added to strength shall march in the van. Do you not believe me, Milo?"

Again the dazzle sprang between them. His thoughts fell into an ordered pattern, so he marveled that he had not realized this all long ago. Yevele spoke the truth, they were the ordained spearhead of the company.

"Do you not understand?" She took one step, a second toward him. "Each of us has a different talent, welded together we make a weapon. Now is the time that you and I, swordsman, must play our own role."

"Where and how?" A faint uneasiness stirred in him. But Yevele before him was not the source of that uneasiness—she could not be. Was it not exactly as she had said? They were each but a part—together they were a whole.

"That it has been given me to see in the foreknowledge." Her voice rang with confidence. "We march—there!" The hand still holding the moon disk swept out, away—and the disk appeared to blaze, giving a higher burst of cold light to her pointing fingers.

"See—" Now the stern quality left her voice. In its place was an eagerness. They might be fronting an adventure in the safe outcome of which she had full assurance. "I have brought the dust shoes. The moon is high and the light full. Also the storm is past—we have the night before us."

She stooped to pick up the crude shoes he knew well. Then her fingers touched lightly on Milo's wrist, below the band of the bracelet. Though she looked so cold in this light, yet a warmth spread upward along his arm from that lightest of touches. Her eyes held his again, commanding, assured.

Of course she was right. But . . .

"Where?" He repeated part of his question.

"To what we seek, Milo. No, you need no longer depend upon that ring of yours with its near-forgotten map. The Lady has given full answer to my pleas. See you!"

She whirled the moonlit disk at the length of a chain, letting it fly free. It did not fall, to sink and be hidden in the dust. Rather there was another dazzle of light and Milo blinked. For in its place a spot of light hovered in the air at the level of Yevele's eyes.

"Moon magic!" She laughed. "To each his own, Milo. I do no more than any who has some spell training can do. This is a small thing of power, it will be drawn to any source of Power that is not known to us, or that is alien to our understanding. Thus it can lead us to that which we seek."

He grunted and went to one knee to tighten the lashings of the sand shoes. Magic was chancy—he was no spell-user. But neither, he was certain, could any agent of Chaos have marched with them undiscovered since they had left Greyhawk. Deav Dyne—Ingrge—both would have known, caught the taint of evil at their first meeting with Yevele.

"The others?" he half-questioned as he arose again. She had moved a little away and there was a shade of impatience on her face. Though she now bore her helmet in the crook of one arm she made no attempt to re-net her hair and place it on her head.

"They will come. But no night is without a dawn. And our guide can only show its merit by the moon under whose blessing it was fashioned. We must move now!"

The disk of light quivered in the air. As the girl took a step forward, it floated on, always keeping at the same distance from the ground and ahead.

One range of dunes was like unto another. Twice Milo strove to check their way with those lines upon his ring. But the veins in the stone were invisible in this light, which gathered more brightly around Yevele. She had begun that trilling again, so that all he had known before this time now seemed as dim as the setting of his strange ring.

There was no change in the Sea of Dust. Dunes arose and fell as might the waves of a real sea. Looking back once, Milo could not even sight any trail that they left, for the powder straightway fell in upon and blurred any track. In fact he could not even tell now in which direction lay the body of the dragon and those others who had marched with them. This troubled him dimly from time to time. When such inner uneasiness awoke in him Yevele's soft trilling struck a new note, drawing him back from even the far edge of questioning what they did— or were to do.

Time lost meaning. Milo felt that he walked in a dream, slowly, his feet engulfed by a web that strove to entangle him. Still that disk floated ahead, Yevele sang without words, and the moon gave cold light to her floating, unbound hair, the carven features of her face.

It was chance that brought a break in the web that enmeshed Milo. Or *was* there such a thing as chance he sometimes wondered afterwards? Did not the priests of Om advance the belief that all action in the world, no matter how small or insignificant, had its part in the making of a pattern determined upon by Powers men could not even begin to fathom with their earth-tied senses?

The fastening on one dust shoe loosened and he knelt again to make it fast. As he pulled on the lacing, his left hand was uppermost. The dull dust clouded the setting of his second ring. But, though it was indeed filmed with dust, it was no longer dull! Milo wiped it quickly across the edge of his surcoat, for glancing at it alerted that uneasiness in him.

No, it was no longer dull gray, without any spark of light. Something moved within it!

Raising his hand against his breast Milo peered more closely at what was shafting within it. What—?

"Milo!" Yevele had returned, was standing over him.

Again (was it some hidden impulse of his own, or was he only the tool or player of some other power?) he put the hand wearing the ring up and out. His grip closed about her wrist.

The dull stone was indeed alive. In its depths there stood a figure. Tiny as it was it showed every detail clearly. A woman, yes—very much of woman—well-endowed by nature. But not Yevele!

Under the fingers that imprisoned her wrist there was no hardness of mail, no wiry arm strengthened by sword exercise to a muscularity near his own. Milo, still keeping that hold, faced her whom he so held. Not Yevele, no. . . .

The hair that floated around her was as silver as the moonlight. In her marble-white face the eyes slanted, held small greenish sparks. Her jaws sharpened, fined to form a mask that held beauty, yes, but also more than a touch of the alien. Now her mouth opened a trifle to show sharp points of teeth such as might be the weapons of some beast of prey.

That change in her jerked Milo free from the spell which had held him. He was on his feet, but he did not loose his hold on her. Save for a first involuntary pull against his strength, she, too, stood quiet.

"Who are you?"

For a moment she stared at him, her slanted eyes narrowing. There was on her face a shadow of surprise.

Her lips moved. "Yevele."

Illusionist! His newly awakened mind, freed from the spells she could so easily weave about the unwary, gave him the true answer. He did not need to hear the truth from her—he already knew. Now he spoke it aloud. "Illusionist! Did you so entice the berserker?" They had been too occupied with danger to question Naile before the coming of the storm, but Milo believed that he now saw the answer to the other's desertion of their party.

She tried to fling off his grasp, her face more and more alien as her features formed a mask of rage. But Milo held her tight, as the once cloudy gem blazed, while the disk that had spun through the air whirled and dove for his face like a vicious insect. He flung up his other hand to ward it off.

It dodged his defense easily, as might a living creature, swooped, and flattened itself against his skin above the wrist of the hand that gripped its mistress. Milo cried out—the pain from that contact, was as intense as any burn. In spite of himself, his hold loosened.

The woman gave a sinuous twist of her arm and her body broke free. Now she laughed. For a moment he saw her waver, become Yevele. But the folly of keeping up such a broken cover of deceit was plain. Instead she turned from him, kicking off the clumsy sand shoes.

She was mistress of more than one form of magic, for she skimmed across the surface of the dust apparently as weightless as the wind, not even raising in her passage the uppermost film of the sea. Above and around her whirled the moon disk, moving so swiftly that its very radiance wove a kind of netting for her defense.

Useless though pursuit might now be, Milo followed doggedly after. He had no way, he was sure, to return to the party by the dragon. If there was any hope to win free of the sea it might be to trail his beguiler.

She rounded a dune and was lost to his sight. Then he came to the point where she had disappeared. When he reached it he saw that flicker of light now so well ahead that he had no hope of catching up.

However, now it kept to a straight line, for the dunes fell away and the surface of the Sea of Dust was as level as it had been in that place where they had found Naile battling with the dragon. There was something else . . . The light flickered, dipped, spun from the dull gray of the sea into what stretched not too far ahead, a mass of darkness rising unevenly.

The blotch of that shadow swallowed up even the moonlight. Milo paused, his head up, his nostrils testing the smells of the night. He lacked the keen sense of the elf and the berserker, but he could give name to what he smelled now—the rank odor of a swampland. Yet to find this in the ever-abiding aridity of the Sea of Dust was such a strange thing it instantly warned him against reckless approach.

That swampland was no barrier for her whom he followed. The light spun on out, wan and pale, into the embrace of the darkness, drew even more rapidly ahead. Milo's dust shoes beat a path for him to the edge of the shadow. He caught a diminished glimmer of what might be a stretch of water; he could smell the fetid odor of the place. For the rest it was only darkness and menace. To follow out into that would be to entrap himself without any profit.

But that he had reached the place they had been seeking, the place of which Lichis had told them, Milo had no doubt. Somewhere out in that quagmire, which defied all natural laws by its very being, lay the fortress of the enemy.

What if he had remained in the illusionist's spell—would she have left him immured in some bog, as treacherous as the dust, to be swallowed up? He looked down at the ring that had given him the warning. There was no light there now, the stone was once more dull and dead. Milo wheeled slowly, to look back, careful of how he placed his feet. There was no returning. . . .

He had no idea how long he must wait for dawn, nor how he might reach the others, draw them hither to face the next obstacle in their quest. Using the dust shoes as a supporting platform, he hunkered down, his gaze sweeping back and forth along the edge of the swampland. There was growth there. He could trace it in the moonlit humps of vegetation. There was life also, for he started once and nearly spun off into the dust, as the sound of shrill and loud croaking made him think, with a shiver he could not entirely subdue, of that horror tale told about the Temple of the Frog and the unnatural creatures bred and nurtured therein to deliver the death stroke against any who invaded that hidden land. That, too, occupied the heart of a swamp, holding secrets no man of the outer world could more than guess.

The line between the Sea of Dust and this other territory ran as straight as a sword's point might have drawn it. None of the vegetation or muck advanced outward, no point of dust ran inward. That line of division was too perfect to be anything but artificial. Milo, understanding that, fingered his sword hilt.

Wizardry—yet not even the wizardry he knew of—if Hystaspe had been right. A wizardry not of this world—and it was hard enough for a fighting man to withstand what was native. He had no spells except . . .

Milo stretched out his right wrist. Moonshine could not bring to life the dice. He struggled to remember. They had turned—or one had—as he had followed the enticement of the illusionist into the night. Then he had been so under her spell that he had not been able to influence the turning. He advanced his other hand, flattened down the thumb to inspect the once more dead stone ring, putting it beside the other with the map he could not see. Where had he gained those rings?

The swordsman fought to conquer memory, seek those passages in his mind that were blocked. He was—

There was a flash of a mental picture, here and gone in almost the same instant. Sitting—yes, sitting at a table. Also he held a small object, carven, shaped—the image of a man! That was of some vast importance to him—he must struggle to bring the memory back—to retain it long enough to learn—He must . . . !

Something flashed out of the air, hung before him. Moonlight glittered on it. But this was no disk—it hissed, shot out a spear tongue as if to make sure of his full attention. Memory was lost.

"Afreeta."

The pseudo-dragon hissed as banefully as had her greater cousin, but his speaking of her name might have been an order. As speedily as she had come to him, she sped off through the night. So the others now had their guide. In so little was Milo's distrust of the future lifted. He tried once more to capture that memory—thinking back patiently along the lines he had followed. He had looked at the bracelet, his rings—before that had been the call that had made him remember the Temple of the Frog. He was . . .

Slowly he shook his head. Something in his hand—not the rings—not the bracelet that tied him to this whole venture. He thought of the scene with Hystaspes. What the wizard had said of an alien who had brought him—and the others—here to tie. . . . Tie what? Milo groped vainly for a clue. What lay away, hidden in the unnatural swamp, was of the highest danger. They were the ill-assorted hunting party sent to ferret out and destroy it. Why? Because there was a geas laid on them. Men did strange things to serve wizards whether they would or not. It was not of Chaos, that much he knew. For a swordsman could not be twisted and bent into the service of evil.

But this tied him! He pounded his wrist against his knee in rising anger. It was a slave fetter on him, and he was no man to take meekly to slavery. His anger was hot; it felt good. In the past he had used anger to provide him with another weapon, for, controlled as he had learned to control it, that emotion gave a man added strength.

Before him lay someone, something, that sought to make him a slave. And he was—

Voices!

He got to his feet, hand once more seeking sword hilt. Now he faced the swells of the dunes. From between them figures moved. More illusions?

Milo consulted the ring. It did not come to life. As yet he had no idea of the range of that warning. He continued to hold his thumb out where he could glance from the setting to those drawing near at the pace dictated by the dust shoes.

Though he could not see most of their faces because of the overhang of helmets, or cloak hoods, he knew them well enough to recognize that they had the appearance of those with whom he companied. Still he watched the ring.

"Hola!" Naile's deep call, the upflung arm of the berserker, was in greeting. He led the party, Afreeta winging about his head. But close behind him trod a smaller figure, helmeted head high. It was toward her that Milo now pointed the ring.

There was no change in the set. Still he could not be sure—not until perhaps he laid hand on her as he had on the singer out of the night. Wymarc drew close to her as if he sensed Milo's suspicion.

"There was the smell of magic," the bard said. "What led you on, swordsman?"

The dark figure of Naile interrupted. "I said it, songsmith. He followed someone he knew—even as did I. That damn wizardry made me see a brave comrade dead in the earth these three years or more. Is that not so, swordsman?"

"I followed one—with the seeming of Yevele." He took three steps forward with purpose, reached out to touch her. No blaze—this *was* Yevele. The battlemaid drew back.

"Lay no hands on me, swordsman!" Her voice was harsh, dust-fretted, with none of the soft warmth that other had held. "What do you say of me?"

"Not you, I have proved it." Swiftly then he explained. The threat that an illusionist could evoke they all already knew. Perhaps Deav Dyne, Gulth (no one could be sure of any alien's reaction to most magic that enmeshed the human kind) or Ingrge might have withstood that beguilment, but he was sure that the rest could not.

"Illusionist." The cleric faced the dark swamp. "Yet you were led here—to what we have sought."

"A swamp," Naile commented. "If they sink us not in dust, perhaps they would souse us in mud and slime. Such land as that is a trap. You were well out of that, swordsman. It would seem those trinkets you picked up somewhere are near as good as cold steel upon occasion."

He was answered by one of those croaking cries from the swamp. But Gulth, who had trudged waveringly at the end of their party, gave now a hissing grunt that drowned out the end of that screech.

Throwing aside his dust-stiffened cloak, the lizardman headed straight for the murky dark of what Naile had so rightfully named "trap."

16

Into the Quagmire

DAWN CAME RELUCTANTLY, AS IF THE SKY MUST BE FORCED INTO illuminating this strangely divided land. Now they could see color in that mass of vegetation, rank, sickly greens, browns, yellows. Here and there stood a twisted and misshapen rise of shrub, some species of water-loving growth maimed in its growing by the poisoned earth and muck in which it was rooted. There were reeds, tangles of bulbous, splotched plants among them. Dividing each ragged clump of such from another lay pools, scum-covered or peat-dark brown, to the surface of which rose bubbles that broke, releasing nauseating breaths of gas from unseen rot.

Some of these pools, in the farther distance, achieved the size of ponds, and one might even be considered a lake. In these larger expanses of water there spread pads of water-growth root-anchored below. There was a constant flickering of life, for things squatted on those pads or hid among the reeds and shrubs, darting forth to hunt. Above insects buzzed—some so large as to be considered monsters of their species.

Yet the line of damarcation between dust and quag must form an invisible wall, for the life of the swamp never, even when being pursued or hunting, came across it. The line between dust and quag was no physical barrier, however, for Gulth had had no trouble in entering the water-logged land and had immersed his dust-plastered body in one of the dark pools, seemingly having neither fear nor distaste for the stinking mud his bathing stirred up, or what might use that murk to cover an attack.

Sharing the lizardman's fearlessness, Afreeta flew ahead to dip, flutter, pursue, and swallow insects whirring in the air. Yet, as the land grew clearer and clearer to their sight in the morning, the rest of the party drew closer together, as if they sought to position themselves in defense against lurking danger.

Though the illusionist had flitted above the swamplands in the night as if provided with a firm road for her feet, Milo could not now understand how she had been able to do that. The clumps of vegetation were scattered, broken apart by flats of mud, which heaved and shot up small, brown-black bits, as if they were pots boiling. Their company had fashioned the dust shoes, which had given them a measure of mobility across the sea, but those would not serve them here. There was no steady footing.

Gulth blew, shaved mud from his limbs with the edge of one hand. With the other he grasped a bloated, pale-greenish body from which he had already torn so much of the flesh that Milo could not be sure what form it had originally had. Chewing this as if it were the finest delicacy offered at some high banquet, the lizardman teetered from one foot to another, facing inward toward the hidden heart of this water-logged, unnatural country.

The quag country was largely hidden. A mist drifted upward, steaming as might the fumes from the bubbling mud pots. They could no longer sight some of the ponds, or one end of what might be a lake. Fingers of fog reached outward towards the partition between dust and mud. If the swampland had seemed nigh impossible to penetrate before the clouding of the land in a shroud that grew thicker and thicker, blotting out one clump here, a stretch of uneasy mud or pool there, now they dared not consider a single forward step.

That creeping mist reached Gulth, wreathed about his mud-streaked body. Before he was lost in it, he wheeled, strode backward to the line change, where he stood facing them but making no move to reenter the Sea of Dust. One of his scaled arms moved in a loose, sweeping gesture, his snouted head turned a little, so one of the unblinking eyes might still regard the quag.

"We go—" His hissing voice pierced the continued buzz of the insects.

Naile, both hands clasped on the shaft of his axe, shook his head.

"I am no mud-sulker, scaled man. One step, two, and I would be meat for the bog. Show me how we can move across those mud traps—"

"That states it for us all," Wymarc said. "What do we do, comrades of necessity? Is there any among us who knows a spell to grow wings, perhaps? Or one that will at least temporarily dry us a path through the murk? What of your ring, swordsman—your map ring? What does it point as a way ahead?" He looked to Milo.

The green stone had no life to illuminate those red veins. It remained as lifeless as the film of dust lying over it and all the swordsman's skin. Milo studied the rolls of mist and knew that Naile was right, the nature of this land defeated them.

"Make road." Gulth's head swung fully back in their direction once again.

"With what?" Yevele asked. She had not spoken since Milo had told his tale of the illusionist. He had marked also that she deliberately kept as far from him as she could during their short rest before the coming of light, sitting herself at the other end of their company, with Naile, Wymarc, and the elf between them. Did she, Milo wondered, now with an awakening of irritation, think that he held her accountable for the trick of spell-weaving? Surely the girl could not be so much a fool as to believe that!

Deav Dyne held up his hand for silence before he spoke directly to the lizardman.

"You have some plan, some knowledge that is not ours then, Gulth?"

There could be no change of expression on that so-alien face, nor did Gulth directly answer the questions of the cleric. Instead he croaked a word that carried the weight of a direct order.

"Wait!"

Without lingering for any reply or protest from the others, the lizardman strode back into the quag with a confidence that certainly the rest of the party lacked. Mists closed about him so he vanished nearly at once.

In turn they drew forward to the line between sea and quagmire. This close, the unlikeliness of finding any path over or through was even more evident. Deav Dyne addressed Milo.

"The illusionist vanished here?"

"Over it—or at least the light of her moon disk did."

"Could be another of her illusions—to make you believe so," Wymarc pointed out.

The elf and the cleric nodded as if in agreement to that.

"Then where did she go?" returned Milo.

"If she ever was." Yevele spoke, not to him, but as if voicing some inner thought aloud.

"She was there. I laid hand on her!" Milo curbed anger arising from both her tone and words.

"Yes." Now Deav Dyne nodded once more. "Once the spell is broken she could not summon it again easily. But another spell . . ." He allowed his sentence to trail away.

Naile went down on one knee, his attention plainly not for his companions but for something he had sighted on the ground before him. Now he reached over that dividing line and poked at a straggly, calf-high bush. From the mass of intertwined twigs he freed a strip of material, jerking it back.

"Someone passed here, leaving a marker," he said. "This was not so twisted by chance."

What he held was a scrap of material—yellow and dingy—about the length of two fingers.

"Cloak lining." With it still gripped in one hand, Naile used his axe with the other, sliding that weapon forward to rest momentarily on the earth beside the bush. The weight of the double-headed blade sank it into the bare spot as soon as it rested there. Hurriedly he snatched it back again. "If it marked anything," the berserker commented, "it must be *not* to enter here. But if this was set to ward off—then there is some place that *is* safe—"

"And that may look enough like this spot," Ingrge cut in,

viewing what they could see in spite of the mist with a tracker's eyes, "to mislead those who would travel here—"

"Or else," Wymarc added wryly, "to play a double game and make us believe just what you have now said. Wizards' minds are devious, elf. Such a double-set trap might well be what we have here."

"Something moving!" Yevele cried out, pointing into the swirling mist.

Milo noted that he was not the only one to draw steel at her warning. But the figure that came toward them at a running pace turned out to be Gulth, a Gulth laden with great rolls of brilliant, acid green under each arm.

One of these he dropped so it flipped open of its own accord, lying directly above the spot Naile had tested with the weight of his axe. It was wider than that axe and its shaft, round in shape. A mighty leaf, rubbery tough, now rested on the treacherous surface as if it had no weight at all.

"Come—" Gulth did not even look up to see if they obeyed his summons. He was too busy laying down the rest of his load, disappearing into the mist again as he put one leaf next to the other to form a path.

Naile shook his head. "Does the scaled one think we shall trust such a device?" he demanded. "How he manages to keep from sinking is some magic of his own people. We have it not nor can a leaf give it to us."

Gulth did not return, though they watched for him. It was the elf who pushed past Naile and knelt to stretch out his bow, prodding at the surface of the leaf with the tip.

"It does not sink," he observed.

"Ha, elfkind, what is your bow, even though you put muscle to your testing," Naile enquired, "against the full weight of one of us? Even that of the battlemaid here would force it down—"

"Will it?" Yevele gave a short spring that carried her over the dividing line to stand balanced on the leaf. It bobbed a little as she landed upon it, but there was no breaking of its surface, nor did it sink into the mud it covered. Before Milo could protest she moved onto the second leaf where the mist began to swirl. Her folly was reckless. Still she had proven that in part Gulth was right. What knowledge of strange life—or alien sorcery—the lizardman had, it would seem that in the quagmire it was of use.

Ingrge went next. He was slight of body as were all his race, yet it was true that he must weigh more than the girl, in spite of her armor and weapons and the pack she had slung over her shoulder before she made that reckless gesture. As he, in turn, steadied himself on the leaf, he looked over his shoulder.

"It is firm," he reported, before he moved on, to be hidden in the mist as Yevele had vanished. Deav Dyne drew his robe closer about him, perhaps to guard against the tangled bush, stepping boldly out and away. He was gone as if walking on a strong-based bridge.

Wymarc shrugged. "Well enough. I hope that that harvest of leaves will hold," he remarked, readying to take the stride that would set him on Deav Dyne's heels. Then Milo and Naile stood alone.

Plainly the berserker mistrusted the green support. Of them all he carried the most weight, not only in bone and flesh, but also in his axe, pack and armor. He shifted from one foot to the other, scowling, his narrowed gaze on the leaf. Finally, as the bard had done, he shrugged.

"What will be, will be. If it is the fate set on me to smother in stinking mud, then how can I escape it?" He could have been marching to some battle where the odds were hopelessly against him. Milo took off his cloak, rolling it into a very rough excuse for a rope.

"Take this." He flapped one end into Naile's reach. "It may not serve, but at least it will give you a better chance." Privately, he thought Naile was entirely right in mistrusting Gulth's strange bridge. Whether he could pull Naile out of danger if the leaf gave way beneath the berserker, he also had his doubts, but this was the best aid he could offer.

From the quirk of the berserker's lips Milo believed that Naile agreed with every unvoiced doubt. Yet he accepted the end of the cloak as he went forward, bringing both feet firmly together on the surface of the leaf.

The green surface did tilt a fraction, bulging downward immediately under Naile's feet. Yet it held, with no further sinking, as the heavy man readied his balance to take a second stride. Then he was gone, still on his feet, and the cloak pulled in Milo's hold. Gritting his teeth and trying not to think of what might happen if the leaf, which must have been badly tried by the passing of the others, gave out under him, the swordsman stepped cautiously onto its surface.

It did shift under his boots, moving as might a soft surface. Still, he did not sink, and he braved the queasy uneasiness that shifting aroused in him. Now the cloak tie with Naile was broken, the other end loose so he drew it to him. Apparently the berserker had been so encouraged he felt no need of such doubtful support.

On Milo moved, standing now on the second leaf, the mist

234 of Andre Norton

hiding from him all but a fraction of the one ahead. He waited a second or two longer, making as sure as he could that Naile had progressed beyond. These leaves, by some miracle, might take the weight of one alone, but Milo had no mind to try their toughness with both him and Naile striving to balance together.

He moved slowly and carefully, though not straight, for the leaves had been laid down to skirt most of the open pools. Thus sometimes, in the mist that so distorted and hid the rest of the quagmire, the swordsman felt as if he had doubled back in a time-consuming fashion.

"Wait!" The warning out of the mist stopped him as he gathered himself for a small leap to carry him over a pool to a leaf lying beyond.

It was harder to force himself to stand there, listening, then to keep on the move from one leaf to another. Now the insects, which he had tried to ignore in his concentration upon his footing, were a torment as they bit and stung his sweating, swollen flesh. Out of the murk of the pool something raised a clawed, scaled paw, caught the edge of the leaf. A second paw joined it. Between them appeared a froglike head. But no frog of Milo's knowledge showed fangs, pointed and threatening. The thing was the size of a small dog or cat. And it was not alone. Another paw reached for support some distance away.

Milo's sword slid delicately out of its sheath. He continued to mistrust the result of any sudden movement. The first of the frog things was on the edge of the leaf, fully clear of the water, its head held at an angle so that the glitter of its eyes reached his own face. Milo struck as he might spear a fish.

The sword point went into the thing's bloated body. It gave a sound more scream than croak as he flung away from him with a sharp twist of his blade, not waiting to see it sink back into the water before he slashed down at the other. More clawed paws were showing along the leaf side.

The leaf quivered under him. He killed the second of the creatures. Now no more climbed from the pool. Instead those paws—and there were more of them than he could stop to count—fastened on the leaf, forcing its side downwards. So the things had intelligence of a sort. They were united in an attempt to upset him. Once in that pool, small as they were, he would be at their mercy. Moving as swiftly as he could, Milo slashed and slashed again. Paws were cut from spindly legs, yet others arose as the mutilated enemy sank out of sight. He was forced to his knees by the continuous shaking of the leaf. And it was slowly but inevitably sinking at the side where the frog things congregated.

Milo could not move from where he already crouched, lest his own weight add to the efforts of the frog things. But he defended his shaky perch with all the skill he knew.

"On!"

The call out of the fog reached him dimly. He was far more aware of his own struggle. He allowed one glance toward the next leaf. There were none of the frog things waiting there. But to reach it meant a leap and that from the unsteady leaf. Now they were no longer striving to upset him. Instead, with those taloned paws, and perhaps with their teeth, they ripped away at the leaf itself; tearing it into strings of pale green pulp. And they no longer climbed high enough for him to get at them. He must move, and now!

Milo gathered himself together and, not daring to pause any longer, (one tear in the leaf had already nearly reached him) he made the crossing. His haste perhaps added to the impact of his landing, for he lost his footing as the leaf moved under him. The toe of one boot projected back over the pond.

As he fought to regain his balance, drawing in his leg, he saw one of the frog creatures had its teeth embedded in the metal-reinforced leather of the boot. With a small surge of something close to panic, the swordsman struck out with his mailed fist, for he had sheathed his sword, and hit the thing full on.

The fat body smashed under his blow. However, the jaws did not open, keeping fast their hold. Milo had to slash and slash again with his dagger, his hands shaking with a horror he could not control. Though he so rid himself of the flattened body and of most of the head, he could not even then loose the jaws.

Those he carried with him as he hurried on, moving from one leaf to the next. Voices sounded ahead, there was a calling of his name. He took a deep breath and answered, hoping that his present state of mind could not be deduced from his tone. Then, as his pulse slowed and he mastered the sickness that threatened each time he glanced at that thing deep set in his boot, he had another fleeting thought.

The bracelet! Milo swung up his arm, almost believing that he must have lost it. There had not been the slightest warning of any peril ahead such as he had come to rely upon. The dice were fixed. He prodded one with a finger—immovable.

Did that mean that they had lost the one small advantage they might have in any struggle to come?

Leaf by leaf he won ahead. The mist did not thin. All he could see was what lay immediately around him. Luckily, though he skirted two more pools, neither had to be directly crossed.

"Take care." Another warning from the curtain of mist. "Bear right as you come."

The leaf before him was set straight. Milo hesitated, looked to the bracelet. It remained uncommunicative. Voices—illusions? If he bore right as ordered would such a shift take him directly into disaster?

"Naile?" he called back, determined for identification before he obeyed.

"Wymarc," the answer came. The mist, Milo decided, played tricks with normal tones. It could have been anyone who mouthed that name.

Sword in hand, Milo teetered back and forth. He must chance it. To do otherwise might not only endanger him but one of the others. He moved on, across the leaf and to the right, skirting the very edge of it and causing it to tilt.

So he came through the mist to where figures stood half-unseen. There was a line of leaves laid out here, so each one had a firm platform of his own. Before them stretched a wide spread of water. Perhaps this was the lake they had been able to view in the first gray time of light before the mists gathered. As he moved up even with the others, he saw that his neighbor was indeed the bard.

"What do we wait for?"

Wymarc made a gesture to the sweep of dark water. "For a bridge apparently—or something of the sort. I could wish that we did it in a less populated place." He slapped at his face and neck, hardly disturbing the insects that buzzed about him in a cloud of constant assault.

"Gulth?"

The lizardman had solved one problem for them. Would he have an answer for this also?

"He was gone when we reached here. But we are not the first to come this way. Look."

It could only be half seen in the mist, but what the bard pointed to was a post made of a tree trunk, its bark still on and overlaid with a thick resinous gum. Caught in it were layers of the insects, so that it was coated above the waterline with the dead and the still-struggling living. But on each side of it, well up above the water, were two hoops of metal, dulled and rusty, standing away from the wood.

"Mooring of a sort." Milo was sure he was right. And, if something had been moored here in the past. . . . Still that did not signify that any such transportation would be available to *them*.

"Something coming!" Naile, beyond Wymarc, gave them warning. Milo could hear nothing but the noise of the insects which, now that he was not occupied with leaf-crossing, was maddening.

Out of the mist a dark shadow glided across the surface of the lake, heading straight for them. Afreeta, who had been in her usual riding place on Naile's shoulder, darted out to meet that craft.

It was a queer sort of boat and one that Milo could not accept at first as being any possible transportation at all. It looked far more as if a mass of reeds had been uprooted and was drifting toward them. Still, no mat would move with such purpose, and this move steadily if slowly, plainly aimed at the shore at their feet.

As it at last nudged the mud, Milo could see that the raft was indeed fashioned of reeds, at least on the surface. They had been torn from their rooting, forced into bundles, and tied together with cords made of their own materials. The bundles did not dip deeply in the water, plainly they rested on another base. Now, below the front edge of this unwieldy platform of vegetation (it did not even promise the stability of a raft) something rose to the surface.

Gulth drew himself up and collected from among the reed bundles his swordbelt with its weapon.

"Come." In the mist his voice took on some of the croaking intonation of the frog things. To underline his invitation-order, he gestured them forward.

There were extra rows of the reed bundles forming a raised edging about the platform. But seven of them on that? Milo, for one, saw little hope. Yet Yevele was not going to lead this time. Since by chance he was the closest, the swordsman jumped, landing on the other side of the low barrier. The raft did bob about, but it remained remarkably buoyant. Milo scrambled hastily to join Gulth. Perhaps with their weight on the other side to balance, the others would have less trouble embarking. One by one they followed Milo's lead, Naile coming last. The raft did sink a little then, some of the water forced in runnels through the raised edge. At Gulth's orders they spaced themselves across the surface in a pattern the lizardman indicated, which, they deduced, had something to do with maintaining its floating ability.

Then, dropping his swordbelt once more, Gulth slid easily into the water and the raft slowly moved out from the shore.

Milo turned his head. Wymarc lay an arm's distance away.

"He can't be towing us, not alone!" the swordsman protested. Magic he could swallow—but this was no magic, he knew.

"He is not," Ingrge, instead of the bard, answered. "Direction he gives—but to others. The scaled ones have their own friends and helpers and those are born of swamps. Gulth has found here such to answer his call. They swim below the surface—as the horses of the land pull a cart, these will bring us across the water."

Their journey was a slow one. And it was, as the mist gathered around them and they could no longer see the shore from which they came, a blind voyage. Nor was there any sign of what or who drew them on. Milo rose cautiously to his knees once to peer over the barrier. He saw lines of braided reeds showing now and again at the meeting of raft and water. They were drawn taut. Save for those and the emergence of Gulth at intervals, his head rising so he might check on the raft, there was no proof they were not alone.

17

Quag Heart

IMPRISONED BY THE WALLS OF MIST, SURROUNDED BY CLOUDS OF insects which even the forays of Afreeta did nothing to drive away, they were caught in a pocket of time that they could not measure. They only knew that the crude raft on which they balanced continued to move. And, since Gulth controlled that journey, they guessed that the lizardman must also know their goal.

"I am wondering," Yevele said, "if we have already been noted and there are those awaiting us . . ." She raised her head, propping herself up on her extended arms, and looked directly at Milo. "Such ones as this shape-changer you have already fronted, swordsman."

"She's no shape-changer," Naile cut in. "An illusionist needs to reach into the mind to spin such webs. And another can break them, when he realizes that they are only fancies." He appeared aggrieved that Yevele equated the stranger with him in such a fashion.

"I am wondering why she came to us." Wymarc shook his

head vigorously to try and discourage the attentions of a flying thing nearly as long as his own middle finger. "It argues that we have been discovered, thus we may indeed meet a welcome we shall not want."

"Yes, the open jaws of another dragon," commented Naile, "or the sucking of a mud hole. Yet there is something about these attempts against us—"

"They seem to be not very carefully planned," Wymarc supplied when the berserker paused. "Yes, each attempt possesses a flaw, does it not?"

"It is," Ingrge spoke for the first time, "as if orders are incomplete, or else they are not understood by servants." He rolled over on his back and held up his arm so that the bracelet was visible. "How much do these control our way now?"

"Perhaps very little." Milo gained their full attention. Quickly he outlined his battle with the frog things and how then there had been no warning spin of the dice.

"It may be because we approach at last the place in which those came into being, that they can operate only beyond its presence," Yevele said slowly, her hand rubbing now along her own bracelet. "Then, if that is so—"

"We are without warning or any aid we can gain from a controlled spin." Deav Dyne finished her thought. "Yet, do you feel released from the geas in any fashion?"

There was a moment of silence as they tested the compulsion that had brought them out of Greyhawk and to this place of water, mud, and mist. Milo strove to break loose, to decide to turn back. But that force was still strong within him.

"So, we learn something else," the cleric pointed out. "Wizardry still holds us, even though the other, this,"—he tapped fingertip against the band about his wrist—"does not. What are we to gather from such evidence?"

"A geas is of this world," Yevele mused aloud. "The band which we cannot take from us perhaps is not. There are many kinds of magic; I know of no one, unless it be an adept, who can list them all. This foul quagmire is magic-born. What kind of magic, priest? There are many fearsome odors here, still I have not sniffed yet the traces of Chaos leaves when dark powers are summoned. Alien forces?"

"So said Hystaspes," Milo returned.

"We are slowing," Ingrge broke in. "Those who tow us want no part of what lies ahead, they protest against Gulth's urging." He raised to look over the edge as Milo had done. More water seeped in and his cloak showed patches of wet.

"How many of these swamp dwellers can be allied for us or against us?" Naile wanted to know. "None answer to my were-call."

So the berserker, without telling them, had been trying to use one of his own talents.

"Who knows?" Ingrge answered. "None have I touched who were not life as we of this world recognize it. Though this swamp has been populated arbitrarily. In some minds I have found fading memories of living elsewhere—in the rest there is only consciousness of the here and now."

"A slice of country transported *with* its dwellers?" hazarded Deav Dyne. "That is wizardry beyond my learning. Yet all things are possible, there is no boundary of knowledge."

"Something there!" Milo picked a dark shadow out of the mist. It was fixed, not moving. Toward that the raft headed, far more slowly now.

"Gulth holds them, those who pull us," reported the elf. "They protest more, but his control continues. He has agreed to release them when we touch that which we see ahead."

The shadow grew and became not just a dark spot in the mist, but a tumble of rocks spilling forward to form a narrow tongue. They looked upon the promise of that stability with divided minds. To the credit side, the solid look of the rock promised firm footing, a refuge from the swamp. On the other hand, firm land would also hold other dangers.

Gulth crawled out of the water, climbing carefully over the side barrier.

"We go there—" He gestured to the tongue of rock.

It loomed high above, its foot water-washed and covered with green slime. The raft bumped gently against it a moment later.

"Push—that way—" Gulth stepped close, leaned over, to set his taloned hands against the rough surface of the rocks, obeying his own order, to edge the unwieldy craft to the left.

Only Naile, Milo, and Wymarc could find room to stand beside the lizardman and add their strength to this new maneuver. The stone was wet and their progress was hardly faster than that of the fat leechslugs that clung to the rocks and that they tried to avoid touching. Little by little they brought the raft around to the other side of that jutting point. There, in an indentation which made a miniature bay, they worked their way closer to some smaller stones that rose from the surface of the water like natural steps.

One could only see a short distance ahead, but Naile had a method for overcoming that difficulty. Afreeta took off, spiraling up, then darting into the mist at the higher level to which that stairway climbed. Milo and Gulth found fingerholds to which they clung as Naile swung over, setting his feet firmly on the first stone.

The berserker climbed up out of sight while they still held so. One by one the others passed between them to follow. Then Milo clambered over, and the lizardman was quick to follow, leaving the raft to drift away.

Here fog enfolded them even more thickly. They could not see those they followed. However, the mist did not muffle a sudden shout or the sound of steel against steel. Milo, sword in hand, made the last part of that assent in two bounds. Nor did he forget a quick glance once more at his wrist. The dice neither shone nor moved. It would seem the phenomenon on which they depended still did not work.

Gulth, moving with more supple speed than the swordsman had seen him use since their quest began, gave one leap that surpassed Milo's efforts and vanished into the mist. The swordsman was not far behind. With a last spurt of effort he broke through the fog, into open space. This lay under a gray and lowering sky to be sure, but one might see his fellows as more than just forms moving in and out of eye range.

What he did witness was Naile, axe up to swing, as if the berserker had fastened on Milo himself as the enemy. Yet— *there* was Naile, further off, confronting a shambling, stone-hided troll!

Illusion! Milo lifted the hand wearing the ring, half-afraid that, in the atmosphere of this alien setting, it, too, might have ceased to possess its spell-breaking quality. But, like the geas, it still served. The Naile about to attack him changed swiftly, in a flicker of an eye, to a man he had seen before—the animal trader Helagret. His axe was a dagger, its upright blade discolored by a greenish stain. Milo swung at this opponent with the practiced ease of a trained infighter.

His sword met that dagger arm, but did not sheer deeply for the edge found the resistance of a mailed shirt beneath the other's travel-stained jerkin. But the force of the blow, delivered so skillfully, sent the dagger spinning from the other's hand, rendered him off balance. Milo tossed the sword to his other hand, caught it by the blade and delivered with the heavy hilt a trick stroke he had learned through long and painful effort.

As the pommel thudded home on the side of Helagret's head, the man's eyes rolled up. Without a cry he slumped to the rock. His huddled body lay now in the way of Naile, retreating from the lunges of the troll, for no matter how skillfully the berserker wrought with his bone-shattering axe strokes, none of them appeared to land where he had aimed them.

"No." Milo threw up his ring hand, dodging past Naile, stooping just in time to escape one of the berserker's wider swings, and touched the troll.

There was again that flicker of dying illusion. What Naile faced now was not an eight-foot monster toward the head and neck of which he had aimed his attack, but rather a man, human as Milo, and well under the berserker's own towering inches. Knyshaw, the thief-adventurer, his lips drawn into a snarl, dove forward, stretching forth both hands as the troll had earlier threatened Naile with six-inch talons. Strapped to his digits were the wicked weapons of the soundless assassin, keen knives projecting beyond his own nails. The tips of two were stained and Milo guessed that the lightest scratch from one would bring a painful death.

The axe arose and fell as Naile voiced a shrill squeal of boar anger. There was no mail here to stop that stroke. Knyshaw screamed, stumbled. The hands with their knives were on the ground. From the stumps of his wrists spouted blood. Again Naile struck. The thief, his head beaten in, fell, the hands hidden beneath his twitching body.

Milo leaped over that body, heading for the rest of the skirmish. Deav Dyne crouched by a spur of rock, his belt knife drawn, but his other hand cradled his beads, and he chanted, intent on keeping his attacker from him while he wrought some spell of his own calling. That attacker slunk, belly to the ground, a scaled thing that might well have issued from the quagmire. Its body was encased in a shell, but the head, swaying back and forth, was that of a serpent, and the eyes, staring fixedly at the priest, were evilly wise.

Milo brought the ring against its shell. This time there was no change. He swung up his sword, only to be elbowed aside by Naile. His axe flashed up, then down, with an executioner's precision, to behead the monster. Through the air spun viscous yellow stuff that the creature had spat at the crouching cleric just before its head bounced to the rock. A few drops fell on the edge of Deav Dyne's robe. A wisp of smoke arose and the cloth showed a ragged hole.

" 'Ware that!" Naile cried. He had turned and was already on the move.

Wymarc and Ingrge stood back to back, alert to those who circled them. A little apart the druid Carlvols paced around and around the beleaguered two and their enemies. The latter were black imps, spears in hand, their coal-red eyes ever upon those they teased and tormented, flashing in to deliver some prick with their spears. To Milo's surprise neither the elf nor the bard strove to defend himself with a sword, though trickles of blood ran down their legs unprotected by mail.

Naile roared and leaped forward, swinging his axe at the prancing demons. The steel head passed through the bodies he strove to smash as it might have through wisps of smoke. Milo, seeing that, understood the strange passiveness of the two in that circle.

Carlvols did not look at either Milo or the berserker. His body was tense, strain visible on his face. The swordsman guessed that, though the magic worker had had the ability to summon these creatures from whatever other plane they knew as home and keep them tormenting the two they encircled, it was a dire energy drain for him to hold the spell in force. None of the demons turned to attack either Naile or Milo. Thus there was clearly a limit to what the druid could order them to do. Yet they were well able to keep up the threat against both elf and bard, and their spear attacks were growing stronger, the circle narrower.

"Stand aside!" Deav Dyne shouldered by Milo. The cleric whirled his string of prayer beads as if it were a scourge he could lay across an imp's back and rump. Even so did he aim it at the nearest.

Milo was content to leave this skirmish to the two priests and what they could summon. Now he looked for Yevele—to find two battlemaids, locked together in combat.

So much was one girl the image of the other that, as he crossed the rock to where sword met sword, shield was raised against blade, the swordsman could not say which of the two was she with whom he had marched out of Greyhawk.

There was a stir in the rocks beyond. From the shadow there

ran a man. He carried a mace in both hands and ranged himself behind the circling Yeveles, striving to use his weapon on one. Yet it would seem that he himself was not sure which was which and that he hesitated to attack for that reason. Milo bore down on the newcomer. Though the stranger stood near as tall as the swordsman, his face under the plain helm he wore had the features of an orc. And his lips were tightly drawn so that his fanglike teeth were visible between.

Milo, sword upraised, was upon him before the other realized it. Then he whirled about with a sidewise swing of the mace, aimed at Milo's thigh. There was enough force in that blow, the swordsman thought, to break a hip. Only narrowly was he able to avoid being hit. The ring on his thumb did not gleam so this fighter was no illusion. Swords could make little impression as this enemy wore a heavy mail shirt, reinforced breast and back with plates of dingy and rust-reddened metal.

For all his squat thickness of body, the orc was a cunning fighter—and a stubborn one. No man dared underrate this servant of Chaos. But no orc, no matter how powerful or skillful, could in turn face what came at him now from another angle while his attention was fixed on Milo.

This was no axe-swinging berserker but the were-boar, near as tall as the orc at the massive shoulder, grunting and squealing in a rage that only the death of an enemy might assuage. Milo leaped quickly to one side, lest the animal in battle madness turn on him also, as had been known to happen when friend and foe were pinned in narrow compass. He could leave the orc to the were. There remained Yevele, locked in combat with what appeared to be herself. Once more he turned to the battling women.

One of them had forced the other back to stand with her shoulders against a barrier Milo saw clearly for the first time—a wall looming from more mist. He threw out his arm to touch the one who had forced her opponent into that position.

There was no flare of the ring. Now Milo's sword swept up between the women, both their blades knocked awry by that stroke they had not foreseen.

"Have done!" He spoke to Yevele. "This witch may answer what we need to know."

For a moment it seemed that the battlemaid would not heed him. He could see little of her face below the helm. Though her head swung a fraction in his direction, he knew she was still watchful.

The other Yevele took that chance to push forward from the wall and stab at him with her blade. But he caught the blow easily on the flatside of his sword, his strength bearing down her arm. She drove her shield straight at him, and he lashed out with his foot, catching her leg with a blow made the crueler by his iron-enforced boot.

Screaming, she staggered back, her shoulders hitting the wall as she slid down along its surface. Milo stooped to touch her with the ring. Her helmet had been scraped off in her fall, showing tight braids of hair beneath it.

They were no longer red-brown—rather much darker. And it was not Yevele's sun-browned features now that were completely visible. The nose was thinner, higher in the bridge, the face narrowed to a chin so pointed it was grotesque. Her mouth was a vivid scarlet and her full lips twisted as she spat at him, stabbing upward with her sword.

Yevele kicked this time, her toe connecting expertly with the illusionist's wrist. The sword dropped from fingers suddenly nerveless. Then the fallen woman screeched out words that might have been a curse or a spell. But if it were the latter she never got to finish it. As deftly as Milo had done in his own battle, Yevele reversed her sword and brought the hilt down on the black head.

The illusionist crumpled, to lie still. Yevele smiled grimly.

"Swordsman," she said, not looking at Milo, rather bending over the illusionist while she unbuckled the other's swordbelt to bind her arms tightly to her body, "no longer will I think that you were telling some tavern ruffler's tale when you said that you had met me in the dust dunes by moonlight." She went down on one knee. Tearing off a strip from the cloak she had dropped earlier, she thrust a wad of the stout cloth into the illusionist's mouth, making fast the gag with another strip. "Now she will throw no more spells of that or any other nature." Yevele sat back on her heels, her satisfaction easy to read.

"Yes," she continued after a moment's survey of her captive, "not only can this one appear before me wearing my face, but look you—she has had some study of the rest of me—even the dents upon my shield and the sifting of dust! Swordsman, I would say that we have been watched carefully and long— probably by magic means."

Yevele spoke the truth. What the unconscious girl before them wore was an exact duplication of her own apparel. When the illusionist had played her tricks upon him in the night— then her armor had also been an illusion, vanishing when he broke the spell. But this time the clothing was real.

"Look not into her eyes, if indeed she opens them soon," the battlemaid continued. "It is by sight—*your* sight linked to theirs'—that such addle a brain. Perhaps"—her tone turned contemptuous as she arose—"this one thought to bedazzle me so by a mirror image that I could be easily taken. She speedily discovered such tricks could not bemuse me. And"—now she swung around, Milo turning with her—"it would appear we have all given good account of ourselves. But—where is Gulth?"

Boar stood, forefeet planted on the body of the orc, a ragged piece of mail dangling from one yellowish tusk. Wymarc and Ingrge were no longer surrounded by any encircling of dancing imps. Instead they backed Deav Dyne who swung his beads still as he might a whip advancing on the black druid who cowered, dodged, and tried to escape, yet seemingly could not really flee. The prayer beads might be part of a net to engulf him, as well as a scourge to keep him from calling on his own dark powers. For to do that, any worker of magic needed quiet and a matter of time to summon aides from another plane, and Carlvols was allowed neither.

Yevele was right. There was no sign of the lizardman. He had been with Milo when they had climbed to this spot—or at least the swordsman had thought so. Yet now Milo could not recall having seen Gulth since he himself had plunged into battle. He cupped his hands about his mouth and called:

"Ho—Gulth!"

No answer, nothing moved—save that Naile performed once again his eye-wrenching feat of shape-changing.

"Gulth?" Milo called again.

Afreeta darted down from the mist above them, circled Naile's head, to alight as usual on his shoulder. Of the lizard-man there was neither any sign nor hint of what might have become of him.

A silence had fallen as Deav Dyne got close enough to his quarry to draw the beads across his shoulder. The black druid clapped both hands over his mouth and fell to his knees, his body convulsed by a series of great shudders. Stepping back the cleric spoke.

"By the Grace of Him Who Orders the Winds and the Seasons, this one is now our meat—for a space. Do you bind him so that he may not lay hand to any amulet or tool he might have about him. Take also that pouch he wears upon his belt. Do not open it, for what it may contain is for his hand alone. Rather take it and hurl it away—into the swamp, if you will. In so much can we disarm him. As for Gulth—" He came to join Naile, Milo, and Yevele. "It might be well that we seek him. Also, be prepared for what else can face us."

The druid, his pouch gone, his arms pulled behind him, the wrists tightly bound, was dragged up to them by Wymarc. Milo went to examine him who had played the role of another Naile. There was a sluggish pulse, but his skull might be cracked. He could be bound and left.

They had two conscious captives, the illusionist and the druid. Perhaps these two were of least use, though they were the most deadly, that since both had defenses that were not based on strength of body or weapon in hand. Over the gag Milo saw the woman's intent gaze as he went to bring her to their council of war. But he knew that Yevele had been right in her warning. The last thing to do was to look into her eyes or let her compelling gaze cross his. He laid her down beside the druid. The man's face worked frantically as he fought to open his lips, yet they remained close-set together.

"I would not suggest we take them with us," Wymarc spoke

up. "To my mind it is a time to move fast, laying no extra burdens upon ourselves."

"Well enough," agreed Naile. He drew his knife. "Give me
room, bard, and this I shall lay across their throats. Then we
need not think of them again."

"No." Milo had seen plenty such blooding of captives on
fields of victory. It was a custom among many of the weres, and
not them alone. Better to leave only dead than to take prisoners,
when to guard such defeated one's purposes. Wymarc was right,
they should not take with them these most dangerous of the enemy. But it was not in him to kill a helpless captive coldly and
neatly out of hand.

18

Roll the Dice

THEY DREW TOGETHER AT THE BLACK WALL, ITS TOP VEILED IN THE mist. With that as a guide they went warily forward, seeking some break in its surface. This was no natural upthrust of rock, but laid by the hand of either human or alien. The blocks were unfinished, placed one above the other, but so cunningly set that it was solid enough without mortar.

Floating wisps of mist drifted above them, sometimes curling down that wall. Milo glanced back. There the mists had closed in, dropping a curtain between them and the recent battleground. Here, a pocket of clear air appeared to move with them. There was nothing to see but the black rock, with clusters of moisture bubbles gathering underfoot, or the wall. While, with every breath they drew, that dankness invaded their lungs, tainted as it was by the effluvia of the swamplands.

Ingrge went down on one knee, intent upon something on the ground.

"Gulth has come this way." He indicated a smear on the rock.

Some of the grayish slime growth, which spotted it leprously in places, had been crushed into a noisome paste.

"How can you be sure that was left by Gulth?" Yevele demanded.

The elf did not look at her. It was Milo who caught the clue—those scrape marks could only have been made by Gulth's forward-jutting foot claws. But why had the lizardman deserted the fight, gone ahead?

"I said it!" Naile broke into the swordsman's thoughts. "To trust one of the scaled ones is folly. Can you not see? It was he who brought us here, delivered us as neatly as a merchant's man brings a pack of trading goods across country to a warehouse."

Afreeta lifted her head, hissed with the viciousness of her kind. Naile raised one hand to rest on her body between fanning wings. With his axe in the other he went on with an agile tread surprising for his bulk.

There was their gate—or door; a dark gap in the wall, waiting like the maw of some great, toothless creature. There was no door or bar—only a dark trough which they could not see. Naile swung his axe, slicing into that blackness as if it were a living enemy. The double-headed blade flashed inward, vanished from their sight. Then the berserker pulled it back once more.

"Look to your wristlet!" Wymarc's warning was hardly needed. A growing warmth of that metal had already alerted them all.

The dice spots blazed, the metal bands themselves took on a glow that fought against the drab daylight of the rocky isle. But the dice did not spin, nor could Milo, concentrating with all the power he could summon, stir them into any action. They were alive with whatever force they had—but they did not move.

"Power returns to power." Deav Dyne held out his own banded arm. "Yet there is nothing here that answers to my questing." He shook his beads.

"Still—the geas holds. We must go on," Wymarc returned.

It was true. Milo felt that, too. The compulsion that had kept them moving ever southward and had sent them into the Sea of Dust here strengthened. Some force stood or hovered behind him, exerting rising strength to combat his will.

Now all the power Hystaspes had summoned to find the geas built higher—as a flame leaps when fresh oil is poured into the basin of the lamp. There could be no arguing against the wizard's will, no matter what might face them in or beyond that curtain of the dark hung across the arched opening of the wall.

Without a word to each other, hooked like fish upon a line, they moved forward, while the warmth from their bracelets grew to an almost unbearable heat. Darkness closed about them—bringing a complete absence of all light. Milo took three strides, four, hoping to so win into a place where sight and hearing would once more function, for here he was blind, nor could he catch any sounds from those who shared his venture.

He was isolated in the smothering dark. It was difficult to get a full breath, though the swamp air had been cut off when he had taken that first stride into the total black. Trap? If so he was fairly caught. The band on his wrist was burning, though here he could not see those flashes from the minute gems on the dice. He tried with the fingers of his left hand to free them, make them swing. It was impossible.

Ever the command that Hystaspes had set on him sent him on and on. If this was all they could sense—how then might they combat an entity blindly? Such a defense as this on the part of the alien was more than they had expected.

Milo shook his head. There was a kind of mist in his brain—slowing his thoughts, perhaps blacking out his mind even as this outer darkness had entrapped his body. He could move freely, yes, but he was not even sure now, in his state of increasing bewilderment and dizziness, that he moved straight ahead. Was he wandering in circles?

And in his head. . . .

A table, voices, something he clasped within his hand. A figure! Milo's thought caught and held that fraction of memory in triumph. He had held a figure, beautifully wrought, of a fighting man armored and helmeted like—like Milo Jagon himself!

Milo Jagon? He paused, enfolded in the dark. He was . . . was . . . Martin Jefferson!

He was . . . was . . . With the beginning of panic he staggered on, his hands going to his head as he fought to control the seesaw of memories. Milo—Martin—Martin—Milo—Absorbed in that conflict, he stumbled on, one foot before the other, no longer aware of his surroundings.

Then, just as the dark had closed about them upon their entrance through the wall, so did it end. Milo blundered out into the open once again. He squinted against a light that struck at him. To his eyes this was a punishing glare, so he blinked and blinked again. Then his sight adjusted.

He stood in a room of rough stone walls and floors. There were no windows in those walls. Above his head the ceiling was the same drab black-gray, though it was crossed by heavy beams of wood. In the wall directly opposite there was the outline of a doorway—an outline only, for it had long ago been filled with smaller stones wedged tightly together to form what looked to be an impassable barrier.

Before this stood Gulth, facing that blocked way, his back to those who had joined him. Milo strove to move forward, nearer to the lizardman. He had taken two strides to bring him out of the darkness into this place where the walls themselves gave forth an eerie glow without any benefit of lamp or torch. But, he now could go no farther in spite of all his willing. His feet might have been clamped to the stone floor.

"Wizardry!" Naile rumbled at his right. "One wizard sends us on, the other traps us." The berserker was twisting, trying to turn his body, manifestly attempting to loosen feet as immovable as Milo's.

"No spell of this world holds us," Deav Dyne said. The cleric stood quietly, his beads coiled about his wrist, carefully looped not to touch the bracelet. On all their arms those still glowed with minute sparks of light.

"What do we now?" Yevele demanded. "Wait here like sheep in a butcher's pen?"

Milo moistened his lips with tongue tip. To be so entrapped sapped his resolution, and he understood the danger of such wavering. Now his voice rang out a fraction louder than he had intended. He hoped that no one of them could hear in it any inflection of uneasiness.

"Who are we?"

He saw all their heads turn, even that of Gulth, though the lizardman was far enough in advance that he could not really see who stood behind him.

"What do you mean?" Yevele began and then hesitated. "Yes, that is so—who are we in truth? Can any of us give answer to that?"

None replied. Perhaps within themselves they shifted memories, strove to find a common ground for the seesaw of those memories.

It was Wymarc who made answer. "In that way lies our danger. Perhaps we have been so split now to disarm us, send us into some panic. While we stand here, comrades of the road, we must be one, not two!"

Milo steadied. The bard was right. But could a man put aside those sharp thrusts of alien memory, be himself whole and one, untroubled by another identity? He glanced at the bracelet on his wrist. Naile had called this wizardry. The berserker was right. Could one wizardry be set against another in a last battle here?

"Be those of Greyhawk!" A sudden instinct gave him that. "The swordsman has made an excellent suggestion," Deav Dyne said slowly. "Divided we will be excellent meat, perhaps helpless before the alien knowledge. Strive to be one with *this* world, do not reach after that which was of another existence."

Milo—he was Milo—Milo—Milo! He must be Milo! Now he strove to master that other memory, put it from him as far as possible. He was Milo Jagon, no one else!

The bracelet. . . . The swordsman fastened his gaze on it, holding out his arm so that he could see it clearly. Dice—spinning dice—no, do not look at that—do not think of them! He fought to drop his arm once more to his side, discovered that it was as fixed in the raised position as his feet were to the stones of the floor. Look away! At least that he could do. He forced up his chin. By an effort that made the sweat bead on his skin, he broke the intent stare of his eyes.

"Well done." Deav Dyne spoke with the firm tone of one who had fronted wizardry of many kinds and had not been defeated. Milo glanced at the others. Their arms, even that of the cleric, were held out stiff before them, but every one had broken the momentary spell that had held them in thrall to the motionless dice.

"This is the magic of *this* time and place," the cleric continued. "Milo has told us—be of Greyhawk. Let us use the weapons of Greyhawk against this alien. Perhaps that is the answer. Each of us has something of magic in us. Ingrge holds that knowledge which is of the elves and which no human man can understand or summon, Naile puts forth the strength of the were-folk. Yevele has some spells she has learned, Wymarc controls the harp, Milo wears upon his hands ancient rings of whose properties we cannot be sure. I have what I have learned." He swung his beads. "I do not think Gulth, either, lacks some power. So, let us each concentrate his mind on what is ours and bears no relation to those bands set upon us against our wills."

His advice was logical, but Milo thought they were trusting in a weak hope. Still the illusion-breaking ring *had* worked during their fight outside these walls. He looked at the two rings, moving his other hand out beside the one held so stiffly straight before him. Now he concentrated, as Deav Dyne had bade, upon them. What other strange powers they might control when used by one with the right talent, he had no idea. He could only hope. . . .

He pressed his two thumbs tightly together, thus the settings touched side by side. Wizards were able to move stones, rocks as heavy as those making up these walls, with mind power alone when it was properly channeled. No, he must not let his mind stray as to what could be done by an adept. He must only think now on what might be done by Milo Jagon, swordsman.

Cloudy oval, oblong green bearing forgotten map lines—he stared at them both, strove to reduce his world to the rings only, though what he groped so dimly to seize upon he could not have explained. In . . . in . . . in . . . Somewhere that word arose in his mind, repeated—it had a ring of compulsion, a beat that spread from thought to the flesh and bone. In—relax—let it rise in you.

What rise? Fear of the unknown tried to break loose. Resolutely Milo fought that, drove it from the forepart of his mind. In . . . in . . . in. . . .

The beat of that word heightened, added to now by a strain of music, monotonous in itself but repeating the same three notes again and again, somehow adding force to his will. In . . . in . . . in. . . .

As Milo had exiled beginning fear, so now he battled with doubt. He was no wizard, no spell-master, whispered that doubt. There could be no real answer to the task he willed. Steel only was his weapon. In . . . in . . . in. . . .

As his world was deliberately narrowed to the rings, they grew larger until he could see only the strange gems. Both were coming alive, not exactly glowing as had the bracelet, rather as if their importance was being made manifest to him. In . . . in. . . .

Milo moved before he was aware that that which had held his feet had loosed hold. He took one slow step, another. It was like wading through the treacherous mud of the swamp. To raise each foot required great effort. Still it could be done.

His shoulder brushed against Gulth's. They both stood facing the wall. On his other side he was dimly aware of Yevele coming up beside them, could hear, without understanding, a mutter of words she voiced. In. . . .

He took a last step. His outstretched hands, held at eye level so that he could concentrate on the rings, came palm flat against the small stones that had been set to block the doorway. Beside him, Gulth had also moved, his taloned hands resting beside Milo's.

Concentrate! He found it difficult to hold that fierce will-to-be on the rings. Then—

The wall barrier, which had looked and felt at his first touch so immovable, began to crumble. The blocks decayed into coarse rubble, which tumbled to the flooring. A brighter light than they had yet seen streamed out. Concentrate! Milo fought to keep his thoughts fixed steadily on the rings and hold there.

Those blocks were gone, their outstretched hands now met no opposition. Milo heard a soft cry from beside him, echoed it with a sharp breath of his own. The bracelet was no longer only warm. It formed a tormenting band of fire about his arm, bringing sharp pain.

However, his feet were not fixed. Aroused to sullen anger by that pain, he moved on, dimly aware that the rest of the party were fast on his heels.

What they faced. . . .

Illusion? Milo could not be sure. But as he stared ahead into that brightly lighted room his surprise was complete. Here were no stone walls, no sign of any dwelling that one might find in this world.

The floor under his boots was wood, only half-covered by a rug of dull green. Planted in the center of it was a table. And on the table was stacked a pile of books—not the scrolls, tomes, parchment he might expect to find in a wizard's chamber—but books that the other person deep within him recognized. One, a loose-leaf notebook, lay open, back flat on the table. Facing it was a row of small figures, standing in scattered array on a large sheet of paper marked off into squares by different colored lines. On the wall behind the table hung a map.

Deav Dyne spoke. "This is the land we know." He gestured to the map.

Milo came to the table. The figures. . . . Once more his hand curled as if he clasped their like in protecting fingers. Not chessmen—no—though these were playing pieces right enough, representations of men, of aliens, each beautifully fashioned with microscopic detail. He eyed them narrowly, almost sure that each of them must be one of the pieces. But that was not true. There were a druid, a dragon, others he could not be sure of without examining them closely—but no swordsman, no elf, bard, battle-maiden, no Gulth, Deav Dyne, Naile. . . .

There was no one in the room, no other entrance save the door they had opened for themselves. Still Milo had a feeling that they would not be alone long, that he who had opened that book, set out the figures, would at any moment return.

Yevele moved around the table, looking down at the papers spread there. She looked up.

"I know these—why?" There was a frown of puzzlement on

her face. "This is . . ." Her mental effort was visible to any watcher as she fought to find words. "This is—a game!"

Her last word was a key to unlock the door of memory. Milo was not transported back in person, but he was in mind in another room not too different from this in some ways. Ekstern should be there unpacking the new pieces. He held a swordsman—

"We—we are the pieces!" he broke out. He swung halfway around, pointing from one of the party to the next. "What can you remember now?" he demanded from them.

"Game pieces." Deav Dyne nodded slowly. "New game pieces—and I picked one up to examine it more closely. Then"—he made a gesture toward himself, toward the rest of them—"I was in Greyhawk and I was Deav Dyne. But how can this be—wizardry of a sort I have no knowledge of? Was it the same with all of you?"

They nodded. Milo had already gone on to the next question, one that perhaps none of them might be able to answer. "Why?"

"Do you not remember what Hystaspes said to us?" counter-questioned the battlemaid. "He spoke of worlds tied together by bringing us here—of a desire to so link two planes of existence together."

"Which would be a disaster!" Wymarc said. "Each would suffer from such a—"

Whatever he might have added was never voiced. There came a flickering in the opposite corner of the room. Then a man stood there, as if the very air itself had provided a doorway for his entrance.

An expression of complete amazement on his thin face was

quickly overshadowed by another of mingled fear and anger, or so Milo read it. The swordsman made the first move. He depended once more on the reflexes of his body, as his blade cleared scabbard and pointed toward the stranger in one clean, flowing act.

Yevele moved as speedily—but in a different direction. She snatched up the open notebook from the table.

"Let that alone!" Anger triumphed over both amazement and the trace of fear in the stranger.

"This is the key to your meddling, isn't it?" demanded the girl in return. "This—and those." She pointed to the row of figures. "Are they to be your next captives?"

"You don't know what you are doing," he snapped. Then he paused, before adding, "You don't belong here. Ewire!" His voice rose in a sharp, imperative call. "Ewire, where are you? You can't trick me with your illusions."

"Illusions?" Naile rumbled. "Let me get my two hands on you, little man!" The berserker strode forward with a purposeful stride. "Then you will see what illusions can do when they are angered!"

The stranger backed away. "You can't touch me!" His tone now held a shrill note. "You're not supposed to be here at all!" He sounded aggrieved as well as impatient. "Ewire knows better than to try her tricks on me."

Yevele leafed hastily through the ring-bound pages of the notebook. Suddenly she paused, and called out. "Wait, Naile, this is important to us all." Steadying the book in one hand, she used a finger of the other to run lightly across the page as she read. "First shipment of figures on its way. Will run periodic checks. If the formula does work—what a perfect game!"

"So," Milo held his sword with the point aimed at the other's throat. Thus far he kept rigid control of his anger. "We have been playing your game, is that it? I do not know how or why you have done this to us. But you can send us back—"

The stranger was shaking his head. "You needn't try to threaten me—you aren't real, don't you understand that? I'm the game master, the referee. I call the action! Oh—" He raised one hand and rubbed his forehead. "This is ridiculous. Why do I argue with something—someone who does not really exist?"

"Because we do." Naile reached out one hand as if he would seize upon the stranger's shirt just above his heart. Inches away from the goal his fingers brought up against an invisible barrier. The stranger paid no attention to the aborted attack. He was staring at Yevele.

"Don't!" his voice reached a scream, he had suddenly lost control. "What are you doing?" Now he moved toward the table and the girl who held the notebook in her hands. She was methodically tearing out the pages, letting them drift to the floor. "No!"

The stranger made a grab for his possession. Even as Naile could not reach him, neither could he reach Yevele. Calmly she moved back and continued her destruction.

Then the other laughed. "You really can't be anyone now but yourselves," he said in a voice he once more had under control. "It's a one-way road for you."

"But not for you?" Deav Dyne asked with his usual mildness.

The stranger flashed a glance at him. "I'm not really here. You might term it 'magic' in this benighted barbaric world. I project only a part of me. I have an anchor—back there. You do not. You serve my purpose by being here. Do you suppose I would have left you any way back? The more of you"—he glanced at the figures on the table and away again—"who can answer to what is set in those figures—because each one holds that which will draw someone of the right temperament here—the stronger my plan will be."

"Thank you for the information." Wymarc reached the table to gather up the figures with a single sweep of his hand. He slammed them to the floor and stamped hard, flattening the metal into battered lumps.

The stranger watched him with a sly smile. "It doesn't put an end to it, you know. There are more of those waiting. I need only bring them through, link them here, and then—" He shrugged.

"I do not think you will do that." From the back of the notebook Yevele drew a single sheet of time-browned paper. Milo caught only a glimpse of a straggle of dark lines across it.

Now the stranger let out a cry. "I—I couldn't have left that here!"

Once more he made an ineffectual attempt to seize what she held but the barrier that lay between them held. Yevele backed farther away, holding out the paper to Deav Dyne. The cleric grasped it and swiftly rolled it up, to be wrapped with his prayer beads. Yevele spoke to Milo.

"The dice, comrade, get the dice! It would seem he has forgotten them also."

Milo lunged for the table, the stranger doing the same from the other side. It was he who overbalanced the board, sent it crashing on its side, barely missing Milo's feet. Dice such as those they wore in miniature rattled among the cascade of books and papers, to spin across the floor. Milo scooped up three, saw that Ingrge and Wymarc had the others.

"Roll the master one, roll it now, Milo! See what will happen," Yevele ordered.

"No." The stranger sprawled forward, on his knees, his arms reaching out in a vain attempt to gather his property.

"Does it work both ways then?" Milo did not expect an answer. But because he was impressed by Yevele's order and was willing at this moment to believe that perhaps magic was at work here, he spun the proper cube.

The result was startling. That man, cursing now in his futility, wavered; table, papers strewn across the floor, they and their owner were gone. Around the party the whole room began to spin, until they caught at one another dizzily. There came a rushing of wind, a chill of freezing air.

Once more they stood in a stone-walled room. Above them there was no longer any ceiling, for that wall ended in the jagged line of ruin. And they were alone.

"He is gone, and I believe I can swear by the High Altar of Astraha, he cannot return," Deav Dyne announced.

"But we—*we* are here," Yevele said slowly.

Milo looked straightly at her. "Perhaps he was right and for us there is no return. Still, there is much strange knowledge in this land that may aid us if we are fortunate. We have this." He tossed the master cube in his hand and caught it. "Who knows what we can learn concerning it."

"Well spoken," Deav Dyne agreed. "And we are free of the geas also."

It was true. Though Milo had not realized it, that faint uneasiness born of the geas no longer rode him.

Naile cleared his throat. "We can now go our own ways with no reason to bow to any other's wish—"

He hesitated and Yevele said, "Is that what you wish, berserker? That we should now part and each seek his own fortune?"

Naile rubbed his chin with one hand. Then he answered slowly. "A man usually chooses his battlemates and shield companions. However, now I say this. If you wish Naile Fangtooth, yes, even the scaled one there, to march your road—say so. I am free of all other vows."

"I agree." Wymarc shifted the bagged harp to an easier position on his shoulder. "Let us not be hasty in splitting our force. It has been proven we can act together well when the need arises."

Ingrge and the cleric nodded. Last of all Gulth, looking from one face to the next, croaked, "Gulth walks your road if you wish."

"So be it," Yevele said briskly. "But where do we now go and for what purpose? From this foray we have gained little—save perhaps the confounding of this player of games."

"We have this," Milo tossed the die. His problem had been solved. He knew now that he was Milo Jagon and in that he took a certain amount of satisfaction. "Shall we roll to see what we can learn?"

"We are wed to that, the bracelets will not loosen." Ingrge had been pulling at his, to no purpose. "Therefore, comrades of the road, take care of those same dice. But as you ask, swordsman, I now say—roll to see what comes of it. One chance is as good as another."

Milo cupped the die tightly in his hand for a moment and went down to one knee. Then, wondering what might follow, he tossed the referee's control out on the rock floor of the ruined keep.